The ... W9-CQH-460

NORMAN PARTRIDGE

"The hottest new writer going." —Joe R. Lansdale

"Partridge writes like nobody else. He's a big talent and he's going to get a whole lot bigger."
—Ed Gorman, *Mystery Scene*

"Partridge is a genuine original: funny, mordant, hard-edged, and altogether his own man. Read his new book, then settle in, like me, to wait for the next." —*Cemetery Dance*

"Probably the most exciting and original voice . . . to have appeared in the last decade. This wonderful writer, always entering from an unexpected direction, instantly claiming his terrain with the authority necessary to take the reader to unexpected places, offers challenges, surprises, and deep satisfactions to anyone willing to think about what they are reading." —Peter Straub

"Norman Partridge, I feel certain now, is the reason rock 'n' roll will never die." —Edward Bryant

The game is
SAGUARO RIPTIDE

Welcome to the Saguaro Riptide Motel, a seedy little surf joint in Arizona where Jack "Battle-ax" Baddalach is about to join in the fight for two million in cash—the biggest disharmonic convergence since the invention of gunpowder.

"The remarkable things here are the energy and the non-stop flow of invention with which the author invests each scene and each character. There is not a scene in this book that sounds as if it might have been written by anyone other than Norman Patridge." —*Cemetery Dance*

"One of the most dependable, exciting, and entertaining practitioners of dark suspense . . . Emphasis on the *dark*. When Partridge is hitting on all eight cylinders, he's one tough contender for any ambitious hot young bravo to beat. Street legal? Yeah, but barely." —*Locus*

THE
TEN-OUNCE
SIESTA

Norman Partridge (signature)

NORMAN PARTRIDGE

FEBRUARY 24, 1998

BERKLEY PRIME CRIME, NEW YORK

THE TEN-OUNCE SIESTA

A Berkley Prime Crime Book / published by arrangement with the author

PRINTING HISTORY
Berkley Prime Crime edition / February 1998

All rights reserved.
Copyright © 1998 by Norman Partridge.
This book may not be reproduced in whole or in part, by mimeograph or any other means, without permission.
For information address: The Berkley Publishing Group, a member of Penguin Putnam Inc., 200 Madison Avenue, New York, NY 10016.

The Putnam Berkley World Wide Web site address is
http://www.berkley.com

ISBN: 0-425-16143-9

Berkley Prime Crime Books are published
by The Berkley Publishing Group,
a member of Penguin Putnam Inc.,
200 Madison Avenue, New York, NY 10016.

The name BERKLEY PRIME CRIME and the BERKLEY PRIME CRIME design are trademarks belonging to Berkley Publishing Corporation.

PRINTED IN THE UNITED STATES OF AMERICA

10 9 8 7 6 5 4 3 2 1

For Mike Chestney,
who will recognize the parts that are almost true . . .

This story includes rattlesnakes, one standard-issue good guy, bikini girls with machine guns, cops with donuts, the heavyweight champion of the world, and one demon from hell. The aforementioned characters are all figments of the author's imagination and are not meant to resemble extant reptiles, humans, or creatures of the supernatural.

I don't believe there's any virtue in understatement.

—KEN RUSSELL

THE
TEN-OUNCE
SIESTA

PART ONE

Bikini Girls With Machine Guns

I met a lady in the meads,
Full beautiful—a faery's child;
Her hair was long, her foot was light,
And her eyes were wild.

—JOHN KEATS
™*La Belle Dame Sans Merci*Ĵ

ONE

THE CHIHUAHUA DIDN'T BARK. IT COUGHED.

"It's the secondhand smoke." The girl sucked on a Marlboro. "I can't quit. Spike's the one who suffers, though. The poor little muchacho probably has lung cancer. He's been coughing like this for a week."

Jack Baddalach stared at the Chihuahua cradled in the girl's arms. There wasn't enough meat on the little sucker's bones to fill a Taco Bell burrito, but it looked pretty happy wrapped in a private cloud of Marlboro smoke. Its goggle-eyed head bobbled back and forth between the girl's breasts. Her breasts were a lot bigger than the dog's head. If the dog was dying, it had picked one hell of a way to go.

"Do dogs get lung cancer?" the girl asked.

A handful of girls stood behind her, but they didn't answer. They looked at Jack, waiting for him to do the job.

Jack looked at them. They were about a thousand miles away from the mental group portrait he'd imagined when he took Freddy G's call.

Cerebral rewind cued the soundbite in Jack's brain, transmitted through the casino owner's gravelly Mafioso voice: *Fly to the coast. We'll have one of our drivers waiting*

3

with a limo. The two of you go to my daughter's house in Palm Springs. Pick up my granddaughter's pet Chihuahua. She's coming to Vegas with a bunch of her friends for a bachelorette party. One of 'em's getting married and they want to watch a bunch of steroid puppies shake their moneymakers or some such shit. Anyway, my granddaughter's got a Chihuahua transport problem. She can fly but the doggy can't. It's sick or something, and she don't let it out of her sight 'cause she ain't done that since her Grandpa Freddy give it to her on her sweet sixteenth birthday. So I gotta put on my thinkin' cap and find a way to keep my grandbaby happy even though I ain't got time for this shit. But that ain't no problemo grande, Jack, 'cause I'll pay you to have time for it. . . .

Listening to Freddy G's encapsulation of the situation, Jack had expected Palm Springs debutantes deluxe. But that wasn't what he was getting. Uh-uh. Because the semienchanting female tableau standing tough before him was a study in torn jeans, black mascara, tattoos, and the very latest in trashcut hairstyles.

Jack shook his head. Man oh man, even punk rock had gone mainstream in the age of raging ennui. No surprise there. After all, Johnny Thunders had been dead a long time and Macy's needed *something* to accentuate that new summer line. This year it was basic black, way too tight, and way too expensive. Not that Jack Baddalach was a safety-pin purist. He didn't care one way or the other. Hell, he listened to Dean Martin records.

The Chihuahua coughed again, reminding Jack that he wasn't one of those erudite hipsters who slagged records for *Spin Magazine*.

"Dogs," the girl repeated. "Can they get lung cancer?"

"I don't know." Jack paused. "I mean, I guess they could.

But I'm sure that's not what's wrong with your dog. He's probably just got a cold."

"Grandpa said you were a veterinarian. But you don't sound like a vet."

Jack nodded, because who knew what kind of bullshit Freddy G had given his granddaughter. "Sure. I'm a vet. But I work with tigers. Those white ones at the Mirage, just down the road from your granddad's casino."

"Which one are you?"

"Huh?"

"Siegfried or Roy?"

She laughed and so did Jack. He kind of liked the way she laughed. The way she talked, too, the way her words crackled over him in that smoky voice she had. And he especially liked the way she gave it right back to him when he dished the sarcasm her way.

"The name's Jack Baddalach," he said. "I'm what you might call a behind-the-scenes kind of guy."

"I never even heard of you."

"Oh, you will. I'm a comer in the white tiger business. Why, just last month *Cat Fancy Magazine* called me a man to watch."

Jack winked.

"*Shit.*" The girl smirked bright and bloody, because her lipstick was a little smeared. "*Bullshit.*" Southern California sun catching spiked blond hair that was jet-black at the roots. "*White tiger bullshit.*" She passed the Chihuahua to Jack, the tattooed rattler on her left arm wriggling like some neon nightmare. "If you're a vet, I'm Sheena, Queen of the Fucking Jungle."

Jack took the dog and returned the girl's smirk. "The truth is that I'm kind of a troubleshooter for your grandpa. I may not look like much, but I'll get your dog to Vegas."

"Normally I'd take him on the plane with me. It's just a

short flight. But with the way he's coughing and everything, and the way his nose is running . . . Well, I don't want his ears to get fucked up on an airplane. I had that happen to me once, and it took the Cramps live to clear 'em out."

"Don't you worry about it." Jack shot a thumb over his shoulder in the direction of the waiting limo. "Your grand-dad fixed me up with one of the best drivers in LA, or so the guy claims. We'll put the pedal to the metal, take Spike straight to Dr. Newman, and I'll bet you green money that he'll be fast asleep in your suite at the Casbah before you and your girlfriends get your club crawl into first gear."

"Is Newman good?"

"Best vet in Vegas. Your granddad had him checked out. Newman handles all the stars. I read about him in the paper one time. He spayed Wayne Newton's bitch."

"And what'd he do to *Wayne*?" The girl laughed. Her breasts danced a little rhumba beneath a tight white T-shirt that said SWEET CHEERY LOVE. It looked like her breasts were penned up in a black lace brassiere, if Jack Baddalach was any judge. Not that he was paying an inordinate amount of attention. He only looked because, hey, the awful truth was that men *always* look.

But truth be told, Jack had another woman on his mind. And the woman who was on his mind wasn't anything like this girl. For one thing, the woman on Jack Baddalach's mind would never in a million years wear a T-shirt that said Sweet Cherry *anything*—

The girl's arms were around him quite suddenly, pulling him close. Jack felt the undeniable warmth of Sweet Cherry Love penning the Chihuahua between her chest and his.

She came closer.

Jack figured he'd better say something, and quick.

Her lips touched his.

So Jack couldn't say anything. Because he was kissing

this girl and thinking of another one, and it was all pretty damn complicated and—

Her mouth was open. And then so was his.

The Chihuahua coughed between them.

"I like the way you look at me," the girl said.

Jack shrugged. He'd finally thought of something to say, only it was a little late: "Be careful. I'm just the hired help."

The way she held on, it didn't seem like she was the careful type.

One of her girlfriends swore. Another one giggled.

"My name's Angel." The girl whispered the words in Jack's left ear. He managed to keep a straight face. Spike panted against his chest. Angel's hands drifted away, traveling south before they gave him up, her right hand lingering on a bulge beneath his coat.

"You expecting trouble?"

"It's not a gun." Jack drew back his coat and showed her the leather holster strapped to his belt. "All I'm packing is a cellular phone."

She opened her purse. Took out a tube of lipstick. Opened it. Held it against her arm.

"What's your number?"

Jack gave it to her. Surprised, even as he opened his mouth.

She wrote it in red, on the neon scales of a tattooed rattlesnake.

The limo driver said, "Had me a woman with a snake tattoo once."

Jack stared at the back of the guy's head. Bald as a cue ball. Bright pink skin. Heavy folds of flesh on the back of his neck that reminded Jack of a pack of Oscar Meyer wieners.

As the big Caddy pulled away from the house, Pack O'

Weenies started talking about the woman with the snake tattoo. "Big old anaconda started at her pussy and wound its way up to her neck, sinking its fangs into her carotid and man, did she have a body in between. Skinny little Mexican thing with little bitty brown sugar titties that stood up and said *Buenos días*. Man, was she something."

Jack didn't say a word. Neither did Spike, who sat shivering on Baddalach's lap.

Pack O' Weenies went on: "This chick ran a credit card scam. Bigtime. Her and her brother Jesus. Jesus worked at the post office. He stole the cards and she ran 'em up. Bought TVs and stereos, stuff she could sell or return to the stores for cash. Got me into it. We'd go out on the weekends like Ma and Pa Suburbs, buy stuff till we maxed out a card, then switch to another. See, doing it on weekends was the way to go, because then the credit card companies don't pick up on it. That's when they expect people to do their big spending. Go out and trot up those charges on Monday, Tuesday, Wednesday and alarm bells go off in the credit card company's computers. But stick to the weekends and you can charge till the wheels come off. Unless it's Christmastime, of course. Christmastime—that's heaven for credit card scammers. Every day is what you might call Santa-*intensive*.

"Anyway, it seemed like an okay deal at first. We made pretty good money. She put me in the driver's seat of a brand new Cadillac. I put a ring on her finger. Then we got caught. Or Jesus got caught, I should say. See, one day the stupid motherfucker has a bunch of cards jammed down his shorts on the way out of work, and the postmaster stops him for a chat, and his ass starts to sweat, and pretty soon those little chunks of plastic start sliding down Jesus's perky little ass cheeks and before you know it he's shitting Visas and Mastercards on the post office floor.

"It was summertime, see, and Jesus wore shorts. The son of a bitch wanted to show off his legs like he was a fucking UPS driver or something. He was always after the chicks on his route. And the fool wore boxers, too. If he would have stuck to long woolies and briefs, he would have been as safe as sunshine. But he just had to play the stud, this boy.

"And Jesus was a tater, too. One hundred percent spud. Me and my wife, we just knew he'd give us up the first time the cops offered him a deal. And these were federal cops, y'know? The post office is a federal institution, and federal cops, hell, you don't even want to take a chance with those motherfuckers.

"So I shot Jesus before the cops could sweat him. Did his tater ass out in the woods, a little meadow in the middle of nowhere—this was up north, you understand. Marin County. Hell. I couldn't see nothing that wasn't green for miles. And the only sound I heard were the birdies singing. I didn't think anyone was around. Not even Bigfoot.

"Turns out there was a group of bird watchers back in the trees. Card-carrying members of the Audubon Society, all done up in their best L.L. Bean camouflage wear so they wouldn't scare their fine feathered friends. They were awaiting the arrival of the palm warbler or some such shit. Some rare fucking bird. Instead, they got me and my .357 Magnum.

"Ten pairs of binoculars were aimed right at me when I pulled the trigger. A half dozen cameras, too. And that magnum made a hell of a lot of noise. I never even heard those camera shutters click when I pulled the trigger.

"The pictures came out pretty good, too. You should have seen me. All dressed in black, my bald head gleaming in the sunshine. I looked like Yul Brynner in *The Magnificent Seven*. After the trial was over, I asked the judge if I could get copies of some of those pictures. They were evidence; it shouldn't have been a big deal. But the son of a bitch made some Fruit Loop ruling so I couldn't have any of 'em. What a tater. He had no sense of humor at all.

"Anyway, I took the fall. Spent the next ten years in Corcoran, which was one bad jailhouse in those days. Ten years without my little brown baby and her sweet anaconda. I couldn't get her off my mind, though. Not even. I read every reptile book in the prison library and dreamed of my sugar's anaconda every fucking night. Snakes, snakes, snakes. Pussy, pussy, pussy. That's all I thought about.

"Then I got out of prison. Parole. My baby's waiting for me. She'd moved to Vegas and I hadn't seen her in three-four years, but we kept in touch with letters. While I was away, she did all right. Went straight. Opened up a donut shop with some of the money she made off the credit cards.

"That was a tough one. Bad enough I'm always thinking about snakes and pussy, now I start thinking about donuts. See my old lady's always writing me about glazed donuts and chocolate bars and big old gooey bearclaws, and I'm lucky if I get some dried-out turd of a cookie in the slams. And not only that, the donut shop is a really different environment for her. All of a sudden she's got plenty of cop friends. Las Vegas cops. They all like donuts.

"Anyway, on graduation day my little *mamacita* sends a limo for me. The driver picks me up at the prison gate. Takes me to a Holiday Inn in Fresno. Man, I'm hard before I even hit the door, thinkin' of my long tall baby and that snake writhing on her belly. That big ol' anaconda traveling those sweet little lumps of brown sugar on her chest.

"I open the door, and there she is. Naked on the sheets. You can't fuckin' miss her. But all I see is the snake. 'Cause it's big now. Thick. Jesus. Some of those scales would dwarf the trunk of a Buick. And somehow I get the idea that the damn thing is a lot longer, too. Gotta be, because since the last time I seen her there's a lot more of my baby to go around . . . and around . . . and around.

"But the worst part is her chest. Those sweet breasts that used to be so little and firm. The snake is even wider there, sort of swollen, like it swallowed a couple of hamsters that it can't quite digest."

Pack O' Weenies sighed. "Well, sometimes you just flat out *know* when something is over. That's the way it was with me and my wife and the snake. I just turned around and closed the door on the both of them, because I knew I couldn't spend the rest of my life making donuts and watching that snake get bigger. Fact is, I ain't never dated a woman with tattoos since, and I never will." The driver glanced at Jack in the rearview. "What do you think of that?"

Jack thought it over. "Tattoos are all right," he said finally. "But donuts and gravity—they'll get you every time."

Jack stared at the back of Pack O' Weenies' bald head as they headed toward Vegas. Physiologically speaking, the contents of one human skull was pretty much like another. Psychologically, it was another story entirely. That's the way Jack Baddalach saw it, anyway.

And Jack met all kinds of people. That was a given when you worked for the mob.

Check that. The fact of the matter was that Jack Baddalach couldn't possibly work for the mob. Because his boss, Freddy Gemignani, was the owner of the Casbah Hotel & Casino, located on the beautiful Las Vegas Strip. As such, Freddy G had passed muster with the Gaming Control Board. And anyone who had done that . . . well, anyone who had done that couldn't *possibly* be involved with organized crime in any way, shape, or form.

Still, Jack had met some interesting people through his association with Freddy G. Then again, he had also met more than a few people like Pack O' Weenies. Jack's experience with cold-blooded killers told him that protracted conversations were generally a minus with same. Verbally speaking, a couple of strangers were bound to step on each other's toes sooner or later. And with cold-blooded killers . . . Well, Jack didn't care how much time a guy like Pack O' Weenies had served; he didn't want to get on the wrong side of a murderer, verbally or otherwise.

If you wanted to understand a guy like Pack O' Weenies, all you had to do was hire a medium to channel the spirit of a postman named Jesus. And then factor in the not-so-stunning revelation that a protracted stay in the slams obviously hadn't done much to change the cowboy who'd delivered the postman with the studly legs to the big dead letter office in the sky. Anyone who listened to Pack tell his story could figure that one out. The guy wanted copies of the photos that showed him plugging the postman, for Christsakes. He probably wanted to hang them over the wet bar in his rumpus room, like a fisherman does with snaps of marlin and trout.

Jack figured there was no reforming a guy like Pack O' Weenies. In Baddalach's opinion, anyone who'd murder a postal employee in full view of the Marin County Audubon Society had to be full-tilt Looney tunes, anyway.

It wasn't a long drive from Palm Springs to Vegas, but it was long enough. Jack didn't want to spend the trip doing the nice-weather-we're-having-today mambo. Fortunately, he knew how to cut a conversation short, even with a cold-blooded killer.

He set Spike on the seat next to him and reached for his jacket, a worn leather thrift shop special with a faded red lining.

His fingers found the inside pocket. In the rearview, Pack O' Weenies eyed him suspiciously. The guy was already sweating. Jack grinned, and that made Pack sweat all the more.

The driver was going to be easy. Jack let the grin grow into a smile. Kind of a frosty smile, lots of incisor showing. Just the way he'd done it in the old days, standing in the ring and staring down an opponent when he was the undisputed light-heavyweight champion of the whole fucking planet.

"Sorry," Pack O' Weenies said. "I didn't mean to go on like that, champ. I'm probably boring the shit out of you. Maybe I better just pay attention to the road. Maybe—"

Jack's hand came away from the coat.

"Hey," Pack O' Weenies said. "What you got there, champ?"

Jack held it up.

The conversation ender to end all conversation enders.

"Don't sweat it," Jack said. "It's only a book."

Outside the limo, the Mojave Desert whipped by. Jack ignored it. Not much of a stretch, actually. He found it inordinately easy to ignore acre upon acre of absolutely nothing.

He didn't have as much luck ignoring the Chihuahua, which had curled up on his lap and fallen asleep. The damn thing was pretty pathetic, taking little rasping breaths, fidgeting now and then as if it were having a doggy nightmare. Jack hoped the dog didn't have lung cancer. Jesus. Just thinking about that gave him a shiver. He didn't want to hear those words from the vet in Vegas. He didn't want to live *Old Yeller*. Not with a Chihuahua named Spike, and not with his boss's punker granddaughter. Complications like that . . . well, Jack Baddalach didn't need them in his life. That was for sure.

Jack tried to concentrate on the book. It was an old Dan J. Marlowe paperback from the fifties. *One Endless Hour*. He'd found it at the same thrift shop where he bought the leather jacket. It was a first edition, a primo score at fifty cents. Not that Jack Baddalach was the type of guy to get his shorts in a bunch over a first edition. No way, Jose. But Jack thought that Dan J. Marlowe was one hell of a writer. That was the thing.

The book was a good one. It pumped right along. But Jack found that his mind kept drifting back to the little scene which had highlighted his morning.

Palm Springs sunshine warm on his back. In front of him, a girl who had to be ten (let's face it, Jack, more like fifteen) years his junior. A girl in a T-shirt that said Sweet Cherry Love.

A girl with her tongue in his mouth.

There was a little fridge in the back of the limo. Jack took a cold Kirin from the compartment and rolled the bottle back and forth across his knuckles. A year and a half since he'd quit the ring, but still his knuckles ached.

He tried to think about nothing at all.

He thought about Sweet Cherry Love.

Suddenly, the cellular phone on his hip felt as heavy as a wedding ring.

Jack swallowed uncomfortably.

Jesus, Baddalach. Get a grip.

He did. He got a grip on a bottle opener, popped the Kirin, and let that golden Japanese beer wash the taste of tarnished virtue from his mouth.

Jack had intended that only one woman have the number for his cellular phone. One woman, and one woman only. Her name was Kate Benteen, and to make a long story short she had saved Jack Baddalach's bacon during the first job he'd ever done for Freddy G. Jack had been waiting for Kate to call him for the better part of a year. Jack thought that the better part of a year was a long time to wait for anything, but he had stuck it out because Kate Benteen had told Jack to stick close to the phone. Jack, a man who tended to take thinks way too literally, had done his damnedest to comply, because if there was ever a woman who was worth a long wait it was Kate Benteen. But in all that time, his cellular phone hadn't rung. Not once. And now he'd given his phone number to another woman. A woman named Angel, who had written his number on her arm with bright red lipstick.

Jack thought about Pack O' Weenies, a guy who knew exactly when things were over. A guy who could close a hotel room door, and leave a woman behind without a word, and never give any of it another thought.

And then he thought about Kate Benteen and Angel Gemignani, and he wondered which woman would call him first.

Spike squirmed on his lap. An anguished little whine escaped the Chihuahua's muzzle. Jack knew exactly how the little bastard felt. Absently, he started petting the dog. Spike stopped squirming almost instantly.

Outside the window, the town of Amboy drifted by. Then Essex. Needles coming up. But the Mojave Desert didn't change a bit. The limo rocketed over a midnight stripe of pavement that split a whole lot of very white nothing. Jack stared at the desert but couldn't see it at all. He found himself staring instead at his reflection in the limo window.

And then, through his reflection, he saw something else. An exit off the highway. And beyond that a gas station. Or what used to be a gas station, because now the broken windows were scabbed over with large slabs of plywood.

Pack O' Weenies took the off-ramp. The limo kicked up a cloud of dust as they crossed the dirt lot and pulled to a stop on one side of the gas station. Pack ratcheted the gear shift into the park position. The ash-colored cloud caught up in a second, and the big Caddy was enveloped in a shroud of swirling dust.

"What's up?" Jack asked.

At first Pack O' Weenies didn't answer him. He stepped out of the car, and into the cloud, without looking back.

"Gotta see a man about a snake," he said.

And then he slammed the limo door.

The door had only been open a second, but in that second Jack caught a mouthful of Mojave dust.

He almost took another sip of beer, but he decided against it. He just didn't want it anymore. He set the bottle on top of the limo fridge, watching Pack O' Weenies disappear around the back corner of the old gas station.

Jack waited, his left hand drifting over Spike's fur as the dog slept easy. Outside, the cloud began to settle around the limo. Lazy dust devils danced in the sunlight. Jack watched them, listening to the limo's big engine ping hotly in the dry desert silence.

A moment later, someone came around the corner of the gas station.

Someone who wasn't Pack O' Weenies.

The woman was dressed in black leather. Black pants, black go-go boots, black bikini top. She was definitely something to see. The cows that had given up their hides for her wardrobe could rest easy in the knowledge that they'd made a much more significant contribution to human society than their brothers who'd given it up for hamburger meat.

The woman came through the dust, ash-colored particles swirling around her, moving forward through it step by step as it settled lower, coming finally into sharp focus as if spied through a camera viewfinder. Everything tight on her long lean body. Everything black save her very white skin. Hair as black as night, and sunglasses that gleamed black as the armor of a carrion beetle scuttling away from the noonday sun, and lipstick as slick and dark as black roses kissed with dew.

She wore braces on her wrists and hands. They almost looked like some kind of medical braces . . . but Jack knew that couldn't be. That was crazy. Because these braces, whatever they were, were covered with black velvet and fringed with black lace.

The slender ivory fingers that escaped the braces ended in long nails polished as black as the inside of Satan's own pocket.

Jack kept his eyes on those fingers as the woman walked toward the limo.

Because those fingers clutched a machine gun.

The woman didn't move fast, but the way she moved was something to see. Sinuous, almost hypnotic.

Much too quickly, the barrel of the machine gun tapped sharply against the limo window.

Spike came awake at the sound. Frightened and wary, the dog whined, shivering against Jack's outstretched hand.

Jack snapped out of his reverie and rolled down the window.

The woman said, "Give me the Chihuahua, and no one gets hurt."

TWO

JACK LOWERED THE LIMO WINDOW. "THERE ARE EASIER WAYS TO GET
a dog, you know. You could always call the SPCA."

The woman in black ignored the wisecrack. "You look
kind of familiar. Didn't you used to be somebody?"

"My name's Jack Baddalach. I used to be the light-
heavyweight champion of the world."

"You don't look like you're exactly in fighting trim,
Jack."

Now it was Jack's turn to ignore her. He set the
Chihuahua on the seat and opened the door. "Take it slow"
was all the woman said, and she kept the machine gun barrel
aimed at Jack's chest as he stepped from the limo.

The desert heat hit him all at once. Jack instantly missed
the limo's air-conditioned cocoon. As he closed the door, he
glimpsed Spike burrowing under his leather coat. Jesus.
Maybe the pooch knew something that its bodyguard didn't.
Jack hoped he wasn't witnessing a display of canine
precognition.

Sweat beaded on Jack's forehead, but the heat didn't seem
to bother the woman. She stood there as cool as a tall glass
of lemonade, watching his every move.

Jack took a final glance at the gas station before turning to meet the woman head on. He was hoping to catch sight of Pack O' Weenies, but his view was obstructed by a rusted tire rack heaped with tangles of twisted metal. Whatever or whoever was behind the station would remain a mystery. At least for now.

Jack wondered what had happened to the driver. He wondered if the Modesty Blaise clone standing before him had already taken Pack O' Weenies down. Or maybe she had some help. Maybe there were a couple others just like her behind the building. Maybe they were aiming machine guns at Pack right now. Maybe he was down on his knees with a gun barrel to the back of his neck, ready to feel the sizzle of hot lead through those pink weenies. Or maybe Pack was—

"The Chihuahua," the woman insisted. "I don't want to drag this out. Hand it over."

"It's not my Chihuahua." Jack stepped toward the woman. "Spike belongs to a friend of mine. And the fact is that Spike's a very sick puppy. He's got lung cancer."

"C'mon. Dogs don't get lung cancer."

"Yes they do. Canine lung cancer. It's the number three killer of Chihuahuas. See, Chihuahuas have a very small lung capacity. Once they get it, it's adios muchacho, PDQ." Jack shot a thumb over his shoulder in Spike's direction. "And the muchacho in question is about two syllables into *ad-i-os*."

The woman's upper lip jerked as if she were about to laugh. Then she cocked her head to one side, just the way a dog does when it doesn't understand something. Jack stared at her sunglasses but couldn't glimpse her eyes through the black carrion beetle lenses, and when his gaze returned to her lips they had clamped into place once more, transforming her mouth into a determined line the color of blood oranges.

"I still want the dog," she said.

"All right." Jack took another step toward her. "Maybe we can work something out. You got a wallet in those tight leather pants? Make me an offer. You'll be wasting your money, but hey, that's your problem, not mine—"

"That's close enough."

Jack took another step.

The machine gun jerked in her hands. "I said stop."

This time Jack did as he was told. He kept his eyes on the machine gun and the braces she wore on her wrists. Braces covered with black velvet and lace.

"Turn around," she said.

"Uh-uh. *Never turn your back on a lady with a gun.* That's what my mama always told me."

"You're not carrying, are you?"

"Carrying?"

"A gun."

"Not the last time I looked."

"Maybe I'd better look for you."

As she one-handed the machine gun and reached for him with her left hand, her right wrist dipped under the weight of the weapon. The gun barrel dipped as well, and it didn't rise for several seconds.

Yeah. The braces weren't for show. There was something wrong with the woman's wrists. She might look like an Amazon, but she had a weakness.

"Arms in the air, Baddalach."

Jack raised his arms, and her left hand eased over chest and explored his lats.

It occurred to Jack that she was playing with him. Enjoying herself. He smiled at her. Shrugged. And she smiled back.

"Pretty good, Jack. Pretty firm. About a forty-four, huh?

At least when you've sucked a lungful of air and you're all flexed up."

Jack didn't say anything. Her hand drifted lower, to his waist, lingering just above his belt.

"Thirty-two," Jack said.

"In your dreams, Baddalach. Thirty-six, at least."

She was only touching him with one long finger now, and that finger dipped below his belt-line.

Jack took a deep breath and closed his eyes.

The woman laughed. Jack opened his eyes. In her free hand, the woman held his cellular phone.

"I guess you won't be needing this, Jack."

"C'mon." Jack reached for the phone, but she pulled away.

"Hey . . . you're wasting your time here," he said. "You should listen to me. I know what I'm talking about. You don't want this Chihuahua. The poor little fella's really sick."

The woman shook her head. The machine gun weaved a little in her right hand, the barrel dipping from Jack's belly to his knee.

Braces or no braces, the weight of the gun was getting to her. If he could catch her just right. She was about the same height, maybe just a hair taller. If he could knock the machine gun out of her hand by smacking her on the wrist, and then clip her on the jaw with his fist—

The cellular phone rang.

The woman in black looked at it, amused.

"You expecting a call, Jack?"

That question was the understatement of the century as far as Jack Baddalach was concerned, but he wasn't up to answering it at the present moment.

Jack was busy doing something else. As the woman in black's lips parted and she spoke the final word of her question, Jack chopped the heel of his left hand against her right wrist. Her hand opened reflexively and the machine gun toppled from her grip. The right hook Jack launched a split second later began at his waist, and by the time it connected with the woman's jaw it was traveling at a felonious velocity. She was biting off the last letter of that last word when the punch hit her, and her jaw snapped closed and the word came out shorter and much less sarcastically than she had intended. Her sunglasses flew off just as her eyes rolled up in her head, and she went down like a femme fatale Halloween costume dropped off a hanger, and she did not move.

The machine gun lay on her left. The phone on her right.

The phone rang again.

Jack snatched it up, reaching for the machine gun almost as an afterthought.

Gunfire stitched the air above his head.

The voice that followed was somehow more intimidating.

"Drop the gun, you miserable cocksucker."

Forty-five years worth of Marlboros, who the fuck cares how many packs, but certainly enough unfiltered cancer sticks to heap several ashtrays Mount Everest high. Cutty Sark on the side, shots consumed per night averaging in the low double digits. An upper denture plate that didn't quite fit no matter how much Poligrip she globbed over it. Vocal chords that had suffered the strain of a lifetime's worth of tantrums, cat fights, and other assorted trials and tribulations.

All those factors had combined to create the voice Jack Baddalach heard behind him, and that was why it was more intimidating than the sound of gunfire.

Jack dropped the machine gun and turned to face the voice's owner. She had come around from the back side of the gas station while Jack faced off with the woman in black. And in the time it took Jack to dance his little dance with the weak-wristed machine gunner, this woman had entered the limo and swept Angel Gemignani's Chihuahua into her hands.

Her hands were sheathed in black leather. So was the rest of her. In fact, she might have been a twin to her weak-wristed counterpart if not for three factors that Jack could not ignore.

First off, there was her voice.

Second, she was wearing a jacket over her bikini top. But the jacket was obviously mostly for show, because she wore it unzipped to her navel.

It was the view Jack spied through that unzipped opening which lead him to difference number three. And that was the simple fact that this woman was much older than the one Jack had punched out. While the younger woman's bikini top was fashioned from nothing but leather, this woman's top was equipped with subtle lengths of supportive wire. The top itself was without question a cantilevered wonder that worked an amazing magic with the woman's breasts. The breasts themselves were deeply tanned globes marred only by a fine dusting of wrinkles— the price often paid by lifelong sunbathers. And while some might remark that the woman's breasts looked like full round grapefruits kissed too long by the warm California sun, even the most jaded observer would be forced to admit that these twin wonders were forced up and out in a way that was in equal parts startling, amazing, and dramatic, and if the image of youth and vitality impressed upon the viewer was indeed an illusion—a mere result of engineering acumen—then, in Jack Baddalach's opinion, the device which provided said illusion was certainly worth every penny the woman had paid.

Jack looked at her face. Tanned skin taut on a skull blessed with a sharply dramatic bone structure, crowned with a bubble of heavily sprayed white hair that from a certain distance might be mistaken for a motorcycle helmet.

Of course, the sight of a little old lady in black leather wouldn't have slowed Jack down for an instant, no matter how amazing her breasts were. No. Not when he had a Chihuahua to protect. What slowed Jack down were the two women who bookended the woman with the cantilevered grapefruit breasts.

Both were redheads. Both held machine guns exactly like the one Jack had so recently possessed. And both were dressed in black leather as well. Together the three women comprised an outlaw gang that would warm the heart of any cattleman—a whole lot of bovine flesh had obviously been shed so they could look way past dangerous.

Three dangerous gringas, and one not-so-dangerous senorita in a horizontal position behind Jack. For a second he imagined the four of them not as a gang of criminals, but as a Phil Spector girl group driven to desperate measures.

Jack was about ready to toss up his hands and ask where the *Candid Camera* crew was hiding. In fact, he almost certainly would do just that, and do it soon. But first he had a bit of unfinished business to attend to.

Because the cellular phone in his hand was still ringing. Ringing insistently.

Jack raised his free hand, smiling at the women as if he finally got the joke.

"Don't do it, cocksucker," the old woman said, and she didn't sound at all like Alan Funt.

The two younger women pointed their weapons at him.

A chill traveled Jack's spine, the kind of chill he couldn't ignore. Still, his hand closed around the speaker panel. Flip it open and he'd know. He *had* to know.

"I've been waiting a long time for a phone call," Jack explained. "Almost a year. I think this might be it. I've got to find out."

The old woman barked laughter. "Answer that phone and you'll *never* find out anything, 'cause you'll be deader'n a paraplegic's dick before you so much as say howdy-do."

The phone rang again. Spike squirmed in the old woman's grasp, barking sharply, worried puppy eyes trained on Jack.

Jack hesitated. It was weird. Like being in some old Lassie movie or something, like the moment when Lassie warns Timmy just before the idiot falls down a mine shaft—

But Jack *had* to know. He *had* to answer the call.

Spike stared at him. No. That wasn't right. Not at him. *Behind* him.

Jack turned and came nose to nose with the woman in black, *sans* sunglasses.

Man, her eyes were something. A real surprise. Clear blue and—

"Don't just stand there!" the old woman yelled. "Take care of him!"

The young woman's irises flashed like chiseled ice as she smashed the butt of her machine gun against Jack's forehead.

He didn't hear the telephone anymore.

But he did hear bells . . .

. . . as if some crazy Quasimodo was ringing in the New Year up there in his head.

Jack knew it was an illusion. Just as he knew that he could get a grip on reality if he could only open his eyes.

Open his eyes and he'd see Freddy G laughing. Pack O' Weenies, too. And the Phil Spector girl group gang singing, backup band chugging to a "He's a Rebel" beat. *Oh, we had you going, Jack*, they'd sing. *We had you going, and good!*

Yeah. That was how it would be.

Jack tried mightily. His brain listed starboard as he got his right eye open, then to port as he raised the lid of his left.

They stood above him like some imposing female forest. Blurry as watercolors running in the bright sunlight that washed them from behind, but Jack could see them just as surely as he could smell all that black leather. Black leather scented with jasmine perfume.

He heard their voices. The younger woman spoke first, the one he'd punched out. Her voice was as smooth as leather and jasmine-sweet.

"I don't want him to suffer, Mama."

"If you would have done your job right, he'd be dead by now."

"But Mama—"

"Don't *Mama* me, girl."

"But—"

A hard slap ended the conversation. Defeated, the younger woman moved away. Another figure replaced her, this one taller . . . rangier. . . .

The stranger leaned over him. A male smell burned Jack's nostrils—the minty stink of Ben-Gay laced with the sickly sweet odor of ginger ale and bourbon.

The old woman's voice again: "Should I do him, Daddy?"

"Don't waste a bullet, sugar pop. I got a better idea."

The man hovered over Jack, wheezing heavy bourbon breaths. Jack worked to see him clearly. He blinked several times and a gaunt face covered with jerky skin came into focus above him. Icy blue eyes wild with frostbitten fire were set beneath the man's heavy brow as if pounded there with a sledge hammer. He wore a top hat and a frock coat and—

Jack's eyelids fluttered. Focus was going. He was fading again.

Something was draped around the man's neck.

Jack fought to remain conscious.

Something shiny encircled the man's neck. Something slick, ends hanging free, like lengths of garden hose—

Like—

The man reached out, shedding wriggling shadows, his scarecrow arms laying midnight stripes across Jack's body. And then the stranger's bony fingers reached into the heavens and closed around a black cloud, and he pulled it down . . . down . . . and further still . . . down . . . until finally the cloud slammed closed over Jack Badd-alach's head.

THREE

THE HEAT WAS THE FIRST THING JACK NOTICED WHEN HE REGAINED consciousness, only the word *heat* seemed too timid a description. Get your ass trussed up in a mummy bag on the hottest day of the year in the middle of Death Valley, and you wouldn't be one degree hotter than this.

Jack opened his eyes, but he couldn't see a thing. Wherever he was, it was completely dark. Completely quiet, too. He lay on his back, knees twisted to one side, right shoulder pressed against something hard. He moved his hands and feet, just a little, and was relieved to find that the dognappers hadn't tied him up.

Jack sucked a shallow breath and immediately wished he hadn't. The air was foul. A single breath made his gut churn miserably. Add to that the mother of all headaches, blooming at the spot where the woman in black had struck him with her machine gun.

Jack reached for his forehead to see if he was bleeding, but his hand struck something hard before his arm could make the trip.

Suddenly he didn't care about his head.

He reached out, palms pressing against smooth metal

barely a foot from his face. His fingers traveled the metal—down to knee level, up above his head—and found no breaks in the wall.

There were walls above and below, too. He was trapped. That was why he couldn't see anything. The women had locked him up.

Inside something.

Claustrophobia. Jack didn't want to even *think* the word.

Instead, he took a deep breath. He knew he needed air and—

He tasted it this time. Actually *tasted* the stink. It was like drinking sewer sludge. He gagged.

He'd hardly moved at all, and already he was covered in sweat. Damn, but it was as hot as Satan's backside. Jack's heart started pounding, a live thing roasting on a barbecue grill. He could almost hear the searing hiss of red hot metal.

He had to get a grip on things. Because if he didn't . . . if he didn't get a grip on himself—

But Jesus, how the hell was he supposed to feel? Maybe the crazy bitches had locked him in a metal box, dug a hole in the middle of the Mojave Desert—in the middle of fucking *nowhere*—and buried him *alive.*

Panic sank sharp hooks into Jack's spine. He pushed against the metal wall above him, then hauled back and rammed it with his elbow. Once. Twice. Three times. Harder, then harder still. Again and again, but the wall did not give.

Jack sank back, sweating like a pig, the imaginary mummy bag tighter now. His breaths came hard and fast, but that didn't bother him because suddenly he didn't notice the stink so much. He was scared and he was hungry for oxygen. No matter how rank it smelled. Whatever he could get he'd take.

He rested a moment.

And nothing changed.

He knew he couldn't rest at all. Not now. Rest, and the heat might drag him down to a place where he couldn't fight it anymore. The mummy bag would get tighter . . . and tighter . . . until there was nothing left for him to do but suffocate in silence.

He wouldn't do that. Wherever he was, he wanted *out*. Right *now*. He slammed his elbow against the metal wall again. Nothing. Pressed against it with his hands and knees until his spine ached. Still nothing.

Okay. He had to stop and think for a minute. Just a minute. He couldn't panic. If he was going to get out of this, he had to figure things out.

His hands drifted over the metal above. It was hot to the touch, like an electric stove notched on LOW HEAT. He slammed his elbow against it one last time, and not very hard. The wall made a flexing sound, a deeper sound than metal would make if dirt were piled on top of it.

If he'd been buried in the desert, metal might very well hold heat like an electric range, but it certainly wouldn't make a flexing sound. No. That fact meant something else.

But if he were locked in something black—say the trunk of a big black limousine—well, a black metal trunk would heat up real nice in the afternoon sun. Hell, if this were August instead of February, you'd probably be able to fry an egg on the sucker. And a trunk would make a flexing sound if you smashed at it like a wildman. Even the trunk of a Cadillac.

Yeah. It had to be. The women had locked him in the trunk of the limo.

Jack relaxed a little. Not much. Maybe a millimeter's worth. Okay. The trunk wouldn't give. And it was dark. He had to get the trunk open, because even if the air held out, he couldn't take the heat forever. Let alone that stink—

There had to be something in the trunk that he could use.
A jack maybe. Or a screwdriver. Yeah. With a screwdriver
he could jimmy the lock from the inside—

Sure he could.

First things first. Things would go much faster if he didn't
have to work in complete darkness. If he could find an
emergency kit, and if it held a flashlight—

Jack reached out, fingers groping blindly across heavy
carpet, until he found something plastic, shaped like—

A water bottle. He tipped it back and forth, and the liquid
slosh he heard was sweet. He twisted the top and drank
greedily.

Jack couldn't tell what he had, not in the dark. Evian or
Calistoga or Perrier. And he certainly wasn't up for any
blindfolded designer water taste test. No way. Jack Baddalach was strictly a tap-water kind of guy.

Jack capped the bottle and set it aside. For the first time
in his life he thanked God for yuppies. If he just kept his
cool he'd be okay. He reached out again, searching for the
emergency kit that *had* to be there.

Was there. He opened it and searched the small compartment—socket wrenches, a screwdriver, a flashlight . . .

With dead batteries. Okay. That wouldn't stop him. He
held the screwdriver in one hand, reaching out toward the
spot where the rear seal of the trunk should be with the other.

His fingers struck something moist and rubbery. Instinctively, he drew back, his mind playing a little riddle-me-
this-Batman game. What the hell would you find in a trunk
that felt like . . . well . . . *lukewarm Jell-O?*

There was only one way to find out. Jack reached out
again, two fingers pressing gingerly against the rubbery
thing, two fingers exploring it carefully.

The thing was slick, and there was a hard casing around
the rubbery part that was also slick . . . *okay, Jack, you've*

found a hole rimmed with something hard . . . and then below that hole was another hole, but this one was more like a slash, a rip in the rubbery surface, and just inside the rip were two hard, curving ridges . . . two rows of—

Two rows of human teeth.

Shock shotgunned Jack's consciousness. He yanked his fingers out of the corpse's mouth and squirmed away, giving in to panic, slamming his elbows and knees against the trunk lid once more, sucking deep lungfuls of fetid air, finally huddling against the rear of the trunk at the place where it joined with the backseat of the limo's passenger compartment.

Jesus . . . Jesus! He was locked in a trunk with a fucking human corpse!

Maybe it was Pack O' Weenies. Yeah. The limo driver, with a hole in his head courtesy of a machine gun-toting gang of Ronettes wanna-bes. Pack O' Weenies, with his mouth welded into a death grimace by rigor mortis, and Jack Baddalach's fingers had almost been on the motherfucker's dead swollen *tongue*—

Oh, man. This was too much. But Jack wouldn't think about it. He couldn't. Because it didn't matter. Not now. What mattered right now was getting to hell and gone out of this trunk.

He clutched the screwdriver in his right hand, afraid of losing it in the darkness. As he shifted onto his side, something rounded and long dug into his ribs. Jack raised up on one elbow and pulled that something free.

It was an emergency flare. In a second he'd have light, and then he'd crawl over Pack O' Weenies dead fucking carcass, and he'd pop the trunk with the screwdriver, and he'd get down on his hands and knees and give the dusty Mojave Desert a big sloppy kiss.

Jack struck the flare.

It sizzled alive, hissing white fire.

The corpse's face was washed in the sickly glow, a twitching mask of shadow and light that would have frightened Stephen King.

It wasn't Pack O' Weenies. The face belonged to a young blond woman dressed in a smartly tailored tuxedo. A bullet hole drilled the spot where her left eye should have been, and Jack knew instantly that he'd touched that spot, just as he knew he'd touched the woman's open mouth, passed his fingers between those full lips that were smeared with lipstick and touched her teeth—

A inescapable wave of horror washed over Jack. Forget wave—this was a fucking tsunami. God, he would have crawled into that suffocating mummy bag right now if only he could have. Crawled into that sucker and zipped it tight over his head. Anything to escape the horror that lay before him.

But he wouldn't do that. No. A minute ago he was ready to crawl over Pack O' Weenies' corpse to be free of the trunk. And now he would crawl over this woman. Dead was dead, after all. And nothing dead would stop Jack Baddalach.

Jack exhaled sharply—a low, rushing sound. But the sound didn't end when he took another breath, it only grew louder in Jack's head, bringing with it a memory, the memory of a man who pulled fistfuls of black clouds from the sky as he locked Jack in the limo trunk, a tall man dressed in a frock coat and a top hat, a man who wore lengths of garden hose around his neck.

No. Not lengths of hose. Seeing the snake curled around the woman's throat with its head nestled in her long blond hair, Jack knew that the things the man wore around his neck were a long way from lengths of garden hose.

The snake drew back, away from the hissing flare, retreating, its head pressing against the hollow of the woman's chin.

And then came another sound, a sound that told Jack he'd made another mistake, a sound that told him the snake wasn't retreating at all—a sharp, angry rattling that played unrelenting counterpoint to the hot hissing of the emergency flare.

Jack pulled the flare away. The rattlesnake slithered forward, its head pressing between the dead blond's small breasts.

Not that the blond seemed to mind. She stared at Jack with that one murky hazel eye, the one that hadn't been shot out of her head, the one that was both unblinking and dead. Her mouth was open and her lipstick was smeared as if from a kiss. She didn't blink, and she didn't move, not even with a rattler coiling around her slim and elegant neck like some hideous living necklace—

You won't have it bad, Jack, she seemed to say. *Just a couple of fangs pricking your skin. Just a little poison pumping through your veins. Not like facing down a gun . . . not like watching a long black barrel spit fire inches from your face . . . not like feeling a couple of ounces of lead blow your eyeball through the back of your skull.*

Cold scales whispered over the woman's silk blouse. The snake began to coil near the corpse's belly. In just a few seconds its rattles would be free of the woman's neck.

Jack coughed. The flare was burning, sure, but it was smoking too, filling the trunk with fumes that burned his lungs and stung his eyes.

Maybe Jack could burn the rattler with the flare. But if he missed. And if the snake didn't. If the reptile sank its fangs into his flesh. He was in the middle of nowhere. Even if he got out of the trunk, he might not get help in time. He didn't know anything about the killing efficacy of rattlesnake venom, and he sure as hell didn't want to find out.

The snake's rattles beat hollowly against the woman's trachea, then slipped free.

Jack dropped the flare, and a shadow curtained the corpse's face, and she seemed to smile, whispering, *Not a bad place to die, Jack. I'm here. At least you won't be alone.*

Fuck no. Jack twisted away from the corpse and the coiling rattler, thinking now of the skinny bastard in the frock coat and the top hat, gas from the flare burning his lungs as he pulled at the rug that covered the trunk compartment, eyes watching the rattler all the while as he tore the carpet free of its Velcro moorings like he was tearing into that jerky-faced man who'd left him locked in a trunk with a corpse and a rattlesnake, crawling under the carpet when it finally came free, putting it between his body and the rattler and he could hear the flare hissing like a whisper as the carpet caught fire, or maybe it was just the woman's corpse inviting him to relax, to stay with her, or maybe it was the hissing sound of the rattler as it sprang . . .

. . . its fanged head sailing over the thick carpet . . .

. . . just missing Jack as it struck the metal fire wall that separated the rear compartment of the limo from the trunk . . .

. . . striking hard, dazed, scales slapping against the metal floor as it fell next to Jack, stunned, slowed, but still a creature of instinct, coiling again . . .

. . . until one strong human hand closed around its throat and silenced its hiss, and another gripped its rattles, and it spit fitfully as its coiled body was pulled to its full length . . . and its scaled belly was ripped open as human teeth tore it in half and then it was nothing . . .

. . . it was dead.

• • •

"Goddamn," Jack said. *"Goddamn."*

The carpet blazed in the trunk. He'd escaped just in time. He beat back the flames with his leather coat, then doused them with the seltzer bottle from the limo's wet bar.

The snake was well done. The woman's corpse was blackened but definitely rare. Jack threw the former into the desert and closed the trunk on the latter.

He put some distance between himself and the limousine. The hot desert wind blew at his back, strong and clean. Cars rushed by on the highway, passengers oblivious, their minds blissfully free from speculative exercises involving kidnapped Chihuahuas, women with machine guns, men with top hats, and rattlesnakes.

Jack wiped rattler blood from his mouth as he walked to the rear of the gas station. There was no sign of Pack O' Weenies. As he returned to the limo, Jack wondered what had happened to the driver.

Pack's fate wasn't important at the moment. Getting to Vegas was. Jack had to explain things to Freddy G.

He was behind the wheel, ready to key the ignition, when he heard his cellular phone ringing.

The dognappers had left it behind.

Jack followed the ringing sound—by now it was surprisingly familiar—and found the phone in a tangle of brush. *C'mon, Kate,* he thought as he picked it up. *I've waited damn near a year. Don't let me down now. Not today. Not after all this corpses 'n' reptiles shit.*

If it's you, I'll take all this shit in stride.

If it's you, I'll forget every damn bit of it.

Jack answered the phone.

Angel Gemignani said, "Where's my goddamn dog?"

PART TWO

Daddy Was A Preacher But Mama Was A Go-Go Girl

And in that town a dog was found,
As many dogs there be,
Both mongrel, puppy, whelp, and
hound,
And curs of low degree.

> —OLIVER GOLDSMITH
> THE VICAR OF WAKEFIELD.
> ™CHAPTER 17, AN ELEGY ON
> the DEATH OF A MAD DOG,
> STANZA 4∫

ONE

Gemignani in the big penthouse office high atop the Casbah
Hotel & Casino, but it was Freddy who held Jack's
attention.

The casino boss furiously crunched a stalk of celery that
wore a sheen of Snap-E-Tom tomato cocktail and vodka, all
that remained of the third Bloody Mary he'd mixed since
Jack walked through the big double doors of the suite of
rooms overlooking the Las Vegas Strip.

"The woman in the trunk was our driver," Freddy said
between bites. "Kitty Crocetti, from Chicago. Jimmy Two-
Nose Crocetti's niece. Christ on a cross, Jack. First someone
does her point blank with a hand cannon, then you set her on
fire with an emergency flare, and now I gotta ship her ass
home in a box. Jimmy Two-Nose is gonna be pissed."

Jack wanted to ask how a guy got a nickname like Jimmy
Two-Nose, but he knew that this was not the time to play
name-that-gangster. Freddy G had been grilling him for
almost an hour, his cohorts watching the action without a
word.

It was plain that Freddy wasn't happy. Neither were his

companions. Their expressions grew sterner in direct pro-
portion with the level of Freddy's unhappiness. Jack
couldn't blame them. As employees of the last old-guard
casino owner on the Vegas Strip, they knew all too well that
an unhappy Freddy Gemignani was a dangerous thing.

When Freddy G became unhappy, somebody usually
ended up taking a dirt nap in a remote corner of the Mojave
Desert. Jack Baddalach did not want to be that somebody.
He looked at the other men in the room and was distressed
to find that none of them would make eye contact. Most
likely they figured there was no use getting attached to a
man who might very soon be sleeping with the prairie dogs.
That's how bad Jack's story was playing out.

Jack massaged the knotted bruise high on his forehead.
Right now he could have done quite nicely without it, but it
was too late to tell that to the woman who'd slugged him
with the butt of her machine gun. If he wanted to keep on
sucking air he'd better start playing detective, and start
playing good. But he had to have a place to start.

Not with the kidnapped Chihuahua. Obviously. And not
with the bullet-ridden, toasted Mafia princess.

"So the driver was a plant," he said, because he had to
start somewhere. "He was working with the dognappers."

Gemignani cringed at the very mention of the last word.
"Yeah. Must be. Most likely he's the one popped a cap on
Miss Kitty, then took her place." Freddy shook his head.
"Christ on a cross. Poor little girl got her head blown off
over a Chihuahua. Thank God it wasn't my grandbaby in
that limo. This crew we're dealing with must be nuts."

"Yeah."

Freddy made himself another Bloody Mary. "Now about
this driver. Let's talk about him. What was he like?"

"Well, the guy seemed a little squirrely. He talked an
awful lot. Told me all kinds of things about himself. Too

many things. Especially for a guy who was a plant. That's the only thing that makes me wonder how he fits into the deal."

"He probably fed you a bunch of bullshit, Jack. Wanted to get you to drop your guard. Make sure you wouldn't suspect him until it was too late."

"Yeah. Could be. But maybe not. Maybe the stuff he told me was true. Maybe he figured I was a dead man, and it didn't matter what he said."

"Slow down, Jack. First things first. Let's start off with the basics." Freddy nodded at one of the other men—a thin guy with a big bunch of stencils and some kind of sketch pad. "Guido here is an artist. Used to work for Vegas PD. Now he works for me. He's gonna ask you some questions about the driver and his gang, then come up with some pictures that we can use to track 'em down."

Jack nodded. Freddy came around the desk. He looked Jack dead in the eye—Jack looking up, Freddy looking down.

Jack got the funny feeling his boss was looking for something specific. A sign of some sort.

The casino owner didn't blink. After a moment he turned away and headed for the doors with his Bloody Mary in hand and the three other wise-guys in tow.

Freddy said, "Do your best, Jack."

The double doors swung open. As they started to close Jack heard the casino owner take a big bite out of a fresh celery stalk, and then all that was left of Freddy was his shadow, a heavy blotch on the white carpet.

The door slammed closed.

Freddy's shadow was gone.

Guido passed a stack of stencils to Jack, who shuffled through them intently.

Every stencil held a different nose. Noses that resembled potatoes or yams or bananas. Roman noses. Hooked beaks. Gnarled W. C. Fields specials, Michael Jackson chop jobs, Dick Nixon ski jumps.

Jack thumbed through the samples, trying to remember the limo driver. The thing he'd mistaken for a sketch pad lay before him on Freddy G's big mahogany desk. It was the kind of pad used by police artists, and the only thing it held was an empty head, round and bald. That part had been easy to remember. But it was Jack's job to fill in the rest of it, and right now he couldn't seem to remember—

Guido coaxed him along. "Just take your time, Jack."

Jack sighed. "I'm having kind of a hard time with this. I mostly only saw the guy from the back."

"Okay. But you must remember something about him. Maybe his eyes. Maybe you saw them in the rearview mirror. Or his mouth." Guido patted Jack on the shoulder. "Try closing your eyes and picturing him. Sometimes that helps."

Jack closed his eyes, trying to remember the driver. The guy's voice was in his head, right there, telling that goofy story about his ex-wife's anaconda tattoo, and Jack concentrated on the voice, reaching out . . . and he felt that he was getting closer . . . closer.

"One thing I remember—"

"Yes? His eyes? His nose?"

"His neck," Jack said. "I remember the guy's neck. The back of it, anyway. He was heavyset, lots of folds on his neck. You know what I mean?"

"I think so. But I'm not sure where this will get us—"

"His neck. You understand what I'm saying? It looked like a pack of weenies."

Jack opened his eyes. Guido stared at him, suddenly as

expressionless as Freddy G had been during the interrogation. Then Guido looked down at his stencils.

"Does that help any?" Jack asked.

"I've got to be honest with you," Guido said, looking over the noses and lips and eyes. "I've got a lot of stuff here. But I don't have any weenies."

Jack didn't like the way Guido took his leave. Stalked off was more like it—the artist tucked the pad with the empty bald head under his arm and went through the big polished doors muttering about packs of weenies. His last words to Jack were: "I think maybe we'd have had some luck if I'd brought along a Mr. Potatohead."

And the hell of it was that Guido was right. Really. Because Pack O' Weenies *did* have a head kind of like Mr. Potatohead's. It was the God's honest truth. Only Pack O' Weenies was white, not Idaho spud brown.

Describing the dognappers hadn't gone any better. Jack did okay with the first woman, the one he'd punched out. He remembered those lace-covered wrist braces she wore, and he remembered her sunglasses and those determined lips that were the color of blood oranges. But when it came to remembering the other women—in particular the older one he'd begun to think of as "Grandma"—well, that was tougher. He did okay with Grandma's white snow-cone helmet of hair, but when he started describing her wizened grapefruit-sized breasts and that cantilevered S & M black leather brassiere, Guido threw up his hands and made some crack about bringing in a comic book artist.

That was when Jack gave up on the whole thing. He sure wasn't going to mention the old guy with the beef jerky face and the top hat, let alone the fact that the guy wore a rattlesnake for a necktie.

Man, it was really something. The only face he remembered really well belonged to the dead limo driver. The poor kid. Jack didn't think he'd ever forget her. Staring at him with that one hazel eye, a scarlet hole blasted where her other eye should have been . . .

Jack went over to Freddy G's bar, opened the fridge, and grabbed himself a beer. He didn't open it. He sat down on a plush leather sofa that ran the length of the window facing the Strip. He ran the cold bottle back and forth across the knuckles of one hand, then the other, watching an animatronic British frigate do battle with a pirate ship at the casino across the street.

A little less than a year ago he sat on this sofa, listening to Freddy rave about two million in mob money that had disappeared along with a mob courier somewhere between Las Vegas and Dallas. Freddy had asked Jack to find that money. And Jack had found it. He'd had some help from Kate Benteen, but he'd brought Freddy's money back all by his lonesome.

Freddy was impressed. Sure. Anyone would be. He'd used Jack a couple of times since then, when he needed a guy he could count on. Used him in "situations," which was Freddy double-speak for trouble.

But "situations" didn't come along every day, even in Vegas. Freddy liked having Jack around. Jack liked being around. He didn't sweat the little stuff.

Not usually, anyway.

But this last thing. This Chihuahua thing. It had grated on him. Just that Freddy would ask him to do something like that hurt. Like he was an errand boy. Sure, Freddy's granddaughter was involved, and maybe it was just that Freddy didn't want to send some tacky little half-a-mozzarella to his daughter's house in Palm Springs, some gumbah he couldn't trust around a young thing like his granddaughter, but still—

Jack shook his head. That last part was a laugh, anyway. After all, Jack Baddalach was the guy who had started the day with his tongue in Angel Gemignani's mouth. He didn't figure that particular performance met anyone's definition of "trustworthy," especially not Freddy Gemignani's.

But Freddy had sent him after a Chihuahua, for Christsakes. And Jack Baddalach was the former light-heavyweight champion of the world. And you just didn't send the former light-heavyweight champion of the world after somebody's dog. Not even if that somebody was your granddaughter.

You didn't send a champ after a mutt.

Jack shook his head. No. You wanted that mutt to come through in one piece, you had to send someone a lot smarter than a champ. You had to send someone who knew how to do something besides get hit in the face, because a champ would fuck things up. He'd get strung along by a guy with a pack of weenies for a neck, and he'd roll over for a bunch of leather girls with machine guns, and he'd end up locked in a limo trunk with a pissed-off rattlesnake and a dead Mafioso-ette.

Jack's foolish pride had its ass down on the canvas. He counted ten over it. If he wanted to make things right with Freddy G, he'd better straighten up.

If it wasn't already too late for that.

Jack rolled the cold beer bottle back and forth across his aching knuckles. Across the Strip, the frigate's cannons spit blinding gouts of flame. Then the pirate ship returned fire, and very shortly great belches of fire and smoke poured from the frigate's belly.

The frigate began to sink. Jack watched it disappear into the concrete deep, the British captain standing proudly on the deck, going down with his ship.

• • •

Freddy's hand closed over Jack's shoulder, and the former light-heavyweight champion nearly jumped out of his skin.

The casino boss sat next to Jack on the sofa. "You're in the clear, champ. None of the boys think you had anything to do with it."

"Okay," Jack said. "But I don't really care what those bastards think. I care what you think, Freddy."

"C'mon, Jack. You and me go back a ways. I've known you since you came out of the amateurs. Most of your title fights were right here at the Casbah. I never figured you'd go dog on me."

"Good. I just want to know where I stand, is all."

"Now you know."

"So what's next?"

"We wait for a ransom note or a phone call. We wait to find out what some crazyass dognapping crew figures a Chihuahua is worth to the mob." Freddy threw up his hands. "Christ on a cross. This business. Sometimes it drives me nuts. Sometimes it makes me wish I could call in the fucking cops."

"Look," Jack said. "I know I messed up—"

Freddy's harsh laughter cut him off. "Yeah. You really screwed the pooch on this one, Jack. Or maybe I should say you wished you'd screwed the pooch. That would have been better than letting the little fucker get dognapped. You should see my Angel. Oh, man, is she pissed. She takes after her grandma, that one. Only difference is her grandma carried a razor."

"As the French say, vive la différence."

"Viva shit, Jack. Angel carries a gun."

The beer was getting warm in Jack's hands. He realized that he was sweating. "What I'm saying is that there has to be a way to track these idiots. The cops do it all the time. So can we." Jack stood up and paced in front of the big window. "Now, it's pretty obvious these guys knew what was going on. I mean, the whole thing was a complete setup. That means they know something about you—"

"Or about Angel."

"Right. Now, if we can figure out how they set up the snatch—"

Freddy G waved Jack off. "We're way ahead of you, champ. My boys are on it. We're checking out the limo right now. The limo company, too. If the driver left a trail, we're gonna find it."

"Like I said before, the driver talked a lot. He told me about a stretch he did for murdering a guy. In California, I think. There's got to be a way we can trace him."

"Don't sweat it." Freddy was up now, patting Jack on the shoulder again, turning the boxer toward the double doors. "I've already got a guy on it. He's a sharp one. Could find Jimmy Hoffa if he had to. He'll probably phone you tonight. You give him the whole story. It's probably bullshit, but it can't hurt."

"Okay." Jack talked fast as they headed toward the doors. "But what can I do in the meantime?"

"Just take your ease, champ." Freddy walked Jack down a corridor, heels clicking over Carrara marble. "Just take your ease."

The casino owner punched the elevator button. The door opened instantly. Jack didn't need Freddy to draw a diagram for him. He stepped inside.

"One thing you can tell me, champ. That rattlesnake. The one that was locked in the trunk with you and Jimmy Two-Nose's dead niece."

"What about it?"

"Did you really bite the damn thing in half?"

"Yeah." Jack pressed "L" for lobby, and the elevator

doors started to close. "And it's true what they say about snakes."

"What's that?"

"The sonofabitches *do* taste just like chicken."

TWO

SPOILED PALM SPRINGS PUNKERS, ARMED AND DANGEROUS DOGNAP-pers cinched in black leather dominatrix gear, rattlesnakes and corpses and irate Mafioso to spare—it didn't matter how much shit Jack Baddalach went through in one day; none of it was as frightening as the prospect of facing a hungry geriatric bulldog.

Jack dumped thirty cans of dog food into his shopping cart. The brand that was recommended by world-renowned pooch breeders. The brand that contained no fillers or harmful additives. The expensive brand.

It didn't seem like he'd be scamming many free meals at the Casbah in the very near future, so he figured he might as well do some shopping for himself while he was at it. He heaped the cart with six boxes of ready-to-heat frozen White Castle hamburgers, three boxes of cherry-flavored Pop Tarts, a couple cases of Diet 7Up (because at heart Jack Baddalach was a rebellious uncola kind of guy), two six packs of the one decent beer that was on special, three huge bags of prepopped popcorn (no palm oil!) that reminded him of the stale stuff upon which he'd gorged as a

movie-going youth, and a couple pounds of coffee beans
that were blacker than sin.

A couple weeks' shopping, done in less than ten minutes.

Four squeaky wheels bore his cart to the check stand,
where he topped off his selections with a *Weekly World
News*. He could have resisted the story about the Nazi
U-boat captain who ruled Atlantis and the one about the
sasquatch recruited by the NBA, but there was a new Bat
Boy story—"Half-Bat, Half-Boy Eludes Air Force Radar
Team!" Jack couldn't pass that up.

He paid for the groceries and the tabloid, skinning several
twenties from his wallet. It had been a bad day. Spending a
fortune on groceries didn't improve things. Neither did the
song spilling from the in-store stereo system.

"Honey" by Bobby Goldsboro.

Jack snatched his change from the checker and exited the
market posthaste, Bobby's trembling vibrato relentlessly
trailing him until the automatic doors shushed closed at his
heels.

Jack opened the trunk of his battered '76 Toyota Celica
and tossed the grocery bags inside. He didn't need to pay a
fistful of twenties for the privilege of hearing a maudlin love
song, and he sure as hell wasn't going to start thinking about
Kate Benteen as a result. He'd suffered enough for one day,
thank you very much.

Jack climbed into the Toyota, keyed the engine, and
turned on the radio.

Ricky Nelson sang "Poor Little Fool."

Jack changed the station. Righteous Brothers. "(You've
Lost That) Lovin' Feeling." He changed it again and heard
Little Anthony goin' out of his head. Changed it one last
time, only to find Sinatra "Learnin' the Blues."

That was it.

Jack punched a cassette into the tape deck and zooma-

zoomaed into the night to the sound of Louis Prima's
blissfully unromantic wail.

About a year ago, the Celica was about two tanks of
unleaded short of the junkyard. Then Jack put some of the
money he earned from the Pipeline Beach job into the car.
Some semi-serious change, but the mechanic had done a
great job. Jack hadn't had a lick of trouble with the Toy
since.

He figured that the Celica was destined to be a classic—
the Mustang of the seventies. He was sure car collectors
would see the light one of these days, and when that
happened he'd score big bucks for the car he'd bought new
in 1976. Then again, Jack was a man who in his time had
predicted a bright future for 8-track players, Sony Be-
tamaxes, and Apple computers.

The only thing the Toyota lacked was some bodywork.
Root beer foam brown in color, its smooth features were
blemished by several dented rust spots that glowed like
pools of dark Jamaican rum when the neon lights of Vegas
shone just right. Jack liked the idea of pools of rum,
especially under a neon glow. He also liked the idea that the
Celica was a little dinged up, because he was a little dinged
up, too. So the bumps and bruises would stay until he
decided to sell the Toy.

He pulled into his parking space behind the Agua
Caliente condominium complex. Agua Caliente was Span-
ish for "hot water." Apart from the fact that every condo in
the complex was indeed supplied with hot water, Jack had
never uncovered another explanation for the name apart
from the fact that real estate developers liked the way those
south of the border phrases sounded almost as much as they
liked undocumented workers.

The swimming pool looked inviting as he passed by.

Empty, peaceful, illuminated with cool blue light. While he walked, Jack's evening became clear in his mind. He'd feed the dog, have a couple White Castles while he read about the Bat Boy's latest escapades, and then he'd blow up his air mattress and float away his troubles on a chlorinated sea.

It seemed like the perfect idea, so perfect that he made a deal with himself—tonight he'd forget everything. The kidnapped Chihuahua. Angel Gemignani. Freddy G and his wise guy minions.

Everything. Even Kate Benteen.

The path to Jack's condo was lined with tiki torches that flickered pleasantly in the evening light. He turned the last sharp corner of the walkway, ready to set down the grocery bags and dig into his jeans pocket for his keys.

He saw that he wouldn't need them.

The door to his condo was already open.

Jack Baddalach owned a gun—a Colt Python that he'd bought after his first job for Freddy G. He'd come up short in the shooting department during that bad bit of business down in Pipeline Beach, Arizona, and he had the scar tissue on his left forearm to prove it.

Jack was pretty good with the Python. He belonged to a shooting range and everything. But the pistol was in his condo, so it didn't do him a hell of a lot of good at the moment.

Still, he wasn't going to turn tail. He'd fucked up enough for one day. Maybe this would be his chance to set things right.

Jack set the grocery bags to one side of the door and entered the condo. Inside it was dark, and quiet. He stopped in the hallway, listening, his hands balled into fists, waiting for his eyes to adjust to the darkness.

The venetian blinds were open in the living room. Slashes of ash-colored light painted the carpet and furniture. Jack scanned the room, searching for any sign of movement. He listened for the slightest sound.

Nothing.

Then he saw it. Underneath the coffee table. Something stirred.

Something that panted, then whined.

Jack flicked on the light switch.

The string of tiki lights that rimmed the ceiling glowed yellow and green and white and red, illuminating a condo decorated in thrift store chic.

From beneath the coffee table, Jack's geriatric bulldog stared up at him.

"I know," Jack said. "We had company."

The bulldog's name was Frankenstein, and Frankenstein had had a rough time of it until he fell in with Jack Baddalach. The dog had the scars to show for it. But just like the dings on Jack's Celica, the scars gave Frankenstein a strong connection to his master. Occasionally, Jack was tempted to get all misty-eyed about it, scratch Frankie behind one battered ear and say, *Like father, like son.*

Jack unfastened Frankenstein's leash from its collar and then untied the leash from the coffee table leg. Whoever had broken into his place had taken care that the dog wouldn't wander out through the open door. America really was a kinder, gentler place these days. Even the crooks were courteous.

The culprit hadn't trashed Jack's place, either. His light-heavyweight championship belt still hung on one wall, bookended on each side by the boxing gloves he'd worn in his first and last pro fights. The bar that separated the kitchen from the living room hadn't been disturbed; the Sneaky Tiki glassware that had served up Singapore Slings and Relaxers at Harvey's Tahoe back in the fifties stood waiting and ready. The drawers to Jack's desk were closed and the desktop seemed undisturbed—the photo of Kate Benteen he'd clipped from an old issue of *Vanity Fair* stood in a silver frame, Kate appearing to look down her nose at a stack of old suspense paperbacks Jack had sifted through before choosing the Dan J. Marlowe book for his Palm Springs trip. The television, VCR, and stereo hadn't been touched, either, and a cursory glance at his record collection assured Jack that his Dean Martin records were still in alphabetical order by title.

If the burglars had left Dino alone, they probably hadn't messed with anyone else. Jack was about ready to check out the bedroom when he spotted the folded note propped near his telephone. He picked it up and unfolded it. The note was computer generated, and it had a handwritten postscript, and enclosed with it was a five-dollar bill:

DOG LOVERS: 1/2 MILLION GETS YOUR GUINEA POOCH BACK. NON-NEGOTIABLE. WE WILL MAKE CONTACT TOMORROW NIGHT. TRY ANYTHING FUNNY B4 THEN AND IT'S SPAGHETTI & CHIHUAHUA MEATBALLS TIME.

YOUR FRIENDS

P.S. The dead pug's dog is hungry. No dog food in kitchen. Enclosed find $. Get something good & don't eat it all yourself, Mr. Gemignani.

Jack held the five-dollar bill in his hands and stared at it until Abraham Lincoln's self-assured expression really started to piss him off.

He planted the dead president in the center of the page and refolded the note. Jack's heart was pounding like he was in the ring again, ready to go to war, listening to the referee give the final instructions before the bell sounded for round one. He was that hyped up. Because it didn't take a straw to break this camel's back. What it took was a five-dollar bill.

Okay. He'd have to call Freddy, give him the note. And then he'd have to figure out why the dognappers had delivered it to him.

Simple explanation—they thought that Jack was dead. Sure. So they delivered the note to his place instead of the Casbah. Because with Jack dead, his condo would be empty. They wouldn't have to risk being caught on videotape by a security camera. They could phone Freddy when they were ready. He'd get the note. And he'd know that this crew had done their homework, right down to casing his favorite gofer.

Jack thought it over. Maybe one of the neighbors had seen someone snooping around. He could do a little door knocking, check that out. His next-door neighbor was a retired keno runner who was deaf as a post, but maybe she'd seen something. If Jack was lucky, maybe he'd get a quick lead and—

Frankenstein rubbed against Jack's ankle. Then the dog sauntered into the kitchen, nudged his empty bowl, and looked at Jack.

"Okay," Jack said. "Not that you deserve it, because you're no kind of watchdog."

He went back to the front door and got the grocery bags. Shit. The other bags were still in the Toy, and it was a hot night. His White Castle Hamburgers were probably thawed and mushy by now.

Well, if they were wrecked, they were wrecked. He'd get them in a minute. He cradled the bag and gave the front door a shove with his foot, but it didn't close all the way. Didn't matter. He'd have to check the lock. The jamb, too. Make sure the dognappers hadn't broken them.

He opened a can of dog food and scooped half of it into Frankenstein's bowl. He might as well have scooped it directly into Frankie's mouth, the way the dog went after it.

Jack's stomach rumbled. Man. He was hungry too. He hadn't had a thing since breakfast. He'd get those White Castles from the Toy, nuke a couple in the microwave and—

The set of Sneaky Tiki glasses exploded behind him, and blue shrapnel slapped his backside.

Jack whirled.

Two guys holding Louisville Sluggers stood in his living room.

And Angel Gemignani stood between them.

THREE

JACK STARED AT THE TWO GUYS WITH THE BALL BATS. FOR THE first time in his life, he knew just what a piñata felt like.

Angel smiled. Even with a couple of troll escorts, she looked damn good. She was still wearing the Sweet Cherry Love tee she'd worn that morning in Palm Springs, along with torn black jeans, Doc Martens, and Calvin Klein's Obsession.

She's a rebel, Jack thought. A punker with a gold card.

Under other circumstances, the perfume might have brightened up Jack's place. It had been a long time since he'd had a woman around. But all too soon the sweet aroma was eclipsed by the stink of beer and marijuana and fatboy sweat that accompanied her companions.

It wasn't hard to figure out where Angel had picked them up. The barroom shine in her eyes gave that away. No beer and dope for her, though. Uh-uh. Jack was sure Angel Gemignani wasn't a beer-and-a-joint kind of woman. She'd sip Sweet Cherry Love drinks—a pink lady, or maybe a cosmopolitan.

Jack wondered if Angel had ever had a mai tai served in a vintage Sneaky Tiki glass. He knew it was a completely inappropriate concern at the moment. But Angel's sparkling green eyes were way past alluring, and he couldn't help wondering.

Jack held tight to the open can of dog food. "You're not thinking straight, Angel."

"Sure I am. I'm thinking that you're a smartass. And that's okay, because I kind of like smartasses. I'm a smartass myself. But I'm thinking that you're also a chickenshit, and I don't like chickenshits."

"Look, I'm really sorry about your dog. I feel pretty awful about the whole thing. But it was a setup. The people who snatched Spike knew that I was coming. They had guns. They locked me up with a rattlesnake, for Christ-sakes—"

"A setup." She nodded. "Sure. And how do I know you weren't in on it?"

"You've just got to trust me on that one, Angel."

"Trust you." She laughed, sharp and hard and bitter. "I don't trust guys who fuck up. I learned that from my granddaddy. You know what he always says about guys who fuck up."

"Yeah: *He who fucks up gets fucked up.*"

"It's a simple rule, Jack."

Jack nodded. "And you just broke it."

The two guys had to be twin brothers. They were both huge bordering on humongous, and they had the kind of faces that would definitely keep them from making it through airport metal detectors on the first trip.

Which meant they were definite pierce-aholics. They'd gone the whole twin route with that particular obsession, too. Identical earrings looped through their earlobes, bejeweled studs dotting the harder cartilage tissue above. Their bristling Neanderthal eyebrows were set off by a startling array of dainty silver loops. They wore nose studs, and an obligatory rod pierced the pouting hollow beneath their lower lips.

Jack figured he'd see identical tongue studs as soon as the twins opened their mouths. The only way he could tell them apart was by their rock 'n' roll T-shirts. Your basic black Gen X-wear, oversized and overpriced, featuring the darlings of sludge lovers everywhere—Mudhoney on the left, and Garbage on the right.

Jack stood up, still holding the can of dog food. "You boys are making a big mistake. This is your chance to back out."

Mudhoney smiled like a jack-o'-lantern, full and yellow, his only answer the percussive beat of a tongue stud against his front teeth.

Jack thought, *Surprise, surprise*.

"Last warning," he said. "I used to be the light-heavyweight champion of the world."

Mudhoney laughed. "We seen you get knocked out. And by a nigger, too."

"We had money on your white ass," Garbage said. "You let down your race, man."

"Yeah. We got us a score of our own to settle with you."

Mudhoney stepped into the kitchen, Garbage backing him up. Jack angled in front of Frankenstein, who had wedged his cowardly ass in the corner where the refrigerator met the wall. There wasn't much room between Mudhoney and Jack. Maybe five feet. Not enough room to throw the can of dog food Jack held in his hand. But throwing it wouldn't do any good anyway—these two behemoths weighed two-fifty a piece at least. A can of dog food wasn't going to slow them down. Unless—

Jack lashed out with the can, open end aimed at the two men. One sharp sucking sound, and a slick gob of Meaty

Treaty flew across the room and splattered Mudhoney from his yellow smile to his eyes.

He dropped his bat and fell back a step, wiping his eyes and blinking furiously.

"You shithouse rat!" Garbage started forward, his bat cocked over his right shoulder. "You're *dead*."

The kitchen was tiny. In cramped quarters, a baseball bat was hardly an ideal weapon. Garbage had maybe one swing. If Jack could elude the punker's first strike, then he could get his licks in.

Garbage grunted. Batter up.

Jack took a quick step forward, careful to keep Franken-stein behind him, then backed off just as fast, hoping to draw Garbage off balance.

But Garbage followed the move beautifully. Jack saw that right away.

The bat rushed toward his head. He watched it come . . .

. . . and heard Garbage's Doc Martens squeal across the linoleum as the punker slipped on the same lump of dog food that had struck Mudhoney in the face.

Garbage went down hard. Jack grinned at the moron. He'd dropped his bat. In a second Jack would have it and then he'd take care of business.

Jack reached for the bat and ran into Mudhoney's knee, which slammed him against the refrigerator. The big punker laid into him before he could recover, fists banging Jack's belly, a dog food–slathered smile on his ugly face, little bits of brown gelatin clinging to the silver rings pinned to his eyebrows.

Jack grabbed a handful of rings and pulled. Mudhoney's scream tore the air like an Axl Rose guitar solo—long and loud, covering several octaves. He stumbled back and Jack followed him, eager to get hold of Mudhoney's bat and finish things.

Jack got the bat, but not where he wanted it. It came up from below and smacked him between the legs, not hard but certainly hard enough, and he dropped to his knees and his right fist opened and silver rings rained down on the tiled floor.

Garbage and Mudhoney towered over Jack, not looking at him, looking toward the refrigerator instead. They didn't say a word, but Jack could hear what they were thinking.

Let's mash the fucker's dog.

Frankenstein could hear them, too. The geriatric bulldog was wedged into the corner, scarred from too many beatings, scared straight through to the bone.

But not too scared to fight back. Bulldog lips curled back over teeth just as yellow as Mudhoney's.

Frankenstein started to growl.

"No!" The word split Jack's lips as Garbage's bat arced down. Jack barely got under it, shielding Frankenstein from the blow. The bat caught him on the left shoulder as his hands closed over Frankenstein. He clutched the dog against his belly, and Mudhoney's bat came crashing down against his left leg as he tried to get up and his foot went out from under him, twisting the wrong way and suddenly he was on his ass.

"Let me have him," Mudhoney said, blood gushing from his torn eyebrow.

"Okay." Garbage nodded, wheezing hard. "But I get the dog."

"You sick bastards," Angel Gemignani said. "That's enough."

Mudhoney and Garbage didn't particularly want to listen to her.

They didn't want to leave Jack's condo, either.

But they did both those things.

Because they had a couple of baseball bats.

And Angel Gemignani had a gun.

Angel smiled. "I never figured you for a dog lover."

"I'm full of surprises," Jack said. "And so are you. Freddy said you carried a gun, but I thought he was kidding. I never guessed that anyone who wore a Sweet Cherry Love T-shirt would pack a .45."

"A girl's gotta *accessorize*, Jack."

Jack nodded. They were sitting in the hot tub near the condo swimming pool. The whole thing was crazy. One minute Freddy's granddaughter was thirsty for his blood, the next they're deep into a witty repartee kind of thing. All because Jack had a soft spot for dogs.

And he was letting Angel get away with it. That was the really crazy thing. But there was something about her. Jack had tangoed with a couple of poor little rich girls in his time. He'd been run through the *slap slap kiss kiss* mill by experts. The whole big-money-breeds-big-emotions routine.

With Angel it didn't seem like a put-on. Of course, Jack had to admit that he really didn't know her at all. But he was beginning to think that maybe he wanted to know her. His phone sure as hell wasn't ringing off the hook. He was beginning to think—

No. He wasn't *thinking* at all. In fact, he was real tired of *thinking* about anything.

Angel was still wearing her T-shirt. Now it was wet and nearly transparent, but no one needed to feel embarrassed because Angel was still wearing that black brassiere, too.

Jack wore a pair of old boxing trunks. The tub jets were going full blast. Hot water bubbled against his sore shoulder and leg. He'd been hit plenty of times before tonight, but never with a baseball bat. The Jacuzzi jets, as well as a stiff drink, were dulling the pain.

"You ever have a mai tai before?" Jack asked.

"This is my first." Angel raised her Fred Flinstone jelly jar glass and took another sip. "Here's to Fred . . . and Barney Rubble, too."

"Don't forget Dino." Jack shook his head. "Sorry about the glass. It kind of ruins the effect, but your friends broke my Sneaky Tiki collection."

"Yeah . . . well . . . I'm beginning to see that I made a mistake about you. And that's not an easy thing for me to admit."

"Hey, you're a rich girl. You can make it up to me. A couple hundred bucks at an antique store and you can replace my entire collection of Sneaky Tiki glassware. Get lucky at the right thrift shop and you might even find a real steal."

"You really like all that old Trader Vic's stuff, huh?" She chewed on a piece of pineapple. "Anybody ever tell you your place looks like the Tiki Room at Disneyland?"

"Yeah. The editors of *Better Homes & Gardens*. They're doing a spread on my place next month. Tiki chic. It's going to be all the rage."

Angel smiled again. Her smile looked really different without the makeup. She didn't exactly look younger, but maybe a little more innocent. And Jack knew that impression was a few clicks south of accurate because—

Angel came across the tub. Jack didn't do anything to stop her. She massaged his bruised shoulder. Jack closed his eyes. A prickle of pain jabbed him to the bone as her strong fingers worked deeper, and then his muscles began to loosen, and the pain went away.

"Feel good?"

"Great."

"I took lessons."

"I'll bet you did."

Angel's fingers departed Jack's shoulder and found his thigh. Again, she went to work on him. Again, Jack felt a prick of pain. Before long, a feeling that was a long way from pain replaced it.

"I really am sorry about tonight," Angel said. "You were really brave, protecting your dog that way. When I saw you do that, I just knew you couldn't have been part of any scam that might hurt Spike."

She took a deep breath. "I really really miss Spike. We've never been separated, not even for a day. He's the one constant thing in my life, the one thing I can really count on. I know it's crazy to feel that way about a dog, but Spike is . . . well, he's a lot more than just a pet."

Jack didn't say a word. He didn't need to. He was concentrating on Angel's fingers as they kneaded his thigh muscles, concentrating on that feeling that was a long way from pain—

Angel whispered in his ear. "They hit you somewhere else, didn't they?"

Jack nodded, settling back, his eyes still closed.

Angel moved closer.

A collage of sound—Angel's throaty chuckle, almost girlish; water bubbling merrily in the hot tub; desert wind whispering through the surrounding palms.

The patter of Bally loafers on concrete.

Jack's eyelids flashed open like a couple of window shades that had been yanked really hard.

Steam wafted from the tub, hiding the lower half of the man who stood at water's edge, but to Jack it didn't look like steam at all. It looked like smoke. It had to be smoke. Because the man staring down at him looked way too much like Lucifer.

"You two look like a lobster dinner."

"Yeah, Freddy. I guess we do."

"Don't be mad, Grandad," Angel said. "It was my idea."

Freddy G stared at Jack, then at Angel. She didn't say another word. The casino owner snapped his fingers, and one of his boys handed Angel a towel. No one got a towel for Jack.

"The boys will drive you home, Angel."

"No. I'll drive myself."

Angel started walking. She was still dripping wet, the towel draped over her shoulders. Freddy's bodyguards trailed her without a word.

When they were alone, Freddy G pulled up a lounge chair and leaned toward Jack. "We had a call from the dognappers." The casino owner's face bore no sign of emotion as he spoke those words, but there was a definite tremor in his voice as he asked Jack, "What's this I hear about you holding a ransom note?"

FOUR

IT WAS A LONG NIGHT, AND JACK SPENT IT THINKING ABOUT PIRANHA.

That was Freddy's fault, of course. Before leaving Jack's place with the dognapper's ransom note tucked in the inside pocket of his Brioni jacket, Freddy told Jack a little story.

Freddy said, "Sometimes I think that Vegas has changed a lot in the years since I first come here, and sometimes I don't think it has changed at all. Like these theme casinos we got lined up and down the Strip—all these little Disneylands. We got pirates and we got New York City and we got the Cowardly Lion and the Scarecrow and that mousy bitch with the braids and we even got her little dog Toto, too.

"But really, we always had that kind of stuff. Vegas has always been Disneyland, only with tits. Jay Sarno knew that.

"Sarno was the guy who started Caesars Palace. You never knew him, Jack. But let me tell you, he was something. The Roman Empire fell a couple centuries ago, but Sarno kick-started the sucker. He not only brought it back to life, he made it pay.

"He had vision, Sarno did. More than these guys today.

That's what made him different. These guys today, everything they do is fake. Plastic. Remote-controlled. It wasn't that way with Sarno. Everything he did was real. He even *dreamed* real. Flesh and blood dreams, if you know what I mean.

"Like for instance Sarno had this plan for Caesars first-class restaurant, the Bacchanal. Jay was gonna have a big pool in the middle of the room, all the tables situated so the pool would be the center of attention. Not that he was gonna forget about the cuisine—a meal in this joint was going to be as close to a Roman orgy as you could get and still keep your clothes on. None of this eat-your-cold-primerib-and-let-me-make-a-decent-turnaround-time-on-your-table shit that maitre d's pull these days. No, Sarno wanted course upon course upon course, the whole experience enhanced by a wine list that would set the most jaded sommelier's little medallion jingling.

"When the diners were reaching their culinary climax, so to speak, the house lights were gonna dim, and the pool in the center of the room would be illuminated, one bright spotlight aimed at a suckling pig hanging over the water by a chain. There'd be dramatic music from hidden speakers. Trumpet fanfares and such. Shit that would make you think of Kirk Douglas in *Spartacus*.

"Then the little oinker would descend, and when it was close to the pool's surface and the water started to churn beneath it and the music hit its crescendo and the piggy started to squeal so loud that those blaring trumpets sounded like whispering flutes, why then the chain would release and that poor little porker would make one hell of a splash.

"At that moment, a hungry school of piranha which had waited patiently beneath the surface of the pool would chow down on our pal Porky the Pig.

"Fuck your bread and circuses, Jack, this idea was the

real deal, the real Las Vegas right there for everyone to see at a hundred bucks a plate."

Freddy sighed. "What a fucking great idea. But that's all it ever amounted to—an idea. As it turned out, Sarno couldn't get permission to import the piranha. Nevada Fish & Game shut him down. But it would have been something, that restaurant.

"I like to think about it, Jack. Fact is, the older I get, the more I think about it, because I can never quite pin the whole thing down the way I want to. I'll start off thinking about pigs fattened for the kill. Then I'll think about guys who do up the chains and the stiffs who pay to watch those chains come loose. And I'll end up thinking about piranha, and how they only do what they're built to do.

"I ain't sure what it adds up to. Not yet. But I'm gonna keep on thinking about it. And I figure the time has come for you to start thinking about it, too."

Jack thought about the story long into the night, long after Freddy had departed. He thought about that suckling pig hanging from a chain, and he thought about the people watching it.

Some of them might see the little porker as a living thing. They might feel their expensive dinner churning in their guts as that chain let loose. Even so, they wouldn't look away. Horrified, amused, or fascinated—every one of them would watch.

And the piranha would do what piranha do, unrestrained by morality or emotion. They wouldn't feel a damn thing for the pig. To them, it wasn't anything more than a slab of bacon with a pulse.

Jack knew he could never be a piranha, but he didn't want to be a pig hanging from a chain, either.

He wondered if there was something in between. He

thought of Freddy and all the things he owed the casino owner, and how his stubborn pride had gotten in the way of those things when Freddy sent him on an errand boy's job. Too much pig and not enough piranha and he'd screwed that job up. Screwed it up for Freddy, and Angel, and a Chihuahua named Spike.

It seemed the more he thought, the less he knew. But the time had come to stop thinking so much. Whether it was Kate Benteen or Freddy Gemignani or Angel or a Chihuahua named Spike, it was time to put the pedal to the metal and get down to business.

Morning dawned, literally and metaphorically. Jack didn't know where he stood on the piranha-pig scale, but he did know that he was hungry.

He wanted donuts.

FIVE

THE LITTLE BASTARD WOULDN'T EAT.

Harold Ticks ran one hand over his bald pate and swore under his breath. What he really wanted to do was yank his .357 and plug the Chihuahua, but he wasn't going to do that.

No. The furry little bastard had to stay alive for one more day. After that Harold knew that little ol' Spike was a goner.

Tough luck, muchachito. Tomorrow night Harold would have a half a million bucks in cold hard cash. Man, what a trip. Harold Ticks rolling in the long green. *Mr.* Harold Ticks, moving among the money men in their Giorgio Armanis, investing in some shit that earned twenty percent. Señor Harold Ticks, a gringo ready for some serious Mexican-style kickin' back while he watched the money roll in just like a warm Pacific tide.

But that was tomorrow. Right now Harold had to take care of business. And that meant getting the fucking can opener and opening another can of dog food.

This Harold did. He flipped the top of the can into the garbage and emptied a gelatin-spackled lump of turd-colored food into the Chihuahua's bowl.

The dog sniffed the food and looked at Harold with its big

brown saucer-eyes. Harold gave the little bastard a big smile and sniffed the empty can encouragingly.

"It's good fucking stuff, Spike," Harold said. "It'll make you a fucking world beater. A couple bites of this and you'll fuck like a German Shepherd. Turn your little *pene* into a ball bat. You'll have hardcore pitbull bitches screaming for mercy, believe you me."

The dog licked its muzzle and coughed feebly. Its spindly legs quivered and shook like pencils at a senior citizens' art class.

The little bastard gave in and settled down on all fours, whining. Swearing under his breath, Harold tossed the empty dog food can into the garbage with all the others. Damn. Ten bucks' worth of dog food wasted.

Harold's ten bucks, too. Every penny. None of the others had chipped in on it. Just like with the tuxedo—the limo driver's outfit he'd used to fool that asshole Baddalach. Harold had spent nearly a hundred bucks on that, every dime straight out of his own pocket. Plus a deposit he was going to lose because things were much too toasty to show his face in Vegas.

Harold wasn't going into town. Not with Freddy Gemignani's greaseballs sniffing around. The odds of getting caught like that were probably pretty fucking infinitesimal, because Vegas was a big place. But Harold Ticks wasn't going to buck those odds. He was going to play this cooler than an Eskimo.

So ten bucks on the pup chow and a hundred-plus on the tux. Plus he'd gassed up the limo on the return trip to Hell's Half Acre. There went another twenty-plus. And this shit wasn't exaclty tax-deductible. Not that Harold had seen many IRS forms, but he was stone fucking sure that there wasn't one for EXPENSES—DOGNAPPING.

But that was okay, really, because if things went the way

Harold wanted them to, he was going to come up kickin' it in the end. Half a million bucks. Hey, we're talkin' thick pockets. Plush. Fresh. Completely frosty.

Harold liked the idea of that. Come drop day his skinflint compadres would learn what was exactly what. They'd find out how a badass alumnus of Corcoran State Prison's gladiator wars cuts up the swag with a bunch of clueless taters who didn't ante up.

Clueless taters. Yeah. That's what they were. Daddy Deke and his big bad Mama, daughters Lorelei and Tura, too. All of them. One big bucket of white trash, their skulls filled with crazy ideas fried up in the Mojave Desert sunshine.

They were expendable, as far as Harold was concerned. Especially the bitches, who grated on him something fierce.

Except for Eden. Eden was different. She was special. She had everything her sisters had and then some, but she wasn't a desert rat. Eden could think. And so maybe the wiring in her head was a little twisted from growing up with a bunch of nuts in the nuke-proof concrete bunker Daddy Deke had built in the middle of nowhere. So what? Get tight with a body like Eden's and a man had to expect to make a few concessions.

But Eden didn't matter. Not now. Not with the damn mutt coughing. Huddled on linoleum the color of a mud puddle, shivering, looking all sick.

"C'mon, Spike." Harold nudged the bowl under the dog's nose. "Those pitbull bitches are waiting. Eat up."

The dog coughed. Harold sweated. Maybe the pug was right. Maybe the dog really was sick. Man. Baddalach had warned them. Maybe Spike really did have lung cancer.

But maybe the dog was really okay, too. Maybe it just had a cold or something. And shit, everybody knew that Chihuahuas were nervous little fucks, almost as bad as

French poodles. Maybe Spike was just freaked out about being dognapped.

Well, it wouldn't matter after tomorrow. As long as the dog stayed alive until drop time, everything would be fine and dandy.

Shit. It was pretty fucking crazy. Kidnapping a Chihuahua, holding it for ransom. But Harold was sure that Gemignani would pay up. Maybe not at first. But once phase two of the plan kicked in and Harold ran a shuffle on the old Guinea . . .

The Harold Ticks shuffle. It was a good one. Harold was going to do an end run around the casino boss. He had set up Gemignani with the first ransom note, but all further communications would go directly to Angel Gemignani's suite at the Casbah.

And Angel would bite. Harold was sure of that, just as he was sure that Angel could get her hands on a half a million bucks in a hot minute. He had the Gemignani tramp cased good. She loved that Chihuahua more than anything. She never went anywhere without her little Spikester. He was always right there in the mix. Even when she visited a man behind closed doors.

Harold almost laughed. Man, that was a good story. The one about Angel and Spike behind closed doors. According to the coconut telegraph, the Spikester was quite the little Hercules. When he wasn't sick, anyway.

Spike whined. Harold knelt, knees cracking under his weight, and patted the little bastard's bony head. Those big brown eyes looked up at him again. Man. Harold couldn't take them right now. He rose and looked out the little pillbox window.

Dirty fucking window, but that didn't matter. This was a dirty fucking land. Nothing but desert and scrub, a useless patch of Joshua trees and tumbleweeds separated from the highway by forty miles of literally bad road. Useless. Hell, the government couldn't even give this shit to the Indians. Hadn't even tried. At the dawn of the nuclear age, they wouldn't even test the fucking atom bomb here, and it was damn sure that the Russians weren't going to waste one on a big hunk of nothing during the cold war. Try convincing Daddy Deke of that one, though. He'd come along in 1966 with a brand new bride and plans for a concrete homestead. What a tater, a big ol' spud who looked at this scab of dirt and saw a grade AAA nuclear-proof Promised Land.

Some fucking promise. Harold called the place the Radiation Ranch. To him, the whole set-up was as useless as tits on a—

Gunfire stitched the silence. Lorelei and Tura were out there somewhere, off behind the rise. Dressed in their leather bikinis, early morning Mojave sunshine baking their finely boned skulls, brains shriveling like apricots in a food dehydrator, machine guns kicking in their hands.

Yeah. Harold had them nailed. Guns but no brains. Sure, they had bodies that wouldn't quit. But grow tits on a tater, and you've still got a spud.

Harold knew how to handle spuds. That's why he carried the .357, a twin to the gun he'd used on Jesus all those years ago. He'd blown the postman's fucking tater head clean off. Just like Dirty Harry. Huge gun kicking up a huge fucking slug, only Harold didn't waste his breath with all that do-you-feel-lucky-well-do-you-punk shit. Hell, no. He was a cowboy, Harold was. A stone fucking killer. A cowboy robot. Forget Yul Brynner in *The Magnificent Seven*; think Yul Brynner in *Westworld*.

Harold stared at the slick lump of dog food and remembered what had happened to Jesus' head out there in the woods. Busted up white bone and raw flesh smearing red as it splattered the green green grass of home.

Harold looked at the dog. Man oh man, what to do?

Harold didn't know what to do. There was too much in the way right now. All this damn dog food. Ten bucks' worth. Every penny gone to waste.

The dog wouldn't eat, and the really funny part of it was that Harold was hungry. Really starved.

All this talk about taters . . .

Harold set the .357 on the counter, where he could get to it fast if danger reared its ugly head. Then he cooked up a mess of hash-browns, bone white and hot, just this side of crispy.

He slathered those taters with catsup.

Lots of it.

A pair of fiery redheads, Tura and Lorelei, inseparable as always. The both of them tall and tan and young and lovely—just a couple of gals from Impanema in their black leather bikinis, enjoying the morning sun.

The sisters were lookers, that was for sure. Except for the machine guns in their hands and the snakebite scars which nestled like marble grave markers on the rich brown earth of their flesh, they might have been models for the Victoria's Secret lingerie catalog.

The machine gun bucked in Lorelei's grasp. She flexed up, taut biceps and forearms rippling, and she gentled that sucker down ASAP, the gun barking the whole time.

Slugs ate metal.

Three cans of pineapple juice spouted thick yellow streams.

"Wish we had tomato juice," Lorelei said. "With tomato juice, the cans look like they're bleeding when you hit 'em."

"Yeah, but you missed the first three. In a real firefight, you don't have time to make adjustments. Waste a couple seconds like you just did and you're the one spoutin' juice."

"Guess I'm lucky that pineapple juice cans don't shoot back. What do you think the problem is?"

"I think your sight is off. You should go back to the Swarovski instead of that Israeli piece of shit you got on there."

"Could be." Lorelei popped the clip and reloaded, then jammed it back in the Steyr AUG. "Well, let me give it another try. If I miss this time, you can call me Swarovski."

A series of sharp blasts erupted behind Lorelei, and the remaining three cans of pineapple juice were blasted airborne. A second later they descended pissing sweet yellow streams.

Tura laughed, blowing on the barrel of a 9-mm full-auto TMP machine pistol. "That's how it's done, sis."

"You bitch."

"Takes one to know one."

"And I know this one."

"You think you do. I got plenty of tricks up my sleeves you know *nada* about."

"You got tricks, all right. And their names are Felix and Raoul and Pablo . . . and then there's your favorite, that doctor who outlived Methuselah." Lorelei wrinkled her brow, a coy little pause. "Now what's his name?"

"You know as well as I do. Just the way you know they *all* used to come to me. You remember that right. Girl, you're lucky we didn't stay in Vegas. If you had to make your living as a lap dancer, you would have starved—"

"You girls stop your chitchat and get back to work!"

Simultaneously, Tura and Lorelei turned toward a little rise to the east. Mama had her old Ford pickup parked up there. Her lounge chair was planted in the bed, which was lined with tinfoil that reflected the morning sunlight on the back of her legs.

Mama slathered cocoa butter on the brown belly that had

once been home to Lorelei and Tura and their younger sister
Eden. That belly was pretty firm for a sixty-two-year-old
woman, but then again there weren't too many women like
Mama. Today she was sunbathing in a black leather bikini
accessorized with a shoulder holster and a Heckler & Koch
USP40. Usually she didn't wear the shoulder holster because it gave her tan lines something fierce. The only reason
she made an exception this morning was because of the
kidnapped Chihuahua and all.

"You girls answer your mama when she talks to you!"

"Yes, Mama." The words came out of their mouths in one
voice, because Tura and Lorelei had spoken them many
times before.

"Now get back to work!"

The twins sidled up alongside one another, nearly putting
their heads together. Lorelei whispered, "The old bitch
doesn't miss a trick."

"No she don't. Look at her, sittin' up there like the
mistress of all she surveys. One eye on us, and the other eye
on the house."

"Probably got a TV hooked up so she can keep her eye on
Daddy, too."

"She wouldn't dare. Not with Daddy."

"Yeah. He keeps her in line."

"I can hear every word, girls," Mama yelled. "Get back to
work! Get them cans set up!"

Tura fed the 9 mm's clip and slammed it home. "Think
she really hears us?"

"If she does, she ain't gonna anymore." Lorelei slipped a
CD into her battered boom box and pumped up the volume.

Joan Jett screamed "Bad Reputation."

Lorelei said, "That'll show the bitch."

"Yeah."

Tura and Lorelei set down their guns and set up the cans.

Mama sure knew how to get them riled. She'd never let things be. Everything had to go her way, right down to the color of their skin.

Eden had it easy. She couldn't tan. All she did was burn. It was hard to believe that Eden was really their sister, because everyone else in the family tanned as brown as nuts.

Tura and Lorelei weren't so lucky. Mama insisted that Eden's older sisters be the same shade—the far side of bronze, not quite as dark as she was. Mama's skin was the measuring stick. She was forever holding her arm against those of her daughters. Her dry saddlebag skin chafed like fine sandpaper. Then she'd tell them *more sun* or *less sun*. They were never *just right*.

Nope. *Just right* wasn't part of Mama's vocabulary. There was no pleasing the woman.

By the time the sisters returned to the firing line, Joan Jett had finished up "Bad Reputation." "I Love Rock 'n' Roll" kicked in as Lorelei took aim.

The gun felt wrong against her shoulder. The damn leather bikini strap was sawing at her skin like a knife. She checked her weapon and adjusted the strap.

"Black leather bikinis and black leather panties. Black leather Wonderbras. Black leather miniskirts and long black leather gloves. I'm so fucking sick of wearing black leather *anything*."

Tura nodded. "Me too. We get that half a million and they'll be no more hijacking trucks off the highway. No more living off whatever we can steal. No more drinking Pabst Blue Ribbon because we got a hundred cases stored down in Daddy's bomb shelter. No more eating tuna sandwiches and tuna burgers and tuna surprise because we hijacked an ocean of canned tuna. No more wiping our asses with pages from the May 1997 issue of *Cosmopolitan* because we've got three hundred of those and toilet paper costs money. And no more wearing black leather just because we knocked over a truckload of S & M gear headed for some kink shop in Vegas."

"Yeah," Lorelei said. "If this deal works out, I'm done with hijacking. I'm sick of playing lot lizard so I can climb up into some trucker's cab. I'm sick of the way the goobers laugh, even when I pull out my gun. And I'm sure as hell sick of cleaning up the mess when we get done with them. It's too damn hard to get goober bloodstains off of black leather."

"Don't worry about it, sis. A half a million, and all those worries are dust in the fucking wind."

"You really think it's going to work out? I can't believe someone would pay half a million dollars for a dog."

"Go figure rich folks. They never have to eat tuna sandwiches or wipe their asses with *Cosmopolitan* magazine. The whole problem with rich folks is that they've lost touch with reality."

"Yeah. I guess."

"And you gotta admit it's been easy so far. That boxer. Shit. Light-heavyweight champion of the world, my ass. Even little ol' Eden could handle him."

Lorelei laughed. "That was something to see. The way she slammed him between the eyes with the butt of her AUG, I mean. Maybe Mama will grow our baby sister a backbone after all."

"Backbone, hell. *Wrist bones* are what that girl needs."

Both sisters laughed now. So hard that their red manes danced, blazing hair brushing their bronze shoulders like wildfire.

"Tura! Lorelei! You girls stop horsing around!"

"Yes, Mama."

"You girls get back to work!"

"Yes, Mama."

They took aim and opened fire.

Yes, Mama.

Eden closed lead shutters over the pillbox window in her bedroom.

She hated waking to the sound of gunfire, but waking to Mama's voice was even worse. At least she didn't have to listen to Mama bark instructions on the shooting range anymore. Mama had excused her from target practice because of her wrists. That was the only good thing about having carpal tunnel syndrome.

Eden stood naked before her closet, looking for her white silk robe. She couldn't find it, and that pissed her off. It meant that one of her sisters had probably "borrowed" it. If she saw it again in this lifetime she'd be lucky.

Eden had many faults, but modesty was not one of them. If her sisters had stolen her robe, why then she'd just do without. The house was empty, anyway. Harold had taken the dog outside. He said the sunshine would probably do it some good.

Naked, Eden padded to the kitchen on bare feet. The room stunk of dog food. A bowl of the stuff waited on the floor. She stepped over the bowl, took a bottle from the fridge, and poured herself a cold glass of pineapple juice. Then she headed for the bathroom, taking small sips as she walked, thankful to be free of the rank, meaty odor.

She got the shower going good and hot and climbed in, turning this way and that, letting the water pulse against the spot on her jaw where the boxer had punched her.

When the soreness was gone, she reached for the soap. The good kind. The honey-oatmeal bar she'd bought at that fancy shop in the mall at Caesars Palace.

The soap was gone.

Eden swore under her breath. She knew who'd used it.

She opened a bottle of shampoo and poured some into her palm, lathering up, soaping her breasts and her belly. The smell of coconuts filled the shower. It was Tura's favorite shampoo.

The bottle was still pretty full when Eden finished her shower, so she unscrewed the cap and poured the remaining shampoo down the drain.

"Bitch," she whispered. "That'll show you."

Immediately, Eden felt guilty. She knew she shouldn't feel that way. Mama and Daddy always said guilt was a trap for the weak. They said a person should take what they wanted from the world, whatever it might be. But Eden couldn't take the way Tura and Lorelei could, leastways not without guilt getting hold of her.

She hated having a conscience. It got in the way and made her angry. She didn't want to be weak. She wanted to be strong.

She went to Tura's room and poked around. Her sister never threw anything away. Dozens of Polaroids lined the frame of her dresser mirror, photos of Tura posing with drunken men when she was a lap dancer at that Fremont Street dive called Harlot's Hollow. Sure, some of the men in the photos were famous. But a lot of them were just scuzbags with money. So they'd peeked at her beaver and given her a few bucks. Was she going to send them Christmas cards every year, or what?

Eden searched through Tura's dresser drawers. Boytoy skin magazines, a bottle of Rio de Plata Tequila Añejo, several unopened packages of nylons—nothing she found seemed equal to her anger.

She came across Tura's vibrator, and that was okay for starters. Eden took the batteries and returned the vibrator to the drawer, but she still wasn't satisfied. She pawed through Tura's cosmetics and perfume, finally turning her search to

Tura's underwear drawer. There she found a package of Fig Newtons hidden in a tangle of black leather panties. Tura loved Fig Newtons. Eden tore into the package and nibbled a cookie as she returned to her bedroom.

She lay on her bed and ate Fig Newtons. The cookies made her thirsty, so she got another glass of pineapple juice. She combed her hair and put on her makeup and sprayed herself with jasmine perfume.

But she could still smell that damned coconut shampoo on her skin. It really bothered her. She dug through her dresser drawers until she found another bar of honey-oatmeal soap.

Then she took another shower.

Damn but she was tired of this. Tired of living in a concrete bunker in the middle of nowhere, tired of hustling for every dollar, tired of living with a mother and father and a couple of sisters who could win the Dysfunctional Family Olympics hands down.

Things were going to change when they collected that fat ransom. Eden called it her good-bye money. She and Harold would use it to make a fresh start. They'd leave Hell's Half Acre together, just like Prince Charming and Cinderella in that old fairy tale.

That kind of cash and she'd have just what she wanted when she wanted it. White silk robes to wear for her man and honey-oatmeal soap for their bath.

She knew Mama and Daddy didn't approve of Harold. They didn't like their daughter devoting her life to just one man. Monogamy went against everything her parents believed. But Eden couldn't imagine thinking of another man. If she even so much as tried—

She felt guilty.

Damn. Eden stood in the shower, hot water pulsing against her lithe body. She was always going around in a circle. No matter how hard she tried to change, she always came back to the same place.

Maybe she could try looking at things differently. The way Mama did. Mama had stayed with Daddy a long time, but she'd had plenty of other men, too. She said those other men made her feel good about herself.

Eden wanted to feel good. She closed her eyes and tried to think about someone besides Harold.

He would have to be strong, Eden knew that much. She liked strong guys. He'd have to be in good shape. Like that boxer. That Jack Baddalach. She remembered the way his muscles danced beneath her fingertips.

But Baddalach was on the wrong side of things. Besides that, he was dead. But that made it okay to think about him. She couldn't feel guilty about a guy who was dead—

Hot water jetted against Eden's skin. She closed her eyes and eased the soap over her belly. Rising steam carried the sweet, sweet honey smell to her delicate nostrils.

"Eden, you in there?"

She nearly dropped the soap. That's how startled she was.

"Eden?"

"Just a minute, sugar. I'll be out in a minute."

A slick laugh echoed through the bathroom. "If you need a lifeguard, just give your Harold a holler."

"Sure, baby."

"Anyway, your daddy's watching the dog. So if you wanna—"

"In a minute, sugar."

She listened to Harold's footsteps as he walked to her bedroom. Then she knelt and picked up the honey-oatmeal soap.

Guilt burned her. She felt awful. Weak. Small.

No, she wouldn't feel that way. It was all wrong. She had to stop it. Right now.

Filled with a newfound determination, Eden rubbed her belly.

She closed her eyes.

She only found one man in her imagination, and his name was Harold Ticks.

SIX

JACK VISITED TWELVE DONUT SHOPS AND ATE THREE BEARCLAWS, two glazed, one chocolate bar, and a hecka lotta donut holes before he found the shop he was looking for.

The place was called True Blue Donuts. Jack set his cell phone on the counter and slid onto a stool between a couple of Las Vegas cops and two plainclothes detectives made obvious by their skin-the-hide-off-a-sofa suits. One thing about cops—they always seemed to come in pairs.

The scent of sugar permeated the shop. Jack figured he'd need a shot of insulin if he so much as started breathing fast. Thank God this was going to be his last stop. The chunky waitress headed in his direction told him that . . . or more specifically, the anaconda tattoo on her neck did.

The snake's electric blue head glistened beneath a sheen of sweat and a light dusting of confectioners' sugar as the waitress smiled across the counter. "What can I get you, hon?"

"Coffee."

"Got some devil's food donuts fresh out of the oven. How about a couple of those?"

"No thanks." Jack tried to look like a man with a serious

devil's food Jones and an equally serious time-management problem. "Just the coffee."

"Maybe a couple donut holes?"

"Well . . ."

"They're the best."

"Okay." Jack raised his hands in surrender. "I give in."

"A dozen?"

"Half a dozen."

The waitress poured Jack's coffee and bustled off. She had to be Pack O' Weenies' ex-old lady. There couldn't be two donut shop owners with anaconda tattoos in town. Not even in a town like Las Vegas.

One of the blue suits—a lieutenant—flashed Jack a grin. "You might want to rethink those devil's food donuts, buddy. We've been waiting for them to come out of the oven."

"Good stuff," said the other uniform, a sergeant. "Damn good."

"Thanks for the tip." Jack grinned. "But I'm trying to cut back a little. Couldn't hurt to lose a few pounds."

"We could too." The lieutenant grabbed a fistful of table muscle. "But, hell, we're both desk jockeys."

Both guys had a little snow on the roof. Probably in their late forties, but for most cops that was close to retirement age. Jack knew that cops could bail early. It was one of the few benefits of the job.

The waitress served devil's foods donuts to the uniforms. One quick turn and she was back with Jack's donut holes. Another turn and she was refilling coffee cups up and down the counter, laughing and joking with the customers.

Jack sipped hot coffee. He had to figure a way to ask about Pack O' Weenies. He couldn't just hit her with questions out of the blue. He had to make her comfortable. If he could do that, she might open up—

"Hey." It was the lieutenant talking. "Shouldn't I know you?"

Jack barely spared the guy a glance. "Well, I've never been in trouble with the law, if that's what you mean."

The waitress bustled by, taking an order from a couple of Clark County sheriff's deputies who'd wandered in. Damn. The place was full of cops. Getting the woman to talk about her ex-con ex-husband in front of this crowd was probably going to be a real stretch.

"I didn't figure you for a con." It was the lieutenant again. "What I meant was, didn't you used to be . . . well, someone famous?"

Jack nodded.

"Jack 'Battle-ax' Baddalach." The sergeant, who seemed to speak only in monosyllabic *Jack Webb-ese*, nudged his buddy. "Former light-heavyweight champion of the world. Five title defenses. Lost the belt to Sugar Ray Sattler by KO."

"That's me," Jack said, keeping his eye on the waitress.

"You look pretty good," the lieutenant said. "Maybe a little husky. You a heavyweight these days, Jack?"

"I'm retired."

"Hey, maybe you should make a comeback. I mean, have you seen the guy who's got the heavyweight title now? Jesus. He makes Primo Carnera look like Muhammad Ali."

"Guy couldn't box oranges," the sergeant said. "Lives high on the hog, too. Mansion by the golf course. Lamborghini sports car. Showgirlfriend."

Jack laughed. *Showgirlfriend*, that was a good one.

"No exaggeration," the sergeant said. "None at all. Guy has big appetites. Big problems."

Jack shook his head. "Man, you know everything."

The sergeant nodded gravely. "I read the tabloids."

"You should think it over, Jack," the lieutenant said. "Why, a guy who can jab the way you can—"

"Like I said, I'm retired."

The lieutenant rattled on. Jack tried to ignore him. If this stuff kept up he'd be signing autographs for every cop in the joint. He'd never get a chance to talk to the waitress with the anaconda tattoo.

She headed his way, a fresh carafe of coffee in her hand. Jack took a quick gulp from his cup, nearly burning his tongue.

"Miss," he said, holding out his cup. "How about a warm-up?"

"Sure."

"Hey, Maria," the lieutenant said. "You know you've got a celebrity in the house?"

The waitress smiled as she refilled Jack's cup. "No kidding? You're famous?"

"Well, I used to be—"

The lieutenant cut in again. "He only used to be light-heavyweight champion of the world, is all."

"Oh." The waitress's voice was a little wary and a little flirty at the same time. "You're a *boxer*."

The last bit came out like a dirty word. "Used to be," Jack said. "I'm retired."

The lieutenant laughed. "You got to excuse Maria, Jack. She's not crazy about boxers. See, her ex-old man used to be cell mates with the guy we were talking about. The heavyweight champ. Tony 'The Tiger' Katt."

"Tiger?" Maria spit laughter. "That's not the way I heard it. The way I heard it, they should call him Tony 'The Pussy' Katt."

Anger flared in the waitress's eyes. Jack could see it. He had to take his chance right now.

"Katt's not that bad," he said. "I saw him win the title. A

lot of people say that he won the fight with a lucky punch.
I don't know about that. If you knock out the heavyweight
champion of the world, it's got to mean something."

Maria shook her head. "I don't know about all that. I only
know that Harold—that's my ex–old man—knew Tony
Katt in the joint. He used to write about Tony in his letters.
He said that Katt was always getting grief about his little
pecker—"

"Don't hold back, Maria," the lieutenant put it. "Give it to
him straight, the way you gave it to me: Tony Katt was
mostly kitty. Without Harold Ticks protecting him, Tony the
Tiger would have been spreading his sweetcheeks for every
fudge-packer on the cellblock."

Maria nodded.

"You're kidding me." Jack laughed. "Your ex . . .
what's his name again?"

"Harold Ticks."

"This Harold Ticks," Jack went on. "In the jailhouse, he
was Tony Katt's sugar daddy or something?"

"Harold didn't swing that way," Maria said. "Or if he did,
I didn't know about it. But he used to say Tony Katt was
hung like a mosquito. He said Katt couldn't find his pecker
with a pair of tweezers."

The donut shop rang with laughter. There was nothing
better than a perpetrator dick joke to get a roomful of cops
howling. For her part, Maria practically burst. She helped
herself to one of the lieutenant's devil's food donuts, and
that finally got her calmed down.

Jack pushed the plate of donut holes across the counter
and sidled off his stool. "I guess I'd better leave these alone.
Maybe I *should* make a comeback."

"You do that, champ." The lieutenant grunted as he rose
and shook Jack's hand. "Then maybe Maria and me can

make back the money we lost betting against Mr. Mosquito Dick."

The waitress blew the lieutenant a kiss. "See you later, honeybunch."

"Sure, angel cake." The cop leaned across the counter and gave the tattooed waitress a peck on the cheek.

Playfully, she shook a plump finger at him.

"Kiss Mama's snake, you bad boy."

He did.

Freddy said, "How's it goin', Jack?"

"Taking your advice, boss. Taking it easy."

"Great. Hey, I'm kind of busy now. What do you need?"

"Wondered if you had any news on our problem."

"Nothing yet. My guy's still working on it. He couldn't find a trail in LA. Checked the limo company and got nothing. Anything new on your end? Anyone show up on your doorstep with another ransom note?"

"Nope. Nothing much here. I went out for breakfast, is all."

"Okay, Jack. Let us know if you hear anything. You gonna be around?"

"Well, I kinda got cabin fever. Thought I might try something different."

"Like what?"

"Like golf."

SEVEN

A YEAR AGO, IN THE SUMMER, EDEN LEFT HELL'S HALF ACRE FOR THE bright lights of Las Vegas.

That summer Daddy realized the Russians weren't going to drop an atomic bomb on Nevada after all. The world had changed quite a bit since he first came to Hell's Half Acre in 1966. What with the Berlin Wall falling and that glasnost stuff and all, Daddy had to face reality. Still, it was hard to let go of a dream.

He had watched the signs for years. They seemed so clear. Like Gorbachev, the Russian leader with that birthmark on his head. Daddy took one look at that big purple smudge and figured it for the mark of the beast. When Gorbachev took power, Daddy battened down the hatches and kept the family inside the bunker for a full month.

But Gorbachev didn't last long. Once his butt met Boris Yeltsin's boot, the prospect of an all-out nuclear holocaust seemed pretty bleak.

Not *entirely* bleak, of course. Yeltsin was a loose cannon. It was rumored that the Russian president was a drunk who pissed on airport runways. There was no denying that the New Russia was a mess—a crazy-quilt of separate states, each one with a vodka-swilling strongman whose finger was poised on his own private nuclear trigger. Imagine Alabama and Idaho armed with fat ICBMs.

It was a volatile situation. Daddy was sure that Barry McGuire's "Eve of Destruction" had arrived at last. The pot was boiling. The end was near. And in a bomb-proof cement and lead sanctuary on a small scab of Mojave Desert called Hell's Half Acre, a new beginning was at hand.

But nothing seemed to happen for the longest time, no matter what George Will said on *This Week with David Brinkley*. Still, the conservative commentator kept Daddy's hope alive.

Daddy was nothing if not a patient man. "Sometimes the wheels of progress turn mighty slow," he'd say. He lay awake many a night imagining some cash-hungry Soviet general selling an atom bomb to a bunch of rug-headed Middle Eastern terrorists or a swarthy Panamanian drug lord, but that kind of stuff only seemed to happen in Tom Clancy novels. In real life the bombs never seemed to make it out of Russia. All they did was rust.

Daddy's faith kind of rusted right along with those bombs. He had always been a man of strong conviction, but that summer he was troubled. Because if there wasn't going to be a nuclear war, then the new beginning he'd prophetized so many years ago wasn't going to happen, either.

And Daddy had seen that prophecy so clearly.

He'd told Eden the story many times. The story about the night he'd met Mama on the Las Vegas Strip back in 1966. A go-go dancer and a preacher sharing a mescaline and neon high. Both of them walking the streets in 1966, but one of them seeing the future.

In his vision, the preacher saw himself as an old man. His

go-go girl bride became an old woman. They stood together, in the desert, with their children.

A blinding blast in the distance. A rushing tsunami of nuclear destruction. Atomic thunder and sharp slivers of neon rain. The Las Vegas Strip, cracked and scalded, a fused mosaic of broken glass. Gamblers bursting into flame as they yanked slot machine handles for the last time, keno girls exploding like ripe sausages in the wild apocalyptic heat, lounge singers radiated to a crisp as they wailed the closing notes of "Volaré."

The true believers would be spared. Daddy and Mama and their children, the lone survivors of nuclear Armageddon. They would stand together and listen for the sound of hoofbeats on that fused glass highway.

They would watch Him claim the earth for His children.

The Lord from below. His Satanic Majesty, Lucifer.

Daddy had served the dark one for many years, preaching His unholy gospel, converting those who had walked too long in the light. And though his faith had been shaken many times, he still believed in Satan, even if he could no longer believe in the prophecy.

The prophecy had come a cropper. Daddy could see that. All that glasnost and perestroika, and then Reagan with his Star Wars, and before you knew it Ronald McDonald was hawking Big Macs on Red Square.

Daddy had to rethink things. Night after night he meditated in the little chapel he had built to honor Satan. Night after night he stared down the old mine shaft behind the altar, the shaft that ran straight to hell.

Night after night he waited for a sign.

Some nights he'd make a sacrifice—a jackrabbit, a prairie dog, a hitchhiker, a coyote . . . something like that. Other nights he'd channel demons through his rattlesnakes. And every now and then he'd get his mind right with a shot of strychnine. Daddy believed in taking a good shot of strychnine now and then. Do that, he said, and you could almost feel Satan nipping at your behind.

Of course, Daddy's people back in Appalachia had been handling snakes and drinking poison since forever, only they were Christians. They claimed to channel the Holy Spirit, but Daddy always said his people were a little mixed up on that point.

Satan, after all, *was* a serpent. And a serpent in the house of God was still a serpent. Once you turned one loose, there was no looking back. It was like trying to close Pandora's fabled box or trap the snake that tempted Eve in Eden.

Eden. That was the name her father had given her. And it was Eden who provided her father with a new vision of the future.

On a hot August night he stepped forth from his little chapel and told Eden that Satan wanted her to find a serpent, because an Eden without a serpent was an Eden unspoiled.

The time had come for his daughters to leave home and honor the dark provider through their carnal appetites. Daddy sent them into the desert with only the clothes on their backs. He told them not to return until they had become as worldly as the whore who gave them birth.

Tura and Lorelei were delighted with the news. They longed to leave home. They dreamed of Las Vegas—the neon kingdom that lay to the east. But Eden was frightened by the idea of leaving Hell's Half Acre. She read books and magazines and watched television, but there was much she didn't know about the ways of men.

The three sisters walked through the desert, following those forty miles of bad dirt road that led to the highway. Tura and Lorelei looked like a couple of innocent flower children from Daddy's day—their complexions a dark nutty brown, the soles of their bare feet toughened from years of desert living.

But Eden was not so tough. She had always clung to the safety of the bunker. Her skin was the whitest shade of pale.

And she could not travel the desert unshod. On her feet she wore a pair of Mama's old white go-go boots. It was, in fact, the same pair Mama had worn on the night she met Daddy back in 1966.

Soon Tura and Lorelei left Eden behind. She stumbled along, all alone, feet kicking up feeble dust devils that were no stronger than a dying man's cough. The sun burned down, and her skin turned red, and the wind stuttered through the dry leaves of the yucca trees with a sound like wild castanets.

The first night had nearly passed by the time Eden found the highway. Sunburned and thirsty, her white go-go boots dusted with white Mojave earth, she put out her thumb.

A trucker stopped almost immediately. Eden said she was headed for Las Vegas. The trucker smiled genially and told her to climb aboard.

Eden did. She felt comfortable around truckers. She'd helped her sisters hijack enough big rigs to know what they were like.

This one liked to sing. Cowboy songs, the ones from TV shows. He knew all the words. "Bonanza," "The Ballad of Paladin," "Rawhide"—he sang them all as the big truck headed east.

The trucker drove toward Vegas and through it. He didn't so much as pull over until he reached an empty valley of towering red sandstone. He parked near a trailer. To Eden it seemed incredibly fragile and somehow tragic, nothing like the concrete-and-lead pillbox in which she'd spent her life.

The trucker dragged Eden inside by her black hair. He didn't even give her a glass of water. He stripped her of everything save her go-go boots and beat her. Eden didn't know why he did that. He didn't have to hit her to hurt her. Her sunburned skin was so raw that the slightest touch was agony.

He took her virginity with his fingers, promising that he would do far worse, and do it very soon.

Eden could not bear the sight of him. Mama had told her about the serpents men carried between their legs and the pleasures that they could give a woman, pleasures as gratifying as a rattlesnake bite. But this man was not like the men Mama had described. The serpent between his legs was weak. Eden soon realized that she had not a thing to fear from it. The trucker's snake cared not a whit for his threats or promises. It did not strike; nor did it bite, no matter how much he coaxed it, no matter how hard he cried.

The trucker tied Eden to a bed that stank of loneliness and despair. He coaxed his serpent through the long night, but it only nestled small and defeated in his big hand.

In the morning he untied Eden's hands and ankles. He gave her an olive-colored work shirt with RANDY stitched over one pocket. She washed herself and dressed. He opened the door when she was ready to go, and when she was gone he shot himself in the head.

She walked to the highway and stuck out her thumb.

It was early and there weren't many cars on the road. She had to wait a while. She sang some cowboy songs. "The Rebel—Johnny Yuma." "Maverick." "Davy Crockett."

She was singing "Happy Trails" when an old Chevy pulled over.

The car belonged to Harold Ticks. He took her to Las Vegas. He put lotion on her sunburn and bought her clothes and let her eat anything she wanted.

He did not show her his serpent. Not at first. But he taught her to satisfy the serpents of other men. He took money from those men, and sometimes he watched the things they did with Eden.

Sometimes Harold filmed the men with a video camera. Other times he would take Eden to a warehouse owned by another man, and the other man would make movies while Eden handled serpents of every description.

Once her sisters joined her for a movie. Eden was happy to see them. It was good to have family around.

But mostly she was on her own. Eden tried to enjoy the other men. She wanted to revel in carnal pleasure to please Daddy and Mama and Satan. But this she could not do.

Eden knew it was wrong to want only one man. It went against everything her parents believed. But she only wanted Harold. She only wanted his serpent.

One night Harold charged a wizened gambler an especially high sum to enjoy Eden's company. When the old man was gone, she confessed her secret desires to Harold. She did not tell him about Daddy and Mama or Satan, because she never spoke of these things with anyone.

Harold gave her his serpent that night, and for the first time Eden understood what Mama had meant when she spoke of pleasures as gratifying as a rattlesnake bite. Eden surrendered to those pleasures, and it was not at all like it had been with the other men.

Harold said it was the same for him. No woman had ever taken him to the places he visited with Eden. He promised that he would never again sell her to another man.

"I have another plan," he said. "A way we can make a lot of money."

"I'll do anything," Eden said, "as long as I can do it with you."

Eden knew it was wrong. Mama and Daddy would not approve. The lone desire that coursed through her veins went against the laws of nature and the drives of the flesh and the teachings of the Dark Lord.

One man and one woman . . . together . . . forever.

It was horrible.

Eden was in love.

EIGHT

THE BADDEST MAN ON THE PLANET STOOD ON A TERRA-COTTA PATIO outside a palatial mansion. A scarlet towel was wrapped around his trim middle, as was the heavyweight championship belt once owned by Evander Holyfield, Mike Tyson, Larry Holmes, and Muhammad Ali.

The champ's name was Tony Katt, but he always thought of himself as the Tiger. In fact, he often referred to himself as such when speaking with the press. "The Tiger trained for this fight with unparalleled ferocity," he'd say, or "The Tiger sprang upon his opponent in an effort to devour the motherfucker like a jungle beast."

While incarcerated in Corcoran State Prison, the Tiger's favorite book had been *Roget's Thesaurus*. That coupled with his habit of speaking about himself in the third person made Tony Katt a great hit with the sportswriters.

The Tiger didn't know about any third person, though. After all, he was just one guy.

The champ eased a pair of Ray-Ban sunglasses high on his nose and checked out the action on the neighboring golf course. The ninth tee was approximately a hundred yards from the Tiger's outdoor Jacuzzi. A group of duffers approached the tee in little white carts while the Tiger studied them with the unbridled intensity of a starved predator.

The golfers tottered out of the carts—a cackle of old chicks, scurrying about, busying themselves with clubs and balls and other accouterments of pasture pool. Four of them, dressed in sprightly outfits that spoke of eternal spring.

These were gold card predators. The Tiger despised them and their kind. Country clubs habitués, they had suckled too long upon the teat of indulgence and grown weak.

No, not weak. Puny. That was a better word. They had suckled too long upon the teat of indulgence and grown *puny*.

One of the women noticed the Tiger's presence. Whispers were exchanged. The Tiger relished such attention. Fingers dared not point in his direction as the women examined him with furtive glances and puny disapproving peeps that registered awestruck disapproval.

To the Tiger, this was the natural order of things. For what more could be expected of mere mortals when confronted by a presence so magnificent as his?

And the Tiger's presence was indeed magnificent— *exalted, great, majestic*—for he was no longer an ordinary man. He was something more.

He was a man *enhanced, augmented, redoubled* . . .

The afternoon sunshine painted the Tiger's bronze skin. His muscles rippled and his tattoos danced, gleaming beneath a brilliant sheen of sweat. The fingers of his left hand stroked the great bronze shield on the front of the heavyweight championship belt, the image of a muscular boxer holding a globe aloft with gloved hands.

Sunlight gleamed against bronze. The Tiger straightened to his full height of six feet two inches, gripping the belt and aiming the shining trophy like a mirror. A slashing beam of reflected light blinded one of the gawking duffers. She shielded her eyes and continued to stare, as if she were braver than all the others who had come before her.

But the Tiger knew that this woman was not brave. She was a fool. She may as well have looked into the eyes of Medusa.

The Tiger smiled his baddest-man-on-the-planet smile.

If she wanted to stare, he'd give her something to stare at.

Dramatically, the way a great artist unveils a masterpiece, the heavyweight champion of the world pulled the scarlet towel from around his waist.

The woman fainted. Her companions, squealing in astonishment, barely managed to collect their friend's supine body as they piled into the golf carts and dispersed as quickly as a herd of startled antelopes, leaving behind nothing save a lone white ball balanced on a tee.

The Tiger stared down—below the gleaming shield that girded his belly, below the nest of dark pubic hair—and smiled.

The operation had been a complete success.

Truly, he was King of the Jungle.

The heavyweight champion's augmented penis bobbed in the hot tub, buffeted by a steady stream of jetting Jacuzzi bubbles.

The champion settled back, uttering a satisfied sigh. It was funny how things worked out sometimes.

First there's the accident, and of course it's frightening but you're treated by the finest surgeon in Vegas, and he refers you to the best cosmetic surgeon, who provides you with a discreet informational video that you watch in the privacy of your own home . . . and before you know it— snip, snip, pull, pull, stitch, stitch—you end up with . . . *this*.

"Oh my God . . . every time I see it . . ." Porschia marveled, searching for words. "Gosh, Tony, it's like a big old barge or something."

"The Tiger sincerely hopes that you brought your tugboat, my dear."

Porschia laughed. She stood at water's edge, wearing a thong bikini bottom and a Tony "The Tiger" Katt T-shirt that was knotted beneath her pert, upturned breasts. Statuesque and strawberry blond, she was a budding star in her own right. Porschia Keyes, understudy to the lead dancer in the big review at the hotel that was sponsoring the Tiger's first championship defense.

Of course, Tony viewed their relationship in completely realistic terms. Cut beneath the hearts and flowers and Porschia was just another perk from hotel management, no different than the big house or the private gymnasium. That didn't mean the Tiger was uncomfortable with the arrangement. Perks like this he could definitely live with.

Tony modulated his voice at a low, sexy growl. "How about fixing us a drink, darling? The Tiger will have a kamikaze. You have whatever you like. We'll spend the whole afternoon together."

"Don't you have to train?"

"The Tiger ran four miles before breakfast. He ate his Wheaties. He hasn't had a cigarette in a month. The fight is not for another three weeks. A day off will do the Tiger a world of good. It will keep him from getting stale."

Porschia thought it over. "Okay. I'll phone the hotel and bag my afternoon rehearsal. But you have to help me come up with an excuse."

"Tell them you tangled with a tiger."

"Yeah."

"Tell them you were mauled."

"Yeah."

"Because you're gonna be."

"Yeah."

"So hurry back."

"Uh-huh."

"And then we'll *luxuriate*."

Porschia flushed. "God, Tony, I just love it when you talk *smart*."

The Tiger offed the Jacuzzi jets and was enveloped by the afternoon silence of a wealthy neighborhood.

A year ago Tony Katt was holed up in a crackerbox apartment in Fresno. Sure the apartment was a step up from the slams, but not much of a step. Then he had that fight on ESPN. Not even a main event. Just a ten round prelim. But Caligula Tate—the guy who promoted the heavyweight champion of the world—watched that fight, salivating over the big white boy covered over with jailhouse Aryan Brotherhood tattoos. When he turned off his television, Tate knew he'd found a pug that would bring in the long green when matched with Alexis Shabazz.

Shabazz was a proud member of the Nation of Islam. Having finally won the title after a long and distinguished career, he was looking for a few good paydays against limited opposition before hanging up the gloves. Which was another way of saying that Alexis Shabazz was over the hill.

His people figured he'd have no trouble taming Tony the Tiger. They were wrong. About that, and about a few other things.

Shabazz trained for a short fight. He knew his old legs couldn't carry him for twelve rounds, so he planned to starch Tony the Tiger as soon as the opening bell rang. Shabazz was a little used up and a little slow, but he still had amazing power. Boxing writers said he had Liston's jab and Foreman's right hand.

Shabazz planned to topple Tony with a big right hand, pocket his check, and be on the next plane to Philadelphia. He warmed up in his dressing room, shadowboxing several rounds in advance of the fight, and by the time he entered the ring he was primed and ready to knock the jailhouse tattoos off the Tiger.

There was only one thing Shabazz didn't count on—the national anthem. Because for all intents and purposes there were two of them.

That was the promoter's fault. Caligula Tate figured he'd do the anthem as a duet to promote racial harmony, because he was taking a real beating in the press for matching a Black Muslim with a guy who had a swastika tattooed over his heart.

Tate hired a redheaded C & W queen with skin the color of Bisquick and a has-been soul mama singer from darkest Detroit to do the honors. What Tate didn't know was that the soul mama had a crack habit and was in desperate need of some serious career revitalization.

The big moment arrived. The cowgirl kicked things off like a true Texican— *"O-ooo say kin yew seeee . . ."* Her pinched wail set every dog within ten square miles to barking, but at least she finished up her part of the tune in under a minute.

Then the soul mama stepped into the spotlight. A vision in purple sequins and scarlet feathers, she was determined to send every member of the pay-per-view audience scurrying to the nearest music store for a copy of her remastered greatest hits CD.

The soul mama wailed. She screeched. She jumped up and down and squinted and stomped her feet, and by the time she reached "the land of the free and the home of the brave" she had stretched the national anthem to a record time of six minutes and fifty-five seconds.

All the while, Alexis Shabazz shadowboxed in his corner, trying to stay warm but actually blowing his load. Like the boxing wits said: Shabazz left his fight in the dressing room. When the bell rang for round one, the champ had nothing left.

Two rounds passed before the Tiger figured it out. When the bell rang for the third, he knew his time had come.

A lot of people said it was a lucky punch, but perfect punch was a better description. The Tiger landed a right uppercut that caught the old champ in the face as he went into his patented bob-and-weave. It was a punch that exploded Alexis Shabazz's nose, nearly driving the bone directly into his brain.

One punch, and Tony Katt had everything he had ever desired. The heavyweight championship of Planet Earth. A mansion in Las Vegas. A showgirl in his bed. And a bigger dick, too.

Life was good.

And sometimes life was one large pain in the ass.

Porschia handed Tony a glass of lukewarm booze.

In such moments, Tony tended to forget himself. And *Roget's Thesaurus*. And the third person. He was liable to say things like, "Goddamn, Porschia. Where's the fucking ice?"

"I don't know. I mean, the ice-maker is broken. And whoever emptied the ice trays didn't fill them up."

"Well . . . Christ. I can't drink a *warm* kamikaze."

"Don't yell at me. It's not my fault. This is your house, not mine. If the ice-maker is broken, it's up to you to get it fixed."

"It's not my fucking house. It belongs to the casino. And even if it was my house, it's not up to me to worry about ice-makers. Jesus, Porschia, I'm the heavyweight champion of the whole fucking planet."

"Yeah. And right now you're acting like a heavyweight asshole."

"Hey—"

"*You* used the last of the ice, Tony. When we had our bath last night. You remember what you did with it."

"Sure, but—"

"And you didn't fill up the ice trays before we went to bed."

"I'm the baddest man on the planet!"

"And I'm understudy to the lead dancer in the *Beauty and the Beast Review* at the Skull Island Hotel and Casino. All it takes is one little sniffle and I'm the one dancing the macarena with that big animatronic King Kong."

"Listen . . . baby—"

"Don't give me that *baby* shit." Porschia threw down her lukewarm cosmopolitan and the glass shattered on the patio. "You can't treat me this way. I've got a career, too."

"Yeah. You jiggle your hooters for a robot monkey and a roomful of idiots who just blew next month's rent on the dollar slots. Move over, Madame Curie."

"That's it. We're finished."

"Not the first time. Won't be the last."

"You're wrong about that, Tony. I won't be back. You can find some other girl to play tugboat with you."

"I'm sure you'll land on your feet, Porschia. Those casino boys at Skull Island will watch out for you."

"You bastard—"

"Who knows: you might even get lucky." Tony grinned behind his Ray-Bans. "Maybe this time they'll let you move in with the robot monkey."

•   •   •

The Tiger boiled with anger. Fuck it. He phoned his trainer. "Get your ass over here. Bring some sparring partners. No chickenshits. Anybody who climbs into the ring today better be prepared to earn his money."

He pulled on a pair of shorts and went to his private gym, a glass and oak vision that was a long way from the canvas and mildew sty where he'd first learned to box.

Everything here was new. Bright sunlight poured into the room from the plateglass windows that constituted the west wall. Chrome and leather gleamed. The Tiger wrapped his immense paws. Then he punched up some hardcore on the stereo system and slammed his fists into the heavy bag.

In Fresno, the heavy bag was filled with sawdust. Hitting it was like hitting a cement wall. The bag in Tony's gym was filled with water, which was much easier on his hands.

The bag had a second benefit. Hitting it excited Tony. It was like hitting a human. He could feel his fists sink into the soft leather the same way they sank into a man's belly when he turned up the intensity.

The Tiger's punches thudded against leather. Jabs and hooks and uppercuts, thrown one at a time as the champ warmed up. Soon the big bag began to swing on a long chromed chain as combinations battered its skin. Three punches, four punches, coming faster and faster as the Tiger found his rhythm.

Tony loved it. The rat-tat-tat of his punches, the chain creaking and groaning and screaming like a woman. These were satisfying sounds. The Tiger concentrated on them, fists flailing, shoulders and back knotted, hips and legs torquing blows that could drive a man's nose bone into his brain.

Sweat rolled off him. Hot droplets pattered against the floor. His muscles were molten steel. His fists drummed leather. Wham, bam, thank you—

Another sound slashed the Tiger's reverie.

The sound of shattering glass. Sharp slivers rained down from one of the large plateglass windows on the west wall. The Tiger barely leaped out of the way as deadly shards sliced divots in the oak floor.

Hot desert air swept into the room, overpowering the state-of-the-art air-conditioning as easily as the Tiger had overpowered Alexis Shabazz. The Tiger rushed to the broken window, his boxing shoes crunching over broken glass.

A man stood alone on the ninth tee. He didn't look like he belonged there. He wore a black T-shirt and black jeans, and he had a baseball bat instead of a golf club.

The stranger tossed a golf ball into the air and hit it in the direction of the heavyweight champion of the world.

NINE

JACK PUT THE WOOD TO ANOTHER GOLF BALL AND THE SELF-described baddest man on the planet jumped away from the windows just in time to avoid a busted-glass shower.

Jack figured he'd made his point. He tossed the baseball bat into the bushes and climbed the fence that separated the golf course from Tony Katt's mansion.

Well, that description was a little short of accurate—the mansion didn't really belong to Katt. It was a corporate cage, a way for the casino fat cats who had signed the heavyweight champion to a multi-million dollar three-fight deal to keep an eye on their investment. As soon as that investment soured, Katt would be out on his ass. He wasn't the first boxer to live at this address. He wouldn't be the last.

Jack twisted over the top of the fence and dropped to the ground on the other side. He crossed a picture-perfect lawn and climbed a staircase that lead to a terra-cotta patio, just in time to see Tony Katt charge through the big empty space that a few moments before had been a window.

"Hey, Tony. I've been meaning to drop by." Jack held out his right hand, ready to shake. "I'm Jack Baddalach. I used to be the light-heavyweight champion of the world."

"What the fuck?" Katt stared at Jack's hand as if it were a turd. "What's the matter with you, man? Are you a fucking lunatic or something?"

Jack smiled at the bruiser. Katt didn't look so much like the baddest man on the planet. Not right now. Right now he looked like a really confused bull that had been beaten to the ubiquitous china shop by a rampaging rhinoceros.

That was just the kind of expression Jack wanted to see on Katt's face. A guy like Katt was used to playing the bully. Bullies couldn't handle it when someone took the bad boy play away from them. Especially bullies who happened to be boxers. For reference check Sugar Ray Leonard defeating Roberto Duran in their famous *no mas* fight, or Evander Holyfield KOing Mike Tyson.

Jack peeked over Tony's shoulder. "Gonna invite me in?"

"Fuck you, pal."

Tony Katt stood his ground, his body a road map of personal insecurities. All those badass jailhouse tattoos on his chest—Nordic maidens and skulls and swastikas— couldn't cover the insecurities of a big guy with a little pecker.

Neither did the tats Katt had added since becoming champ. Friedrich Nietzsche covered one shoulder, his impassive face above the philosopher's best-known quotation: "That which does not destroy us makes us stronger."

Having Freddy Nietzsche on his shoulder probably made Katt feel like an intellectual or something, but Jack had no idea what insecurities the tattoo on Katt's other shoulder stroked. He couldn't understand why the heavyweight champion of the world would want the smiling face of Colonel Harlan Sanders, the Kentucky Fried Chicken king, etched on his hide, let alone what bizarre personal kink had driven him to add the famous slogan: "Finger Lickin' Good."

You'd have to buy the Tony Katt Cliffs' Notes to figure that one out, and Jack didn't want to pony up the bucks. So he left it alone and got back to business.

"Tony, I really want this to be friendly," Jack said. "I need to ask you a few questions."

"Look at this." Katt gesticulated wildly in the direction of the broken windows. "Look what you did to my fucking house."

"I wanted to get your attention. I wanted to let you know I'm serious. I wanted to be sure that when I ask you a question, you'll give me a straight answer."

"Fuck you, man. You'd better get out of here. Right now. Or I'll—"

"Don't tell me you'll call the cops, Tony. I know you won't do that. And don't tell me you'll call the corporate headhunters at Skull Island. Because if you do that I'll have to call my corporate headquarters. And I work for Freddy Gemignani over at the Casbah. You know about Freddy, don't you?"

"He came to one of my fights. Sure. I met the wop. But I don't see—"

"You don't need to see, Tony. All you need to do is give me a straight answer."

"About what?"

"About a guy named Harold Ticks."

Katt jerked like someone had hit him in the ankles with a hatchet.

"This conversation is over," he said.

Then the baddest man on the planet retreated into the gym, cussing a blue streak. He didn't sound the way he did on television. He wasn't talking like a cut-rate Don King. He sounded like a convict who was about to take it hard from a guard who had his number.

Jack followed the heavyweight through the broken window. "About this Harold Ticks."

"I don't know anybody by that name."

"Yes, you do. He's a thief. He stole something from me, and I want it back—"

"Look, I don't care if he stole the steam off your shit. I'm telling you I don't know any fucking Harold Ticks."

"Okay," Jack said. "You had your chance."

Jack's black T-shirt was loose around his waist. There was a reason for that. He reached behind his back and beneath the shirt, and his hand reappeared holding a Colt Python.

The gun was his ace in the hole. His last chance. Because if a Colt Python shoved under his nose didn't get Katt's shorts in a serious bunch, nothing would.

"Harold Ticks," Jack said. "Tell me where he is or you're gonna have a big problem."

"Calm down, man." Katt's lips trembled. "*Calm down.*"

Jack cocked the pistol. "Harold Ticks. You remember. He was your saddle pal in Corcoran State. The way I heard it, he was the stud and you were the—"

"*Fuck you.*" Katt stiffened. "You're not getting anything out of me, Baddalach. And put away that gun. I'm no kid. I'm not gonna shit my pants. I don't care who you work for. I know you're not gonna shoot me. I'm the motherfucking heavyweight champion of the world."

They stood there for a moment, trying hard not to blink. Broken glass all around, but the china shop bit hadn't worked. Jack could see that. The moment had passed and then some. Tony Katt wasn't intimidated anymore. He'd slammed a lid on his fear.

Now he was starting to boil.

Jack glanced around the gym. He hated this kind of place. Everything was new. Hi-tech. Sanitized.

There was only one other way to play it.

Jack nodded toward the boxing ring. "If you won't give me an answer," he said, "I guess I could always beat one out of you."

Katt smiled his baddest man on the planet smile. "You tangle with me, runt, you'd better pack a lunch."

Jack took off his T-shirt. Katt made a point of laughing. "Looks like you've been enjoying the good life, Baddalach."

"Lately I've been eating a lot of donuts."

Katt tapped his forehead. "Some knot you've got there. Someone take after you with a ball bat or something?"

"No. I got butted with a machine gun." Jack pointed to the bruise on his left shoulder. "This one's from a bat, though."

"You should take it easy, Dad."

"Usually I do. I'm retired."

"That's why I'm going to be merciful." Katt threw a pair of sixteen-ounce training gloves to Jack, pillows that wouldn't hurt a consumptive kid. "I promise I'll go easy."

Jack tossed the gloves aside. "Don't do me any favors."

"Okay. It's your call, champ."

"Make it easy on yourself. How about some ten-ouncers?"

"Owww . . . Jack, you are a brave boy. I guess a couple of testosteronic terrors such as ourselves don't need any stinking headgears, either. Huh?"

"Unless you're worried about that pretty little nose of yours."

"I'll be okay." Katt tossed a pair of ten-ounce gloves Jack's way, then selected one for himself. Jack wrapped his hands with protective bandages while Katt shadowboxed in the ring. The Tiger was slow, even for a heavyweight. Ponderous. Like Godzilla on Quaaludes.

But Godzilla was dangerous. One swat of his tail and half of Tokyo crumbled, 'ludes or no 'ludes.

Jack climbed between the ropes and pulled on the gloves. They were red leather with white labels around the wrists that bore the name of the manufacturer.

"Reyes," Jack said, reading the label.

Great. Jack had worn Reyes gloves the night a guy named Sugar Ray Sattler cut him to ribbons and took his title. The brand had always been bad luck for Jack Baddalach.

"Puncher's gloves." Katt smiled, throwing a series of short hooks in the air. "You said that I should make it easy on myself."

"I guess I did."

"You want rounds? This ring has a computer set-up. I can activate a clock from my corner. The computer will ring the bell and everything."

"Let's just do it the old-fashioned way. Come to scratch and let fly."

"Suits me."

They slipped mouthpieces between their lips—Katt's was custom-made, while Jack's was a gum-buster straight out of the package.

Well, beggars couldn't be choosers. Not when they were calling out the heavyweight champion of the world. At least Katt hadn't given Jack a mouthpiece with another guy's slobber on it.

Katt rang an imaginary bell. "Ding ding."

The heavyweight lumbered forward. Jack shook out his arms and bopped back and forth from one leg to the other. His bruised shoulder was pretty tight, but at least his left leg wasn't bothering him. No thanks to Mudhoney's bat. Plenty of thanks to Angel Gemignani's talented fingers.

Katt slammed his gloves together and smiled his baddest man on the planet smile as he crossed the ring. Coming in, the champion flicked a left jab toward Jack's head. The punch was pathetically slow. So slow Katt could have sent it by Western Union. Jack had no trouble getting under it.

He cut to the right, avoiding Katt's power hand. If he could stay away from the champion's right cross, he figured he'd be okay.

Jack juked around the ring, shuffling a little, his legs nice and loose now. Katt turned, thudded his gloves together again, smiled his ridiculous smile, and followed.

Jack nearly laughed. The heavyweight's footwork was horrible. Tony the Tiger dragged his back foot behind him like it was stuck in a bucket of horseshit. Two more Western Union jabs and Jack was gone. He was wearing a pair of Wolverine work boots, but Katt made him feel like the Flash.

Katt slurred words through his mouthpiece. "You want to fight or what?"

"Bring it on."

Katt did. Thudding his gloves, smiling his baddest man on the planet smile, he crossed the ring faster this time. Jack stood his ground, catching the champion's jabs on his gloves, but he couldn't stand in with the big man forever.

A wild right slammed his bruised shoulder as he moved away. Jack felt the power in the punch right down to the bone. Katt could bang, and then some. That was for sure. Barroom rules, he'd probably take anyone. But this was boxing. And until someone designed a ring that included a juke box and a pool table, Tony the Tiger was going to have to play it the Marquis of Queensberry way.

Katt turned, gloves down, ready to give chase. But Jack jumped in, surprising the heavier man before he could set himself, driving a series of hard jabs into Katt's face before moving out.

Katt touched his nose. His Reyes glove came away stained with blood.

"You little bitch," he said, slapping his gloves together one more time.

Smiling his smile beneath a scarlet curtain.

Jack waved him on. The heavyweight came at him just as before, swinging wildly. Against opponents his own size, Jack had never been very fast. But with Katt he felt like a welterweight. He double-jabbed hard to the champion's face, dipped low, and ripped a right hook to the big man's ribs, following up with a hook to the head that missed by a whisper.

And then he was gone.

Jack grinned around his mouthpiece. This was the guy who was pulling down millions for every fight. Jack had never made that kind of money. He wasn't even in shape, and he was boxing rings around the chump—

Katt wasn't going to quit, though. Jack had to give him that. The heavyweight snorted and wiped fresh blood from his nose. Another slap of his gloves, another smile, and the big man really came on, a blur of suntanned flesh and neon tattoos. Aryan Brotherhood swastikas, grim reapers, grinning skulls wearing Nazi helmets. Jack laid leather on all of them, but his punches didn't slow Tony Katt.

The jab that had seemed so pathetic moments before caught Jack dead in the face. Once, BAM, twice, *BAM*, like a jackhammer rattling his skull. Suddenly Jack couldn't remember how to get his mouth open, and he needed to breathe . . . because his lungs were burning and the jab was coming again—

BAM! BAM!

And then Katt's right hand slammed Jack's bruised shoulder. His entire arm went numb. He needed to move. He had to get out of the way—

But he couldn't. The ring ropes burned his back as he fell against them. If he couldn't get off the ropes before he lost his balance . . . If he couldn't slip away before Katt had a chance to launch another punch . . .

Katt grunted as he set himself. Again the right hand, but this time it was whistling toward Jack's head, and the smaller man did sink back against the ropes because there was nowhere else to go.

The punch grazed Jack's nose and Katt's momentum forced him off balance. He stumbled toward Jack . . .

. . . and Jack remembered how to breathe . . .

. . . and he spun away from Tony Katt, leaving the champion hanging on the ropes . . .

The heavyweight was tangled up. He dropped to one knee, then pawed his way up the ropes until he was on his feet again. Jack needed the break. He still couldn't feel his left arm, but he wasn't going to need it. He had spotted his opening. As long as he could catch his breath—

Katt's trainer came through the door with a couple of sparring partners. The old guy nearly had a coronary. "Tony!" he yelled. "What the hell are you doing!"

Katt waved him off and turned toward Jack. The heavyweight's hands were down. He didn't raise them right away. Instead, he launched into that chump move, banging his gloves together for the fifth time in as many minutes.

In just a second he'd smile that stupid smile.

It was a robotic move. Predictable as it was necessary, like a kid winding up a toy soldier before sending it into battle.

This time, Jack was ready for it. As Katt's lips twisted upward, Jack banged a hard right against the champion's skull.

Once. Twice. Three times.

BAMBAMBAM!

Blood geysered from the champion's nose. The lower half of his face was draped in red, and the upper half was all startled eyes.

The Tiger went down hard, his lips contorted in pain.

His trainer's expression was worse. After all, Tony Katt was supposed to defend his title in three weeks. If his nose were broken, none of his corner men would be getting a check anytime soon.

"Oh, Jesus!" The trainer moaned. "Oh, Jesus!"

The baddest man on the planet writhed on the canvas. He wasn't smiling now. Jack watched him. He didn't smile, either. No one in the gym smiled.

Except for the man on Tony Katt's left shoulder.

Colonel Harlan Sanders.

He wore a chicken-eating grin.

TEN

HAROLD KISSED EDEN LONG AND DEEP. "HOW DOES IT FEEL TO almost be rich, sugar?"

"It feels good," she whispered, "to be in love."

They stood next to the bed in Eden's room. Over Harold's shoulder, through the pillbox window's open lead shutters, Eden watched heat waves undulating off the belly of the desert. Outside it was hot, even for the Mojave. A real scorcher.

And it was a scorcher inside, too, in this cool room lined with thick cement walls.

Eden's fingers drifted over the tattooed SS lightning bolts on Harold's neck, across his hairless chest, down his white belly. A thick purple scar puckered low on his left side, a permanent reminder of the bullet Harold had taken for his friend while they were in prison.

Eden knelt and kissed the scar tenderly. When they had the ransom money and things cooled down, Harold was going to introduce her to Tony Katt. She couldn't wait to meet him. Not because he was heavyweight champion, but because he was the person Harold cared about most in the world.

Next to Eden, of course.

Her tongue darted between her lips, and she teased the rough purple circle on Harold's side with a slow lick as her long black hair brushed his thigh.

"Oh, baby," Harold said, and more than once.

Eden smiled up at him. "Looks like I didn't wear you out, after all."

"Uh-uh."

"Guess I'll have to try again."

"Guess you will."

Harold closed his eyes. His fingers drifted through Eden's black hair, knotting at last into a fist as he pulled her closer. Eden was glad they were alone, glad Daddy wasn't in the next room listening at the heat register, glad Mama wasn't peeking through the pillbox window. This was the way she wanted Harold, all to herself. Just the two of them. No interruptions. No distractions—

The question flashed in her mind quite suddenly.

"Where's the Chihuahua?"

Harold sighed. "I couldn't get the mutt to eat anything. Your daddy took it out to the chapel. Said he had some herbs or something that would give it an appetite."

Eden trembled. Kneeling before her lover, staring straight at him—

"The snake," she said. "*The snake.*"

From the distance it was just a tumbledown shack abandoned by a silver miner who had shuffled off into eternity many moons ago. But if you got a little closer you noticed the crudely fashioned sign that hung between two bleached-white steer skulls just above the weather-beaten door. Letters made of rattlesnake hide seemed to writhe on a background of black enamel that had blistered in the desert sun:

HELL'S HALF ACRE CHURCH OF SATAN
DEKE LYNCH, PASTOR & PROPHET
& THE DEVIL'S LEFT HAND

Inside the chapel, Daddy Deke stood before the altar, dressed in his old frock coat and the top hat with the snakeskin band. Trickles of heat slashed cracks and knotholes in the three wooden walls, offset by a cool breath of air rising from the abandoned mine shaft that pitted the dirt wall at the rear of the structure.

Cool air, but Daddy Deke knew that there was fire down below. He had seen it in a strychnine vision, and his strychnine visions always proved true. The mine shaft led straight to hell. Daddy had walked those tunnels in his dreams. He'd seen the black river flowing . . . Cerberus, the three-headed dog guarding the gates . . . the whole nine yards.

Deke knew that his vision of hell was a tough one to swallow. Men, by their very natures, were a skeptical lot. But so was Deke Lynch. He had trouble believing in some things until he saw them for himself. Like demons, for instance. He was skeptical about them right up until the moment he summoned one for himself. Summoned it from the black pit that yawned behind him and watched it stalk off into the desert night leaving nothing in its wake but the sour stink of sulfur.

Of course, some folks said that a man who handled rattlesnakes and drank strychnine was liable to see all sorts of things. Deke figured it this way: if a man couldn't believe his own eyes, what in hell *could* he believe?

Once Deke saw something, he believed it. But there were still a few things he had to see about.

Like this Chihuahua being worth half a million bucks, for instance. Deke had a real problem with that one. And he figured he was going to keep on having a problem with it until someone showed him all that money.

One thing Deke was sure of—if the Chihuahua died, he would never see that money at all. He couldn't let that happen, because he sure could use that cash. Score a half a million and he could do a whole lot. Maybe start spreading Satan's word again. Get hisself a television ministry, do it that way. Nobody had made much of a splash with Satanism since that Diablos Whistler fellow had died down in Mexico a couple of years ago. The country was ripe for a fresh dose of the Devil. Deke could feel it in his bones.

Wheezing miserably, the Chihuahua looked up at Deke from its place on the altar. A full bowl of Alpo rested untouched before the little critter.

Deke closed his copy of *The Necronomicon* and scratched his head. The incantation hadn't worked.

"Maybe you should try it again," Mama suggested. She knelt before the altar, taking little sips of strychnine from a silver chalice. "Or maybe it wasn't written to work on a dog. Maybe you gotta change it around a little."

"No," Deke said. "I don't believe that would work, Mama. And even if it would, I ain't got no idea how to say *Chihuahua* in Latin."

Mama's dark skin gleamed like a freshly polished cowboy boot, the way it always did when she drank poison. She had been drinking strychnine for thirty-two years, and she hadn't been sick a single day. Plus she'd been snakebit forty-six times. Mama never got sick from that, either. She trusted in Satan, and Satan looked out for her. Her faith had always been strong.

Until now. She took the daintiest little sip of strychnine and said, "Maybe we should go ahead and take the little bastard to a vet."

"Don't blaspheme, woman."

"Well, ain't you the sanctimonious one all of a sudden? All I'm sayin' is—"

"Still thy tongue, bitch!"

Mama did as Daddy ordered. But only because it was Daddy. Another man talked to her like that, she'd cut off his balls with a straight razor and feed them to him.

The desert heat cut through those cracks in the walls and set Daddy's blood to boiling. It was too damn hot today, even for a Satanist. He lifted his silver cup and drained it of strychnine, but the poison did nothing to cool his unease.

His blue eyes burned beneath the sharp ledge of his brow as he scanned the chapel for an answer.

His gaze fell upon the inverted cross on the far wall . . . bones bleached of flesh, and those that were not . . . the old leather-bound books heaped upon a leaning bookshelf . . . the potions and balms that were useless to him now.

Daddy Deke threw the silver goblet across the room and it banged against the weather-beaten door. The answers he required were beyond his reach.

Before he could find them, he needed to get right with Satan.

He needed to feel the dark one's unholy power in his very grasp.

He needed to handle Cthulhu.

Eden ran through the bunker.

How could Harold do it? How could he give the Chihuahua to Daddy? How could he be so blind?

Harold just didn't understand. She couldn't blame him for that. He hadn't grown up around Daddy and the snakes. He'd never seen Daddy try to heal the sick—

Eden had seen that. Mostly, Daddy's spells worked. But
sometimes—

And if this was one of those times. If it was already too
late. If the dog had been bitten—

No . . . no . . .

If the ransom money slipped through their fingers. If they
lost half a million dollars to a rattlesnake's venom—

No!

Eden banged through the door and into the heat.

Oh, please, no . . .

Illnesses were demons. This Daddy Deke knew. And Satan
held sway over every demon. His power could pluck the
little pissants from a body as easily as Eve had plucked the
apple from that tree in the Garden. If a man truly believed,
he could channel that power. He could master demons. He
could hold sway on earth, just as Satan did in hell.

Daddy steeled himself to the notion. The door to Satan's
power covered a black box beneath his altar. With his right
hand, he bent low and brought forth the box. It was hinged
with gold and bore a knob of clear crystal.

Like Pandora of old, Daddy Deke feared not to open the
box. He did this with his left hand, the hand he had given to
Satan many years ago.

The dark one's will would be done. Daddy Deke reached
into the box with long bony fingers, giving himself over to
the power of the Lord of Flies.

"Hail Satan!" Mama shouted.

Daddy stroked the rattlesnake. Corpse-cool flesh came
alive beneath his fingers. Keeled scales rippled along the
serpent's thick body as it stirred, forked tongue flicking the
hot air, yellow eyes alive with evil, slit pupils identical to
those of serpents that had crawled the earth long before man
trod upon it.

"Hail Lucifer!" Mama screamed.

Daddy drew the serpent from the black box. Nearly six feet in length and thick as a truck driver's wrist, it was completely white save for those yellow slits that slashed its eyes.

A herpetologist would identify the serpent as Crotalus atrox, or an Albino Western Diamondback Rattlesnake. Daddy called it Cthulhu.

"The dark one is king!" Mama shed tears. "The dark one reigns omnipotent!"

On the altar, the Chihuahua began to whine. Fright shone in its brown eyes. It tried to rise on weak legs.

"Mama! Hold this beast!"

Mama placed her hands on the little dog and held it still. Cthulhu's great tail encircled Daddy's forearm. The snake's enormous head writhed and twisted, facing Daddy, a white diamond made of flesh. Spike's whine cut the silence, but Daddy ignored it. He stared into the serpent's eyes, and he began to fall, and tumble, and spin . . .

Mama cried, "Satan! Lucifer! Beelzebub! All one! All eternal!"

. . . descending into yellow slits in eyes unblinking. And the heat of hell poured through those slits the same way the desert heat slashed through the cracks in the chapel walls, and Daddy was scorched by hellfire, and he burned in the pit, and when he began to rise anew the power was burning in his blood, blistering his flesh, because his eyes were yellow . . . he knew they were . . . he could feel it. His eyes were yellow slits and Satan was a comin' . . .

SATAN WAS A COMIN' . . .

SATAN WAS A COMIN' . . .

. . . AND SOON!

. . . AND SOON!

Eden threw open the door. Mama screamed. The dog squirmed in her grasp. The great snake's head hovered over it.

"Daddy," Eden said. "No!"

Her father's eyelids fluttered. He looked at his daughter as if she were a ghost. His blue eyes were glazed with ecstasy or fear . . . and Eden didn't know what to say, and for a millisecond all was silent.

Then came the dry cadence of Cthulhu's rattle. The snake sprang, jaws spread wide, fangs glistening as they ripped Daddy's cheek.

"No!" Mama screamed as she tore the serpent from Daddy's face and flung it into the mine shaft.

Daddy collapsed on the floor and the Chihuahua scrambled away, escaping between Eden's legs.

The dog scrambled past Harold, too. He gave chase, naked and pink under the hot Mojave sun.

Eden wore a robe. Nothing else. She ran to her father's side. He studied her with that same strange expression on his face, as if he were looking at a ghost whose presence stirred anguish and fear and love. And then a great spasm rocked him, and his eyelids fluttered closed, and he sank into Mama's arms like a sickly child.

"If he dies, I'll kill you," Mama said. "I'll burn you down. I'll rip your heart out."

"Mama . . . I'm sorry—"

"You're *always* sorry!"

Eden started to cry.

"Don't you dare do that in here!" Mama spit the words. "Don't you dare shed tears in your daddy's church!"

Eden couldn't help it.

"You're so weak!" Mama's voice was ice. "You can't be no daughter of mine!"

Shaking with unrestrained fury, Mama cradled Daddy

Deke in her arms. "I never wanted you. But your daddy said it was prophetized that we have three babies. He said it was Satan's will."

Eden stumbled back as if shot. Unable to speak, she could only listen.

"If I had it to do over again I'd rip you from my belly with a coat hanger. That's what I'd do. By Satan, I would."

Eden turned to flee but it was much too late. Her foot tangled in the rib cage of a tramp Daddy had sacrificed three winters past. She couldn't move a lick, but she had to. She had to escape before Mama could say another word.

She smashed the bones with her free foot and kicked the rib cage into a corner. Twisting toward the light, she nearly stumbled but righted herself at the last moment and pitched through the open door.

Into the desert.

She ran.

Harold was dressed now. Night had fallen.

"She still out there?" he asked.

"Yes." Eden stared at Daddy's chapel, absently stroking the Chihuahua's head.

"This is fucked," Harold said. "I don't want to leave you here alone. But I gotta go out. I gotta call Angel Gemignani. I gotta do it from a pay phone. Otherwise they'll trace the call. And I can't take you with me, because the dog is sick and someone has to take care of it." Harold punched the air. "This is *fucked*."

Eden said, "Yes, it is."

"Here." Harold held out his .357. "I want you to have this. Just in case."

Eden took the gun. She wanted to cry. She knew she couldn't.

Harold said, "Don't let anyone touch the dog."

Eden nodded.

"I mean it, Eden. Really. Don't fuck this up. You understand? *I mean it.*"

"Yes," she said.

She watched him go.

He was leaving her. Alone. With them.

Don't fuck this up. You understand? I mean it.

And he had never spoken to her . . . *like that.*

PART THREE

Cherry Bomb

Elysium is as far as to
The very nearest room,
If in that room a friend await
Felicity or doom.

—EMILY DICKINSON
POEMS III

ONE

ABOUT TWENTY MILES OUTSIDE OF VEGAS, OFF HIGHWAY 95 AS YOU headed west toward California, was a freeway exit. It connected to an overpass and a narrow dirt road that headed toward a place no one wanted to visit.

At least that was the way it seemed to Harold Ticks. Harold was parked on the north side of the overpass. He'd parked here plenty of times in the last few months, and in that time he'd seen drunks stop to take a piss and newly-weds pull off for a quick bang in the back seat and college kids pile out of dinged-up vans to light off fireworks that they'd bought at the Paiute reservation store seventy miles to the east.

But no one other than Harold ever took that dirt road. Not too surprising, really. Drive forty miles on that road and you reached the home of satanic patriarch Deke Lynch and his family. Deke called the place Hell's Half Acre, but Harold preferred to think of it as the Radiation Ranch.

Spend some time with the Lynch clan out there in the middle of nowhere and your perspective was bound to change. Listen to Deke ramble on night after night about Satan and the government and a man's responsibilities to his blood kin, and you'd begin to think that the Manson Family might have survived if only they'd been a little stronger in the family values department.

It got so that every time Harold drove down that dirt road and hit pavement, he'd get to feeling pretty strange. It was like visiting a world he had forgotten about, a world that had nothing to do with Deke Lynch and his wild brood.

Harold sat in his old Chevy. He was parked in a dirt lot about twenty feet short of the pavement. He always used this spot when he had to schedule a rendezvous. After a few months in the desert, the glitter and noise of Las Vegas made him as jittery as a caffeine fiend.

This place was so quiet. Tonight there were no drunks or newlyweds or college kids. And that was good. Safe. A place where a couple of guys could meet without being disturbed.

Harold popped the top on an Olde English 500 and looked at his watch. Tony was twenty minutes late. Where was the motherfucker?

Tonight of all nights . . .

Tony would show, though. Harold knew it. Tony wouldn't let him down. Because Tony was his brother.

Not in a biological sense. They weren't connected that way.

But just like Deke Lynch and his family, Harold and Tony were connected by blood.

Harold sipped the Olde English and thought about the old days.

Corcoran State Prison. The badass unit. The one they called the Shoe. The one where they put prisoners who caused trouble.

Harold Ticks was in the Shoe for beating up some nigger queen who tried to turn him into a bitch. Harold broke every finger on the hand the nigger tried to slip up his ass, snapped each one at the knuckle joint just like fucking chicken bones while the nigger screamed like James Brown.

Tony Katt was in the Shoe for fucking up a runty guard who liked to give him shit about his little dick. Tony hit the hack while he was talking, hit him so hard that the hack's teeth slashed through his upper lip, nearly severing it.

A couple of the hack's teeth broke off, ending up embedded in Tony's hand. The prison doctor dug those teeth from between Tony's knuckles with a pair of tweezers. The word around the campfire was that Tony didn't even flinch.

That was Tony. It didn't matter how big his dick was—Tony Katt was nobody's punk. Harold knew that from jump.

Everyone knew it. Even the runty guard with the ripped lip that never healed right. And all the other guards knew it, too. They knew that Tony Katt was a natural for their private gladiator wars, same way they knew that Harold Ticks would make one hell of a tag-team partner for the big white guy with the little bitty dick.

· It worked this way: the Shoe had a brick-walled exercise yard. A control booth with a big barred window overlooked the yard, and video cameras were mounted everywhere. When the guards needed some entertainment, they gathered together in the tower and set up a fight between the prisoners. With the paychecks the hacks were pulling, it wasn't exactly like they were up for pay-per-view boxing matches on TV. Besides, the fights at the Shoe were better. Bloodier. For the hacks, it was just like having a ringside seat in the Roman Colosseum.

Starting a fight was easy. All you had to do was mix the dark meat with the white meat. Toss a couple of Aryan Brotherhood boys into the yard with some cons who belonged to the Mexican Mafia or Black Guerrilla Family.

Toss four guys like that into the yard, and make sure every one of them was wrapped tight as jailhouse TNT. The cons might as well have been sweating nitro. The slightest little shove and someone was bound to go BOOM!

Harold remembered the day he got shot. Waiting in the yard with Tony. The hack with the ripped-up lip that wouldn't smile anymore escorting a couple of Mexican Mafia guys into the yard. The hack pointing at Tony, whispering some little dick joke to the spics, who laughed their hard spic laughs.

The guard laughing, too, laughing through that frozen lip while he took his post with a rifle in his hands . . .

The fight . . .

The guard with the ripped-up lip trying to smile while he watched the Mexicans take it really hard—

Headlights washed Harold's face. He glimpsed himself in the rearview mirror. His face was very pale.

A car drifted across the dirt lot. Harold hadn't even noticed it take the exit.

But that was okay because he recognized the car as Tony's Lamborghini.

Harold drained the Olde English, crumpled the can in his fist, and tossed it out the window. Tony's headlights went out.

The ripe, pale moon hung behind the Lamborghini. Tony had paid $446,820 for the car. It was a 1971 Miura SVJ. There were only three others like it in the world.

The car looked too low to the ground to hold a guy the size of Tony Katt. But it did. Tony hauled himself up and out of it. He came around the passenger side of Harold's old Chevy, holding a six-pack in one hand.

Olde English 500. Had to be. These days Tony might drive a Lamborghini, but some things never changed.

Tony opened the door and slid inside. He popped a brew and handed it to Harold.

Harold said, "You're late."

"Yeah. I had drouble gedding away."

"Hey," Harold said. "Are you okay? You sound like you're sick or something."

Tony flicked on the overhead light. The skin around his eyes was black and blue. His nose was a mess of thick white tape and Popsicle sticks. Bloodstained cotton poked from his nostrils.

"Dip me in shit and roll me in sugar," Harold said. "What happened to you?"

Tony said, "Jack Baddalach."

Harold could believe in a lot of weird stuff. Space aliens visiting Area 51. The Loch Ness Monster. Demons in Daddy Deke's mine shaft. But Jack Baddalach, alive? When he'd been locked up tight with a rattlesnake? No way, man. No fucking way.

"Yes way," Tony said. "No fugging ghosd did dis do my nose."

"Maybe we should call the whole thing off," Harold said. "I told Baddalach some stuff that I probably should have kept to myself. Just started talking, because I figured he was a dead man and I wanted to get him relaxed so he wouldn't guess what was coming when I pulled off the highway. Anyway, he must have remembered the stuff I talked about. That must be how he connected me to you."

"Spilt milk. Like you said, you figured the guy was a corpse. No use worrying about it. So the motherfucker showed up on my doorstep. So he got lucky and broke my nose. No way can he make me talk, no matter what he does."

"It's not just Baddalach." Harold shook his head. "It's this fucking family I'm dealing with. They're getting nuttier by the minute. The only one I really trust is Eden, and I think she's at the end of her rope."

"For a chick you turned out, she sounds pretty special. I can't wait to meet her."

"Yeah. But this fucking family. I swear to God, Tony, it's like *The Hills Have Eyes* out there—"

"We're close," Tony said. "Real close. Just one more day and we'll both have what we want."

Harold drained his malt liquor and reached for another. It was hard to understand Tony with his nose all busted and everything. Jesus, this asshole Baddalach was something. Harold wondered how in the hell the motherfucker had gotten past that big fucking diamondback. And now this—

"I don't know," Harold said. "This Baddalach is a bulldog. And he's only one step away."

"He's only one guy. And I've got a sure fire way to keep him busy. Believe me, the last thing he'll be thinking about tomorrow is a kidnapped Chihuahua."

"Okay, then. I'm still up for it."

"The whole nine yards?"

"Right down the line, brother."

"Good," Tony said. "Did you call the Gemignani bitch?"

Harold nodded. "You should have heard her. Man, she was scared shitless. Especially when I told her that she was going to have to make the drop alone if she wanted to see Spike alive."

"Think she'll tell her grandfather?"

"No. She's got no reason to. She's already got the money." Harold sipped his Olde English. "All she's got to do is unlock a safe-deposit box, right?"

"Right. Granddaddy gave her the key on her twenty-first birthday. It's her own personal stash of Gemignani Family swag, and the taxman doesn't know anything about it. The rich bitch. She makes a withdrawal now and then, parties down with her little friends. They all know about it."

"Thank God for girl talk."

"Pillow talk's more like it," Tony said.

"Don't rub my nose in it, stud." Harold laughed. "Anyway, I told Angel I'd call tomorrow and tell her where to deliver the ransom. Eden's sisters spent the day getting the place ready. As long as Angel gets out of the casino without her granddaddy noticing, we'll be in the clear."

"And you'll have a half a million bucks."

Harold whistled through his teeth. "And you'll have Angel Gemignani."

"Yeah." Tony sniffled blood. "And her little dog, too."

Tony killed his Olde English and popped another. "This Eden's really special, huh?"

"Yeah." Harold looked out the window at the big ripe moon. "She is. Man, she's a keeper."

Harold really liked times like this. Hanging with his blood brother. Tony didn't put on airs around Harold. He didn't talk all that fancy talk that he talked on TV. Nights like this, it was just like rapping on the block in the slams, rapping all night to keep the fucking loneliness far, far away.

Tony popped a couple of Percodans and chased them with malt liquor. He was quiet for a couple minutes. Then he said, "Porschia walked out on me today."

"Again?" Harold was really surprised. "What happened this time?"

"I think maybe I fucked up. Everything's so fucking complicated lately. Little shit gets in the way. Little shit all of a sudden becomes big shit, and it's like I don't know where I stand anymore. I can't see anything clearly."

"Things used to be easier."

"Yeah."

They both thought it, but neither one said it.

Things used to be easier . . . in the Shoe.

In the Shoe, you knew just where you stood. There was you and your blood brother, and that Mexican Mafia tag team, and that guard with the lip that wouldn't smile. And when you took down your spic, you checked on your blood brother. And if he needed some help with his spic, you gave it to him.

And even if he didn't, you watched his back. You kept your eye on that fucking hack with the lip, because you knew he had it in for your bro. And if you saw that hack shoulder his rifle and take aim when your bro wasn't even looking . . . well, you got in the way of the bullet is what you did.

And you wore your brother's scars.

That's what brothers were for.

"That bitch Porschia," Harold said. "I can't believe she left you."

"Yeah. I thought maybe we were going somewhere. I guess she saw things differently."

"Her loss, amigo. Her loss."

They sat together in silence, drinking Olde English, watching the icy white moon rise in the night sky. Harold knew he should be getting back. Eden was wrapped way too tight. She was probably worried about him. And then there was the dog, and Eden's snakebit daddy, and her crazy mama . . .

But Tony was all fucked up. Harold could tell. That bitch Porschia. Why she had to leave him, today of all days—

"You gotta get back?" Tony asked.

"No, man," Harold lied. "Not yet."

"Good," Tony said, and the word echoed through the Chevy as if it had been spoken in a cell made of cement and steel.

TWO

THE KID'S NAME WAS JOHNNY DA NANG, AND ONE OF THESE DAYS HE was going to be famous.

He had the talent, that was for sure. He fronted Johnny Da Nang and the Napalms, the world's best Vietnamese soul band. The Napalms were Johnny's brothers, and the band had a regular gig at the Casbah Hotel & Casino, where they partied down at the Sheik's Lounge five nights a week. Rocked the house and set the slot grannies to dancing in front of damn near every one-armed bandit within earshot. There wasn't a Motown song that Johnny and his boys couldn't do. They had sixties and seventies soul covered, and then some. Didn't matter if the song had come out of Muscle Shoals or Philadelphia or Detroit or LA, the Napalms had 'em all knocked.

Hell, a Saigon-born boy like Johnny could even sing 'em in Vietnamese or French if he wanted to. Do Marvin Gaye's "Sexual Healing" en Français: *Quand j'ai cette sensation . . . Ohhh la la . . .* no translation necessary. *Not even.*

Multiculturalism. It was a big thick slice of all right. Up-tight and outta sight. Ditto for the Casbah gig. But the gig was just a stepping-stone. Johnny wanted his own shot at the brass ring. He wanted his own hit records. Somewhere down the line, he wanted to walk into the Sheik's Lounge and catch some kid doing one of *his* songs.

The big time. That's what Johnny wanted. It was one reason he enjoyed living at the Agua Caliente condominium complex. Lots of show people did. And they were social types, too. Everyone hung out at the pool. Drag down a six-pack and some chips, and you had all the advice you could ask for. Actors, musicians, dancers, athletes—you could find 'em all at Agua Caliente.

Some had enjoyed fifteen minutes of fame. A few had stretched it out a little longer. But for damn near every one of them, celebrity was a past-tense kind of thing.

Except for the guy who was about to knock on Johnny's door.

He was the man of the hour.

Johnny handed Baddalach a Tsing Tao. Right away the boxer started rolling the beer bottle back and forth across his knuckles. Johnny had known Jack for a couple years—after all, they both worked at the Casbah and lived in the same condo complex—and he'd seen Baddalach do that rolling thing with a beer bottle plenty of times. The boxer hardly ever popped the cap and drank one. Kind of a weird habit, but hey . . . Johnny Da Nang was not a judgmental type of guy.

"Whatcha been up to, Jack?"

The boxer sighed. "Well, yesterday I lost the boss's grand-daughter's Chihuahua to a bunch of dognappers dressed in black leather. Then I got locked in the trunk of a limo and had to bite a rattlesnake in half before I could get out. Last night I beat up a couple of punk rockers who tried to smash

Frankenstein with baseball bats. And today I KO'd the heavyweight champion of the world."

Johnny nearly dropped his beer.

"Oh yeah," Jack added. "Somewhere in there I ate a lot of donuts, too."

"Jack," Johnny said. "*Jack . . .*"

Like, Johnny couldn't *even* think of anything to say. But Baddalach seemed pretty unfazed by the whole deal. He said, "Here's the thing, Johnny. A pack of TV reporters has my place staked out—"

"No way!" Johnny peeked through the venetian blinds like some spy on *The Man From U.N.C.L.E* or something. Baddalach wasn't kidding. A TV truck from Channel 13 was parked next to Johnny's Corvette, and a local reporter was doing a remote setup over by the pool. Another TV reporter had staked out the hot tub. He was getting ready to interview a couple Agua Caliente residents who were pretty close to parboiled. No way they were giving up a chance to be on TV, though.

Johnny recognized the hot tub reporter as a sports guy.

For CNN! You couldn't buy exposure like this. *Not even.* CNN meant *national* play. Like, *everyone* was going to know about *this*.

Johnny said, "You're not shitting me, are you Jack? You really knocked out Tony Katt?"

"Like I said—"

"Like, in the ring? You knocked out Tony the Tiger *in the ring*?"

"Kind of. We were in his private gym. See, he lives in this big mansion over by the golf course. First I broke a couple windows hacking at golf balls. I wanted to piss him off, and the whole thing kind of got out of hand. And then we put on the gloves and had this fight—"

Johnny was practically drooling. "Jack, you know how

big this is? I mean, the guy is the heavyweight champion of the world. He's *undefeated*. The baddest man on the planet. And you just *knocked him out*."

"To tell you the truth, the whole thing is a pain in the ass. Katt's trainer is really pissed. He threatened to sue me. And then I come home and find all these reporters hanging around. I had to park my Celica down the street and sneak in on foot. I can't even go home."

Baddalach rolled the beer back and forth. Johnny peeked outside again. The CNN guy was going live.

Like Quick-Draw McGraw, Johnny snatched up the TV remote. He aimed and clicked and the big Sony television came on. There was the reporter, on screen in living color, standing in front of the Agua Caliente swimming pool. He was talking about Jack Baddalach. Talking about Johnny's neighbor like he had stepped down from Mount Olympus or something.

And forget that "Battle-ax" stuff. Jack's nickname of choice was suddenly very five minutes ago. The reporter had a new tag for the light-heavyweight who'd chilled the baddest big man alive.

Jack "The Giant Killer" Baddalach.

Two minutes of air and the blow-dried sports guy was still going strong. Live. In prime time. On fucking CNN.

CNN rolled clips from Jack's old fights, but he wasn't paying attention. "So, Johnny, I'm wondering if maybe I can sleep on your couch tonight," he said. "I know it's a lot to ask. But I'll make it up to you. You want to order a pizza or something, I'll pick up the check."

Johnny looked at the guy. Sitting there in a black T-shirt and jeans, wearing those same old work boots he always wore come rain or shine, rolling a frosty Tsing Tao back and forth across his bruised knuckles.

Johnny couldn't believe it. Man, all Baddalach had to do was open his hand and look.

It was right there, nestled in his palm.

The brass ring.

And Jack didn't know it.

Not even.

They ate Popeye's Fried Chicken for dinner. That was Johnny's idea. He figured Jack could maybe get a commercial gig with Popeye's since he'd KO'd a guy with a Colonel Sanders tattoo.

All through the meal Johnny talked about name identification and product placement and pay-per-view and the talk show circuit and a whole bunch of other stuff that Jack didn't need to hear. All he wanted was a little sliver of peace and quiet so he could think. But the only time Johnny Da Nang shut up was when he was asleep. And he hardly slept at all.

But Jack was in luck, because Johnny had to go to work. The singer managed to slip in an offer to be Jack's manager before he left, though. Jack said he'd think it over.

Man, he couldn't believe all this stuff on the TV. His ruckus with Tony Katt had turned into the hot sports story of the night. Tomorrow morning the newspapers would be full of it.

As it stood, the reporters had pretty much run the initial story dry and were shifting into speculative overdrive. Of course Katt was going to have to cancel his next fight, they said. The champion couldn't do battle with a broken nose. And the nose couldn't heal in three weeks' time.

No one would want to see Katt fight some no-name contender, anyway. A fight like that wouldn't draw flies at the box office. No. Only one opponent loomed large in Tony Katt's future.

Jack Baddalach.

Jack the Giant Killer.

The Giant Killer shook his head. Man oh man oh man. All this crazy adrenaline was burning him down. It really did feel like a fire, the same hungry fire that had torched his belly when he climbed into the ring with the heavyweight champion of the world.

Jack hadn't felt that fire for a very long time.

And there was the money, too.

Money like Jack had never seen.

Heavyweight money. Millions.

Jack lay in the darkness, his face bathed in the dull blue glow of the digital clock on Johnny's VCR. The hours slipped by. One o'clock. Two. Then three. And still Jack was the same guy he'd always been. In the darkness, his beef with Tony Katt didn't seem like such a big deal. By the glow of a VCR clock, it was easy to believe that the whole thing would blow over by the time he finished breakfast.

And what would he do with a couple million bucks, anyway? Trade in the Celica for a cherried-out Mustang? Buy more Dean Martin records? Track down every paperback Dan J. Marlowe had ever written? Replace his busted set of Sneaky Tiki glasses?

Jack's tastes weren't exactly expensive. A couple million bucks . . . hell, he wouldn't even know what to do with it. And if having that much money meant dealing with investment counselors and lawyers and accountants and IRS agents, Jack figured he was better off without it.

Around four, he peeked through the venetian blinds. The bushes seemed free of lurking reporters. Frankenstein was waiting at home. The surly old bulldog was probably hungry. So was Jack.

He left Johnny's place and crossed the courtyard. He'd

eat some breakfast. Get some sleep. And then he'd figure another way to track down Harold Ticks.

That plan went out the window when Jack checked his answering machine.

There were forty-three messages.

Most of the messages were from reporters—TV, print, radio, even some guy who did a boxing website on the Internet.

And it seemed like everyone Jack had ever met had left a message, too. Well, everyone except Kate Benteen.

A friend in Hawaii said Jack could chill out at her place as long as (1) he didn't mind her dog and (2) he understood that everything would have to be platonic because her new *kahuna* wouldn't have it any other way. Freddy G wanted to know where to commit Jack's crazy ass. The tattooed waitress from True Blue Donuts called to say that there was a bag of devil's food donuts waiting for him, on the house. Even Jack's mother checked in—she wanted to know when her son had taken up golf.

The important messages didn't come until the end of the tape. The first one sounded like it was made from a pay phone. Cars rushed by in the background, and the speaker's words seemed garbled and indistinct. But that was understandable, because it was hard to talk when your nose had been taped to a Popsicle-stick splint and your nasal passages were stuffed with a couple yards of cotton.

Tony Katt did his patented King of the Jungle rap: Jack Baddalach had disturbed the balance of nature. Jack Baddalach had upset the natural order of the universe. Jack Baddalach knew not what disaster he had wrought upon mankind. Jack Baddalach now walked the road of death, and that road was paved with misery and pain and suffering eternal.

Another call followed quickly on the heels of Katt's poetic diatribe. This one was from a man Jack thought of as the greatest leech of all time, boxing promoter Caligula Tate. Let's let bygones be bygones, Jack-o. There's money to be made. Millions. Plenty for everyone. Come one, come all. Bathe in the spotlight of riches and glory.

You want riches, Jack-o? Just do what you did this afternoon. Today you did it for free. Do it again for a pay-per-view audience and the world will be your oyster. Do it again and dollars beyond counting will be yours.

Do it again and you'll be heavyweight champion of the world.

You'll have the belt, Jack. Your name in the record books right along those of Dempsey, Marciano, Ali . . .

Jack thought about it. He really did. He didn't hear the next three or four messages. That's how hard he was thinking.

But he heard the last one.

Angel Gemignani said, "I heard about what happened today with you and Tony Katt."

Jack sensed desperation and confusion in Angel's voice. He listened intently as she continued. "Anyway . . . if you think Tony is involved in Spike's disappearance, then there's something I need to tell you . . . and it's something that I can't tell you over the phone."

A pause, fearful and wary.

"Call me, Jack. Please."

THREE

THEY CALLED IT THE WOLF'S HOUR, THAT TIME OF NIGHT WHEN FEAR held dominion over the wicked and the pure.

Eden stared through the open pillbox window. Dead blue moonlight bathed the desert. Daddy's chapel stood in a grove of twisted yucca trees. From inside, the harsh glare of kerosene lanterns slashed cracks in the walls and streamed across the desert, as if the night had been gutted and was bleeding afternoon.

The stock of Harold's .357 Magnum was slick with Eden's sweat. She held tight to the pistol and watched the chapel door. Mama and Daddy were still inside. They had to be. Eden had watched the chapel for hours, and she'd seen nothing. The only sign of movement was an occasional flicker as someone—Eden imagined it was Mama—passed in front of a kerosene lantern.

Anguish whipped Eden as she remembered bursting through the chapel door. The whole thing happened so fast. Of course she didn't want Daddy to get hurt. She only wanted to protect the Chihuahua.

Daddy was surprised. His concentration was broken

when he needed it most. His link with Satan vanished in the wink of an eye and the big albino rattler sprang, biting Daddy's face, pumping its venom into his blood.

Mama tore the viper loose. In the time it took her to do that, Eden's entire world changed.

Because Eden no longer had a family. Mama disowned her, speaking those horrible words that gouged and hacked like the blade of an ax. If Daddy lived, he would do the same. Eden couldn't blame them. Everything Mama said about her was right. She *did* cry too much. She *was* weak.

And there was nothing she could do about it. She had tried so hard—beseeching Satan night after night, asking him for power. She had taken the fork in the road that lead to wickedness, taken it willingly. Her body was a temple to sin.

But through it all Eden's heart remained pure, and that was her great downfall. Guilt was the horse she rode, and she lashed it with a quirt called conscience.

In the end she always surrendered to her weaknesses. In the end she always surrendered to her tears.

Eden's head dipped. Where was Harold? He should have returned long ago. She couldn't stay awake much longer. Her eyelids were so heavy. And so was the gun. Her wrist was killing her. It felt like someone had jammed hot coals between the bones in her forearm.

Maybe she could set down the Magnum for a minute. Just a minute. Give her wrist a rest. Maybe she could take a little break, remove her braces, run some cool water over her aching wrist—

Or maybe she could lean against the wall and close her eyes. Just for a minute. The cement was so cool against her sweaty skin, and she needed to rest her eyes really badly.

After all, the window was open. If Mama or Daddy left the chapel, she'd hear the creaking door. She could rest her eyes for a minute. She could trust her ears . . .

The sound brought Eden sharply awake.

Someone breathing heavily, behind her.

Eden whirled, snatching up the pistol.

The Chihuahua lay on the bed, muzzle open as it drew rasping, tortured breaths. It was so sick. It couldn't sleep at all, not with that horrible cough. Eden tried to look at the dog and see only money. If she could only trust in Satan, truly trust in Him with all her heart, then she could see the dog clearly.

Spike whimpered. Guilt slashed Eden's heart. She reached out, pain jolting her forearm as she bent her wrist. Lightly, with feather touches, she stroked Spike's fur.

Tears welled in her eyes. It wasn't fair. Spike was just a stupid dog. An animal not even worthy of sacrifice in Daddy's chapel. If only she could see the Chihuahua through Mama's eyes. Then she wouldn't care one little bit about the dog.

Eden curled up on the bed, pulling the Chihuahua to her belly. Spike's breathing slowed a bit as he snuggled against her. "It's going to be okay," Eden said. "It's going to be okay."

She would only close her eyes for a minute.

She wouldn't fall asleep.

Harold was counting on her. She had to stay awake.

She would only close her eyes for a minute . . .

Drifting . . . drifting . . . sleep . . .

Mama's face . . . Mama's words . . . *You're so weak . . . You can't be no daughter of mine . . . I never wanted you . . . If I had it to do over again I'd rip you from my belly with a coat hanger—*

Someone was shaking her.

"Wake up, sweetie."

By the time Eden clawed her way up from the pit of sleep, the intruder had already handcuffed one of her wrists to the bedpost.

A moment later the other wrist was handcuffed, and none too gently. The pain was supersonic, as if someone had squirted lighter fluid on those burning coals between the bones in her forearm. Still, Eden struggled against the pain. She kicked with all her might as hands closed over legs, but the intruders—for there were two of them—overpowered her, cuffing her ankles as well.

Spike jumped off the bed and crawled to the far corner of the room. Eden twisted and turned, but there was no escaping her bonds.

Tura and Lorelei stared down at her. With all that had happened, Eden had nearly forgotten about her sisters. They'd spent the day setting up the drop site out in the desert. They probably had no idea what had happened with Mama and Daddy—

Eden had to tell them. There wasn't time for sick practical jokes. "You can't do this," she said. "Not now. Mama's gone crazy. And Daddy is—"

Tura slapped Eden's cheek. "Save it."

Lorelei stuffed a pair of panties into Eden's mouth. "We're gonna teach you a lesson, Eden."

"Yeah." Tura plastered a square of duct tape over Eden's mouth. "You crossed the line this time, princess."

Eden stared up at them, unable to speak. They knew. They had to know. They must have talked to Mama while Eden slept. And Daddy . . . why, the way they were acting . . . Daddy was probably *dead*.

"We're going to make you pay," Lorelei said.

Again, Tura's hard fingers whipped Eden's cheek.

"You shouldn't have stolen my Fig Newtons, bitch," Tura said. "And if you ever touch my vibrator again, I'll kill you."

When they finished with their sister, Tura and Lorelei noticed the Chihuahua.

The dog could hardly breathe. Hacking and coughing—it sounded like a death rattle or something.

Lorelei said, "The little fucker's really sick."

"Yeah. And if he dies, we're screwed. Nobody's gonna pay a half a million for a dead dog."

"What should we do?"

Tura glanced at her watch. "We've got another twenty hours until the drop. That's a lot of time. Maybe we should take the little fucker to a vet."

"Where are we gonna find a vet at this hour?"

"You remember that guy in Vegas. That old Methuselah you were kidding me about? The one who used to come to the club almost every night?"

"You mean Dr. Gooddoggy?" Lorelei asked.

"Yeah. Frank Newman. He's the best vet in Vegas. When we quit he gave me his home number. Said if I ever wanted to take him to obedience school, all I needed to do was call."

Lorelei passed the telephone to her sister. The conversation was short and to the point. "He says his wife is a light sleeper," Tura said. "He'll meet us at his office."

Lorelei grabbed Spike. Tura set the handcuff keys on the edge of Eden's dresser. "Harold can let you loose when he comes home," she said. "Unless he wants to have some fun with you, too."

"Tell your boyfriend we'll be back by noon," Lorelei said. "That'll leave us plenty of time before the ransom drop."

"And tell Harold that he's paying us an extra share for this," Tura added. "He should have had a backup plan in case the pooch got sick. We shouldn't have to do all his thinking for him."

Eden tried to tell them about the Harold Ticks Shuffle. Tura and Lorelei didn't know about Harold's real plan. But with the duct tape over her mouth, she couldn't say a word.

They didn't need to take the dog to a vet. It only had to live until tomorrow. After that it would be dead, anyway.

Eden watched her sisters walk down the hall. The front door slammed. Tura's old Chevrolet Apache truck rumbled alive. Tires chewed hard-packed desert earth as Tura, Lorelei, and Spike headed for the highway.

It was quiet for one hour . . . then two . . . and finally Eden slept.

The sun began to rise. The pillbox window framed a hard square of light that traveled Eden's naked body.

She squinted and came awake.

She heard Harold's car.

Satan, she prayed, give me strength . . .

Harold said, "This is fucked. The dog is gone. So are your sisters. Your mama's gone nuts and your daddy's probably a corpse." He shook his head. "And you want to know what else? That asshole Jack Baddalach is still alive, and he knows that Tony has something to do with the dognapping."

Eden didn't say a word. She just sat there. Harold couldn't believe it. She just fucking sat there.

Naked. Rubbing her wrists. Crying.

Jesus Christ. Always with the tears.

She wasn't going to make him feel guilty, though. No way. It wasn't his fault that he was late getting back. Tony needed him. His *brother* needed him. Tony was hurting.

Man, he couldn't just walk out on Tony when he was like that. No way.

So they drank two sixes of Olde English. So they took some Percodan. So what?

He wasn't going to feel guilty. *No way.*

And this crying shit. It had to stop. Right now.

"Eden, I told you . . ." he began. "I told you not to let anyone touch the dog. I told you that, didn't I?"

She nodded. Big heavy sobs now. Oh, man.

"Fuck," he said, banging his fist against the door. "*Fuck!*"

Eden cringed as if he'd hit her. Jesus. *His* hand all of a sudden felt like it was busted, and *she* was acting hurt.

"I told you it was important." Harold tried to stay calm. "I asked if you understood. I told you not to fuck things up."

Eden looked up at him. Her icy blue eyes were wet with tears, like the irises were melting or something. She opened her mouth, but no words came out.

Harold picked up his .357. "I even gave you my fucking gun, Eden."

She opened her arms to him, spread wide, palms open.

Oh, man, he couldn't take this. Seeing her all fucked up. It was like everything was changing right before his eyes. Like getting out of Corcoran all over again. Like going to that hotel room, opening the door, and seeing that familiar anaconda tattoo on a woman he didn't even recognize . . .

Turning around. Walking out . . .

"I've got to go set up the drop," Harold said, even though it was way too early for that.

He couldn't get out of there fast enough.

"Don't go," Eden said. "Don't go."

But he did. Harold was already gone when she said it. He had left her behind. And she loved him. She really did.

She couldn't stop crying. It seemed she would never run

out of tears. She had enough for everyone—for Harold, for Tura and Lorelei, for Mama and Daddy, for the little dog . . .

Eden cried for all of them.

She did not cry for herself.

It was much too late for that.

FOUR

JACK WAS JUST ABOUT TO PHONE ANGEL GEMIGNANI WHEN SHE knocked on his front door.

"I just got your message," he explained. "What's going on? You didn't sound so great."

Angel didn't look so great, either. Her eyes were red and puffy. She had obviously spent the night crying instead of sleeping.

Jack showed her to the living room. "I couldn't stand waiting around the Casbah," she said. "I had to get out. I figured maybe you didn't return my call because of the other night. I know you and Grandpa Freddy are friends and everything . . . and I know I must seem like some kind of schizo to you. I guess I came on pretty strong, and then when my granddad showed up—"

"It takes two to dance that dance," Jack said. "Don't be so hard on yourself."

Angel smiled one of those peculiar smiles that holds no pleasure. "Anyway, I thought maybe you were mad at me. I'm glad you're not, because I really need to talk to you. If Tony Katt has something to do with Spike's kidnapping . . ."

"I'm not mad," Jack said. "And I *was* going to call you. I just got in. As for Tony Katt, I'm not sure what part he plays in all this. All I know for sure is that one of the dognappers is an old friend of Tony's."

"Okay." Angel yawned. "God . . . what time is it, anyway?"

"Almost five."

Angel sat down on Jack's couch. "I can't *even* remember the last time I was up this early."

"You mean when you weren't still up from the night before."

Jack had intended the comment as a joke. Judging from Angel's expression, she didn't take it that way. She looked as if she'd been slapped when she least expected it.

"Hey," Jack said. "I'm sorry. Whatever I said—"

"It's okay." Angel wiped her eyes. "I'm just really tired. This whole thing with Spike has me seriously screwed up."

Jack handed her a Kleenex. "I was just going to make some coffee. Feel like a cup?"

"Sure."

Jack ground some French roast and got the coffee brewing. From the kitchen, he kept an eye on Angel. The way she was fidgeting, he got the feeling that she wouldn't be able to sit still for long.

He was right. Angel rose and sorted through the old suspense paperbacks piled on his desktop, laughing softly at overblown cover copy hacked out in the fifties.

At least she could still laugh. Jack poured two cups of coffee and returned to the living room. Angel was looking at the framed picture of Kate Benteen that he kept on his desk, the one that he had clipped from an old issue of *Vanity Fair*.

"Is this your girl?" Angel asked.

"Well, she's nobody's *girl*." Jack smiled.

So did Angel. "One of *those*, huh?"

"Yeah. One of those."

"So what's the story?"

"I'm waiting to see if she calls me or not."

"How long have you been waiting?"

Jack blushed. He suddenly felt like looking at his shoes.

Angel asked again. "How long?"

"Almost a year."

"Uh-huh." Angel smiled. "So, like I said, what's the story?"

The question hit Jack between the eyes. He had to think about it for a minute. The whole thing with Kate was so complicated. But Angel's question was really simple.

So was Jack's answer, though this was the first time he had ever articulated it. "I guess the story is that I'm in love with her, and I'm waiting to see if she's in love with me."

"Do you know how long you're going to wait, Jack?"

"No, I don't. If I put a date on it, and she didn't call . . . well, I guess I don't want to think about how I'd feel the day after that."

Angel set the picture on Jack's desk. "She's a lucky girl. I mean *woman*. She may not know it, but she's lucky."

Jack didn't say anything.

"I guess I've spent a lot of time not being lucky," Angel said. "I guess in a lot of ways it's my own fault."

Jack said, "Don't be so hard on yourself."

"Oh, I think I'm way past due being hard on myself." Angel sipped her coffee. "Let me tell you about me and Tony Katt . . ."

Angel thought pink ladies were the prettiest cocktail going. She loved the thickness of the drink and the way the taste of gin and cream and grenadine lingered on her tongue.

The gin warmed her inside and made her glow outside. Angel was usually kind of nervous, actually. She didn't have a whole lot of self-confidence, and she knew it. Oh, she acted tough enough. Hell, she had a rattlesnake tattoo and a closet filled with black clothes, and having those things made it easier to act like she actually was the way she wanted to be.

But Angel knew the difference between acting tough and being tough. You could buy a tattoo. You could buy black clothes. But you couldn't buy confidence.

That was why she took Spike everywhere she went. He made her feel better and gave her something she could talk about if things got uncomfortable. Spike was especially good at parties. Get a stranger talking about your cute little dog and you wouldn't have to talk about yourself at all.

But back to the pink ladies. The pretty pink color, the taste, the warm glow—that was all good. But the best part came when a guy asked her if he could get her a drink. Tell a guy you wanted a pink lady, and he kind of looked at you in a different way. Angel really believed that was true.

And that was the first thing Tony Katt asked her. "Can I get you a drink?"

Angel said, "A pink lady would be lovely."

"How about for your dog?"

"Oh no, he's driving."

Ha ha ha ha. They had a real good laugh over that one. Tony went for the drink. He was gone for quite a while. The party was really slammed. A big New Year's Eve deal at the Skull Island Hotel & Casino. Angel had lost track of all her friends at the celebrity wingding at the Mirage. Way too many mellow LA rockers at that one for her taste, so she'd cut out on her own.

Along the way she had a couple more pink ladies. And now the heavyweight champion of the world was getting her another. She couldn't fucking believe it.

She waited for Tony to return. God, he was the heavyweight champion of the world. And in a room filled with women who would probably sit up and beg just to talk to him, he was getting a drink for Angel Gemignani.

Angel felt the glow. Suddenly she felt really pretty, which she usually didn't. But right now she knew that she *was* pretty, wearing a little sleeveless Versace number that was as black as sin.

The dress was very expensive. Anyone would look hot in it.

Image was everything. Image could cover up a lot.

And here came Tony with her drink, and he was staring at her. Like, right at the rattler tattoo.

"Watch out," he said. "A buddy of mine gave me a serious warning about girls with snake tattoos."

"Yeah," she said, all throaty like Lauren Bacall. "You'd *better* watch out."

Tony gave her biceps a little squeeze and she kind of laughed. "You're Angel Gemignani, right?"

"Yeah," she said, all surprised. She couldn't believe that the heavyweight champion of the world knew who she was.

"Angel," he said. "That's a pretty name."

"Thanks." Angel's real name was Angela. But she hated it. Angela sounded so clunky.

"We've got a few mutual friends." Tony ticked off five or six names, mostly guys Angel had dated at one time or another, a couple girlfriends, too. "Vegas is really a small town, isn't it?" He took her hand and kissed it. "I'm surprised we haven't met before." He held her fingers in his. "By the way, my name is Tony Katt."

"Like I don't know who you are." Angel didn't know what else to say.

But that was okay because Tony did. He could really talk. He sounded like he'd been to college and then some. He sure didn't sound like a guy who'd come out of a state prison in California.

But Angel knew that Tony had done just that. She'd seen him win the heavyweight championship. Grandpa Freddy was a big boxing fan. He went to all the fights. He took Angel to see that one.

She remembered watching Tony in the ring that night. She remembered his muscles, and his tattoos, and the way he looked so tough, so . . . confident.

But he didn't seem egotistical at all. Not now. Not like he did on TV. Maybe that was all an act, because he seemed really nice.

They danced a little, but it was hard to hold Spike and dance at the same time. Tony got Angel another pink lady. She didn't really want another drink. She barely sipped it. Tony set Spike on his lap and started petting him. He talked and talked.

But then Tony started glancing at his watch, and she couldn't help but notice that.

"Sorry," he said finally. "I realize that it's terribly rude of me. But I'm supposed to meet my fiancée at another party before midnight. And it's almost eleven now."

"Oh," Angel said. She didn't know what else to say, because she had started to think that . . . well, maybe . . . but if Tony had a fiancée and—

"Hey," Tony said. "Why don't you join us?"

Angel wasn't sure. Tony seemed like a really nice guy. But going off with him when they'd just met—

"I'm sure my fiancée would love to meet you," Tony said. "Her name is Porschia Keyes. She's a dancer here at Skull Island."

That was different. If Tony's fiancée was going to be at the party—

"It's mostly a celebrity crowd. Nothing but fun people. So you know you qualify on both counts."

Angel felt that glow. He really did like her.

"C'mon," he coaxed. "It'll be fun. Really."

"Sure." She rubbed the rattlesnake tattoo like it was Aladdin's lamp. "Why the hell not. I'm always up for fun."

New Year's Eve on the Las Vegas Strip was really slammed. No way you could drive anywhere. Still, Angel was really surprised when Tony took her to the roof of the hotel, where they boarded a Skull Island corporate helicopter.

They flew above the lights of Vegas. It was really special. All those people partying down on the Strip. Soon they were over a neighborhood Angel didn't recognize. A golf course surrounded by super-nice houses. Mansions, really.

The chopper hovered lower, passing over the roof of a mansion. Angel was kind of surprised. It didn't look like there was a party here. Only two cars were parked in the driveway.

Angel was a little worried. Her Versace dress was riding up, and she pulled it low on her thighs. As low as it would go, anyway.

"Is this the right place?" she asked.

"This is my house," Tony said. "I need to pick up a few Christmas gifts that I haven't had a chance to deliver. Then we'll drive over in my car. The party isn't far."

The chopper touched down on the golf course next to the house. Tony opened the door and stepped out before Angel could say a word.

He offered her his hand.

Just like a real gentleman.

The Christmas tree that stood in the domed living room was nearly twenty feet high. Angel stared at the twinkling white lights and decorations, cradling Spike in her arms. She wished Tony would hurry up. It was almost midnight. Even if they left his place right now, they would probably be late for the party. Angel was worried about that. Tony's fiancée would be really mad. She'd probably take it out on him, but she might take it out on Angel.

Either way, Angel didn't want to be with a bunch of strangers right now. But how could she get back to the Strip? The chopper was long gone . . .

Maybe Tony would call a cab for her. She'd say that the pink ladies were hitting her a little too hard, and that she wasn't feeling especially well . . .

No. That wouldn't work, either. The Strip was jammed with people. Getting to the Casbah by cab would be impossible. Tony knew that as well as she did. No way she could get back home until—

A pair of strong arms encircled her from behind.

"Tony. Hey . . . Tony. Don't."

Tony didn't listen. He pulled Angel against his belly, and she was so surprised that she nearly dropped Spike.

"Tony . . . stop!"

His hand was under her dress, between her legs and—

"Surprise, surprise," Tony said. "The Tiger didn't figure you for the panty-wearing type, bitch."

"No!" Angel shouted, and Spike jumped from her arms.

She spun away from Tony. He let her go. She gasped for breath. Spike was over by the Christmas tree. In a second she'd pick him up and head for the door—

Tony was wearing a black silk robe. Nothing else. He let the robe fall open. "You might as well get down on the floor and spread your legs, Angel. It'll go a lot easier that way."

She was still a little drunk. She tried to think logically. She said, "But your fiancée . . . the party—"

"There is no party. Except for the one we're having here."

He smiled. "I do have a fiancée, though. I didn't lie about that. The bitch walked out on me last night. It's not the first time she's done it, and it won't be the last."

Angel backed toward the Christmas tree. "You know who I am. You know who my grandfather is. If he finds out about this—"

"He won't find out." Tony slipped off his robe and followed her. "You won't tell him. Just think how it would sound: Grandpa, I got drunk with the heavyweight champ on New Year's Eve. You know, the jailbird with all the tattoos. I let him take me home. And then he—"

"Stop it. Just stop it."

But Tony didn't stop at all. He grabbed her and tossed her against the wall. She had nowhere to run. And then his hand closed around her throat.

"Stop it, Angel," he said. "Stop acting so innocent. Everyone in town knows your game. Those guys I mentioned . . . they told me all about you. Even your girlfriends are wise to you. You're a little starfucker."

"No . . . I'm not—"

"Come off it. I've been in the best bars in Las Vegas, honey. And I've seen your name written on the restroom wall in every damn one of 'em."

"That's not true."

Tony smiled a really awful smile. "Tell me it's not."

His hand slid under her dress. Angel slammed her fists against his chest, but he only laughed and shoved her back against the wall.

Spike scampered around his ankles, barking. He kicked the dog away. Then he came at Angel again.

The point of her shoe smacked his shin and he grunted. He slapped her and called her a bitch. She slapped him back and then he caught her hand and turned her around and suddenly she was on the floor, her face buried in the thick shag carpet, and Spike was barking again and Tony's hands were between her legs and he roughly parted her thighs.

"No!" she screamed. "No!"

Tony laughed. Spike growled . . .

. . . and then Tony screamed.

Suddenly he was off her. Angel rolled over fast and gained her feet.

Tony lay on the white carpet.

Spike was between his legs.

There was a lot of blood.

"Spike!" Angel shouted. "Spike . . . no!"

Spike ran to her side. She scooped him up and stumbled to the door and didn't look back. As she ran down the driveway, she heard Tony Katt's screams.

The cool night breeze cut through her Versace dress as she hurried down the street. Gunfire exploded behind her. She ducked into some oleander bushes, clutching Spike to her breasts.

Not gunfire. Firecrackers. It was New Year's Eve. It was midnight. All over Las Vegas, women were kissing men that they loved. And here she was, cold and shivering, hiding in some stranger's oleander bushes, hoping that no one would see her at all.

When it was quiet, Angel started down the street. Spike whined in her arms, but she wouldn't set him on the ground. She was afraid that he might run off.

There were no pay phones in a neighborhood like this one. Angel had to keep walking, even if she had no idea where she was. Every time a car approached, she found a place to hide.

She didn't know how badly Tony was hurt. She was afraid that he would come looking for her. And Spike.

Finally, Angel found a way onto the golf course. She wandered toward a building that turned out to be the pro

shop. She was circling it, looking for a pay phone, when a
security guard stopped her.

He took her to an office. Angel paid him fifty dollars for
one phone call and another fifty to forget the whole thing.

Angel phoned a girlfriend who agreed to pick her up as
soon as the traffic died down. Then she sat in the office and
waited, petting Spike. The guard didn't say a word. He
didn't have to. The way he looked at her said it all.

When her friend arrived a few hours later, Angel left as
quickly as she could.

The guard stuffed two fifties into his pocket and laughed
at the girl in the little black dress as she crossed the parking
lot, clutching a dog to her bosom like it was a baby.

"You two have a Happy New Year," he yelled.

"The guy who drove the limo is an ex-con from California,"
Jack said. "His name is Harold Ticks, and he did time in
Corcoran State Prison with Tony Katt."

"They're after more than money. If Tony Katt's involved
in this, he wants revenge."

"Maybe. But we don't know that for sure. Maybe the
money *is* the revenge."

"I don't think so, Jack. One of the kidnappers phoned
me . . . probably this guy Harold Ticks. He said that I was
going to deliver the ransom, alone. He said if I didn't come
alone, Spike would end up dead. He's supposed to call back
with the details later today." She shook her head. "The guy
wants me to get the money from a safe-deposit box
Granddad set up for me a couple years ago. But if they want
me to deliver the ransom . . . well, then I think they want
me as much as they want the money."

Jack nodded. "The thing with Tony Katt . . . you never
told Freddy what happened?"

"He's my grandfather, Jack. I couldn't tell him about it.

Freddy Gemignani is the kind of man who thinks there are two kinds of women in the world—those with rings on their fingers and whores. He wouldn't understand."

"I don't know. Maybe he would. Maybe you owe him that chance."

"No. I'm not telling my grandfather anything. It was hard enough to tell you." Angel rose from the couch and carried her empty coffee cup to the kitchen. "There's got to be another way."

Jack sipped cold coffee. Angel was right about one thing. It was hard for her to tell him about Tony Katt. But it was harder for her to talk about herself—the private things she kept inside and the insecurities she never revealed to anyone.

Jack knew that, because he'd heard Angel's voice tremble when she spoke the word that cut her to the bone.

"Starfucker."

That word wasn't important to Jack Baddalach. He wasn't going to judge Angel Gemignani's past. Only Angel could do that.

But no matter what Angel had done in the past, she didn't deserve Tony Katt.

No woman deserved Tony Katt.

"What do you think we should do?" Angel asked.

Jack told her. It was kind of involved, but none of it mattered.

When the phone rang a second later, everything changed.

The voice on the other end of the line was cold as ice cream but twice as sweet. Jack recognized it right away.

He said, "You're the one with the wrist braces, right?"

"That's right, Jack. I never thought I'd be talking to you again. How'd you handle that rattler, anyway?"

"I ate it."

She laughed. "Well, I guess I don't want to tangle with you . . . or maybe I do."

"Yeah . . . right . . . how's the Chihuahua?"

"Sick. That's why I'm calling."

"Look, if Spike needs a vet—"

"We're way ahead of you, Jack."

"You've got a vet?"

"Yes, we do," she said, "and he's in Las Vegas. In fact, Spike's in for an office visit even as we speak. Want the address?"

"Sure." Jack laughed. "But first I'd like to know why you'd give it to me when I haven't given you half a million bucks."

"Because there's trouble in paradise, Jack."

"Huh?"

"Look," she said, "do you want your Chihuahua back or not?"

"Sure I do, but—"

"Then get a pencil. Here's the address . . ."

Jack slipped the Colt Python into his shoulder holster.

"This is all pretty complicated for a guy who's used to get hit in the head for a living," he said. "But I'd better check it out, anyway."

"You're not going alone."

"Yes, I am. Listen, Angel, these nuts kidnapping your dog is bad enough. If they snatch you, Freddy will kill me."

"One thing I decided after my night with Tony Katt—nobody's going to make me do anything I don't want to do. And I don't want to sit around waiting to see if some refugee from a Russ Meyer movie ambushes you or not."

"Angel, these people . . . they're *nuts*."

"So is Tony Katt. And I handled him, didn't I?"

Jack laughed. "Well, you had some help. If I remember the story right, it was Spike who chewed on Tony's balls."

"That's right." Angel slipped her .45 out of her purse. "And now Spike is in trouble. Which means that it's time for me to return the favor."

Jack wanted to argue the point.

But he didn't know how.

FIVE

"WHAT WE'RE LOOKING AT IS MOST LIKELY A CASE OF CHRONIC bronchitis. That's what the endoscopic examination indicates. We'll start Spike on some corticosteroids to reduce the inflammation. In addition I'll give you some cough suppressants, but don't use those unless Spike has trouble sleeping."

The vet handed the Chihuahua to Tura. "I did a bacterial culture, too. Just to be certain there's no infection. Why don't you give me your phone number, and I'll contact you when I receive the test results."

"I don't think that would be such a great idea." Tura smiled. "We'll call you, Doc."

Dr. Frank Newman, veterinarian to the stars, pushed his thick glasses high on his nose. Casually chic in a summer suit and bow tie, even at five-thirty in the morning, Newman was tall and cadaverously thin. Nearly seventy, he enjoyed playing the part of the kindly country doctor. His clients recognized that, and he knew he owed a good percentage of his business to the image he had created.

People needed to trust their veterinarian. They wanted a

sense of old-fashioned American values when they brought
Spot or Rover in for treatment. And who better to provide
that than Dr. Frank Newman, who looked as if he had
stepped out of a Norman Rockwell wall calendar?

Of course, Dr. Newman did not own a Norman Rockwell
wall calendar. No. He had a Harlot's Hollow wall calendar,
featuring twelve of the finest lap dancers known to man. It
was posted in the private bathroom adjacent to his office.

The only problem with the calendar was that it was a year
out of date. That was Dr. Newman's fault. He could never
get past October, for that was the month that featured a
startling erotic pose by none other than Tura Lynch. My, but
she knew how to make a pumpkin look good.

Harlot's Hollow wasn't the same since Tura quit. Dr.
Newman was sure that he missed her more than any of her
other former customers.

He *really* missed Tura. If only she'd stayed in Vegas . . .
anywhere. There were plenty of other lap dancers in town,
but none of them equaled Tura Lynch. None of them had
her confident take-no-prisoners attitude. And none of the
other girls called the man with the Norman Rockwell
manner "Dr. Gooddoggy."

This was why Dr. Newman came to the office as soon as
Tura called, even though the hour was late (or early,
depending on your point of view). It didn't matter that his
exit from home required a ridiculous excuse invented for his
wife's benefit. That was a small price to pay. Infinitesimal.
If Tura Lynch wanted to see him, he would cross the Sahara
barefoot.

"On second thought, maybe I should keep Spike for a
couple of days." Dr. Newman tried to keep his voice calm
and professional. "I could run some tests. Just to confirm
my diagnosis, you understand."

"Oh, Dr. Newman," Lorelei teased in a throaty little-girl voice. "You're not just looking for an excuse to see my sister again, are you?"

"Well." The vet loosened his bow tie. "The fact is—"

Tura slipped off her leather coat in one smooth move. "The fact is that I'd like to pay my bill in full, and right now." Her slim fingers traveled long leather strips that clung to her voluptuous body like a black highway with dangerous curves. "Sit, Dr. Gooddoggy."

She didn't have to tell him twice.

"Good boy." Tura snapped her fingers. "Music, maestro."

Lorelei cued their boom box. Framed diplomas, veterinary science certificates, and autographed photos of celebrity clients swayed on Dr. Newman's wall to the ear-splitting beat of Generation X's "Dancing with Myself."

Tura slithered forward and straddled Dr. Gooddoggy like a hungry jaguar, her thighs brushing his. Her brown skin glowed, and, oh . . . her milky white scars did too. Tura had explained that the scars resulted from rattlesnake bites. Dr. Gooddoggy didn't know if she was lying, but . . . oh, he liked the idea that she might be telling the *truth*.

The music pulsed. Doctor Gooddoggy could feel it in his blood. His heart throbbed to the drumbeat. Suddenly the office was very hot—

Tura's exhalations fogged one side of his glasses. His perspiration fogged the other.

Tura removed the glasses and tossed them away. "Are you ready to dance, Dr. Gooddoggy?"

Dr. Gooddoggy didn't say a word.

He sat up and begged.

Tura howled and pulled Dr. Gooddoggy's head between her breasts.

Then she started to move.

• • •

Tura stroked the doctor's angelic white hair. "You're a good little doctor, aren't you?"

"Oh, yes. I'm very good." Dr. Gooddoggy . . . er, Dr. Frank Newman, said.

He straightened his bow tie and cleaned his glasses. Lorelei collected the boom box and the Chihuahua while Tura dressed.

"Well, it's been fun, Doc," Tura said. "But that old highway's a callin'."

Dr. Newman couldn't surrender so easily. He had to give it one more try. "I really think I should run those tests, Tura. If you'll just leave your phone number—"

"No way, Doc. Like I said, we'll call you if the medicine doesn't work."

The doctor trailed Tura and Lorelei through the office door. Black go-go boots beat a hard rhythm on the tiled floor as the Lynch sisters walked down the corridor. In a moment they'd be gone. Dr. Newman couldn't allow that to happen. He might never see Tura again.

The sisters passed the door to the operating theater. In a few moments they'd be in the lobby. Dr. Newman hurried after them. Once again, Tura was walking out of his life. Maybe forever this time—her lithe leg muscles dancing with every step she took, bone-colored snakebite scars glowing ethereally on her chestnut thighs . . .

"Wait a minute, girls." Dr. Newman opened the operating theater door. "I've got a patient in here that you really must see."

Tura paused. "Sorry, Doc. We don't have time."

"I think you'll have time for this, my dear." Dr. Newman squinted, staring at the Lynch sisters through lenses as heavy as hockey pucks.

A playful grin crossed the veterinarian's lips. "I know

you girls like snakes . . . but have you ever seen a dragon?"

Jack said, "Angel, how about you just leave the tape deck alone?"

"Jesus," she said. "I can't believe the stuff you listen to. Dean Martin, Louis Prima, Frankie Laine. Anybody ever tell you that the twenty-first century is right around the corner, Jack?"

"C'mon . . . we're almost there—"

"Yeah? Let me see that address . . . This doesn't look like the right neighborhood."

"It is. Newman's office is around here somewhere. It has to be."

Angel laughed. "Don't tell me. You're lost, aren't you?"

"No," Jack said. "I'm not lost. It's around here somewhere. If you just give me a couple minutes—"

"You're fuckin' lost. I can't believe it."

"I am *not* lost."

"There's a gas station. Why don't you pull over and ask."

"Angel—"

"Jesus, Jack. I can't fuckin' believe you. You're such a fuckin' *guy*. Just pull over and fuckin' *ask*."

"Wait a minute. There it is. That office building over there."

Angel thumbed the safety on her .45. "I hope you shoot better than you drive, Jack."

"Don't you worry about it."

"No—you worry about it. Because if you shoot my dog by accident, I'll forget all about what a good listener and all-around nice guy you are."

"You'd shoot me." Jack was incredulous. "After all I've done, you'd blow me away."

"Yeah. *Especially* after all you've done."

Jack parked the Celica. "You ready?"

Angel looked at him. Really looked at him. Dead in the eye. "This might be a trap, you know."

"I know." Jack stepped out of the car. "That's why I'll go through the door first."

Dr. Gooddoggy was pleased; Tura was excited.

"What is it?" she asked.

"A Komodo dragon," Dr. Newman explained, "the world's largest lizard."

"What's its name?"

Dr. Newman chuckled. "Bruce."

Tura stared into the steel cage. Dr. Newman placed a hand on her shoulder, rather instructively, and was delighted to discover that she was trembling with excitement.

The reason was obvious. Bruce was an amazing specimen—two hundred and twenty pounds of carnivorous reptile. With thick skin the color of bloodstained concrete and hard black eyes that gleamed with cold reptilian intelligence, the huge monitor lizard would send a shiver up anyone's spine.

Bruce turned in the cage, razor-sharp claws clicking against the metal floor. The lizard looked at Tura for a long moment, pale yellow tongue flicking in and out of its mouth.

"Is he dangerous?" Tura asked.

"Very," Dr. Newman said. "Just look at those claws. And his teeth are razor-sharp."

"What does he eat?"

"Komodo dragons eat meat, alive or dead. I once saw Bruce devour three suckling pigs in the space of twenty minutes. He ate so much that he literally couldn't move for several hours."

"Where'd you get him?" Lorelei asked.

"Bruce belongs to a couple of magicians who have quite a menagerie."

"What's wrong with him?"

"Bruce is getting a little old. Last year he started to develop cataracts. I've been monitoring his eyesight since then, and we've decided that it's time to operate and correct the problem. Later today I'm bringing in a veterinary ophthalmologist from Virginia to perform the surgery. She's the best in the country." Newman laughed, pushing his Coke-bottle specs high on his nose. "In fact, if my eyes get much worse I might have her take a crack at me."

Dr. Newman glanced at Tura and Lorelei. He thought his joke was uproariously funny, but the Lynch sisters weren't laughing at all. Obviously, they weren't listening to a word he said.

Tura knelt and peered into the cage. "Daddy would just love him."

Lorelei nodded. "And he's got a birthday comin' up at the end of the month."

"You get him anything yet?"

"Nope. How about you?"

"Nope."

Lorelei chuckled. "Could you imagine the look on his face if we brought him one of these?"

"We'd have to change his name, though. Daddy wouldn't want a dragon named Bruce."

"Yeah. Maybe we could call him Yog Soggoth."

"Works for me," Tura said. "How about it, Doc?"

Dr. Newman didn't know what to say.

But there wasn't a doubt in his mind that he had to say something.

"Tura," he began, "you have to understand—"

The world's greatest lap dancer leaned forward and removed Dr. Newman's Coke-bottle glasses, placing them atop Bruce's cage.

Suddenly, Dr. Newman's throat was uncomfortably dry. "No, darling, you really must listen. I just can't let you do this—"

"Sure you can," Tura said. "You want my phone number, don't you?"

Dr. Newman couldn't see a thing without his glasses, so he didn't see Tura's hand moving toward him. But as soon as he felt it, he made his decision.

He would tell the magicians that the dragon had been stolen. Or kidnapped. Yes, kidnapped. That would be better. He'd send the magicians a ransom note—

"The dragon is yours," he said, and suddenly his bow tie seemed very tight indeed.

Tura kissed the vet. He had just consigned himself to hell. He was sure of it. But at the moment he didn't care—

Until the door to the operating theater burst open.

Until someone yelled, "Get your hands in the air . . . and give me that Chihuahua."

Tura couldn't believe her eyes. The asshole was dead. *Dead.* And dead didn't come back with a Colt Python in its hand and a blond bimbo sidekick armed with a .45.

"C'mon," Jack Baddalach said. "Just give us the dog and no one gets hurt."

"Yeah." The bimbo aimed her .45 at Tura. "Like he said."

Tura raised her hands, just slightly. "Okay," she said. "Okay."

She angled behind Doc Gooddoggy. He was squinting in Baddalach's direction. Obviously, he couldn't see a thing.

Tura sucked a deep breath. So far so good. Her heart was out of the line of fire. So was her left hand. She reached into her coat pocket and pulled the Walther PPK.

Lorelei saw her do it. She had a firm hold on Spike, cradling the dog over her heart. Baddalach and his bimbo wouldn't shoot her. Not when they might hit the dog.

"I'm not going to wait forever," Baddalach said. "Bring me the dog. Now."

"Okay," Lorelei said. "But don't shoot."

Quite suddenly, Tura grabbed Doc Gooddoggy by his prissy white hair. Using him as a shield, she aimed the Walther over his shoulder and started shooting as Lorelei dumped the mutt and yanked a Heckler from the shoulder holster concealed under her coat.

Badalach and his bimbo dove behind a metal counter near the operating theater door.

They rose a moment later, guns blazing.

Warm blood splashed Dr. Newman's face. He heard a few stumbling steps, and then something thumped to the floor in front of him.

He heard a dog barking, claws scrabbling over tile floor.

The pistol next to his ear barked several times, and then he couldn't hear a thing.

"No," Dr. Newman moaned. "Oh please God . . ."

Tura yanked his hair. At least he thought it was Tura. He couldn't see a thing without his glasses.

She pulled him backwards, hiding behind him, until they were on the far side of the Komodo dragon's cage. Then she yanked his hair again, and he dropped to his knees behind the cage.

People were shouting. He knew they were. But his ears were ringing with the sound of gunfire.

He couldn't hear a blessed thing.

• • •

"You killed my sister," Tura shouted.

Jack and Angel crouched behind the metal counter. Angel was holding Spike. Her .45 lay on the ground. Suddenly, she had forgotten all about it.

"You blond bitch!" Tura screamed. "I'm going to make you pay!"

Angel glanced at Jack, her face creased with worry. He shrugged. "You *did* shoot her sister," he said.

"Either I walk out of here," Tura said, "or the vet dies."

"Oh, man," Jack said.

Spike coughed, and Angel held him tight. "What are we going to do?"

"We've got the dog," Jack said. "The vet probably doesn't have anything to do with any of this. I don't want him to get hurt."

"Yeah, but we can't just let her go."

"So what do you want to do? Shoot it out? That's great. Maybe one of us will plug the vet by accident and save her the trouble of killing him."

"Yeah. But if we let her go, do you really think this will be the end of it?"

On the other side of the room, a door slammed.

"Shit," Jack said. "*Shit!*"

Dr. Newman couldn't see a thing. The gunshots had rendered him as deaf as Beethoven, but at least Tura had stopped pulling his hair.

He undid his bow tie and wiped the blood from his face. Then, scooting along on his ass, he moved away from the Komodo dragon cage. He didn't want to be too close to the bars. Bruce's claws were sharp as a samurai's blade. One slash and Medicare wouldn't begin to cover all the reassembly Dr. Frank Newman would require.

There. That was better. Bruce couldn't reach him now. And no one had grabbed his hair to stop him from moving. That was better still.

Dr. Newman reached out tentatively. He couldn't remember where Tura had put his glasses. Maybe they were on the floor.

His fingers drifted across the tile and touched cold metal.

The door to the Komodo dragon's cage . . .

. . . and it was open.

Dr. Newman couldn't hear the scream that spilled over his own lips. But he could feel the dragon's long slithering tongue as it slapped against the back of his hand.

And he could smell the stream of urine even as it spilled down the leg of his summer trousers.

The vet was scooting around the floor on his ass.

The redhead lay by an open door, half her skull splattered on the wall behind her.

The door swung shut slowly. And then Jack noticed the other door. The one to the big metal cage.

A fucking monster came out of the cage, moving fast, little black eyes gleaming like eight balls.

A Komodo dragon. Jesus. Jack had seen one of the big lizards on an old *Johnny Quest* cartoon. The damn thing had tried to devour Race Bannon, who had outsmarted it through good old American ingenuity.

The vet might be an American, but he wasn't in Race Bannon's league. He just sat there on his ass, looking kind of like Pa Kettle dressed up for the county fair. Jack couldn't understand it. Even if the vet didn't see the big lizard, he'd have to hear the thing's claws clinking over the tiled floor—

The monster's long yellow tongue flicked against the back of the vet's right hand. Then its jaws opened wider.

Jack raised the Colt Python and opened fire.

· · ·

Once again, blood splashed Dr. Newman's face. Only this blood was colder.

He reached out and touched a long, slimy hunk of flesh.

Bruce's tongue. Only the tongue wasn't attached to anything.

Bruce was dead.

Bruce had been shot in the head.

Along with an exotic dancer.

All of it had happened in Dr. Newman's operating theater.

Dr. Newman began to cry, because none of these events could possibly occur in a Norman Rockwell universe.

His career was over.

And, worse than that, he would probably never see Tura Lynch again.

The vet sat on the floor, holding the dead lizard's tongue and crying.

"What's wrong with him?" Jack asked.

"I think he's deaf, for one thing. And blind, too." Angel picked up the doctor's Coke-bottle glasses and handed them to Jack. "He probably can't see a thing without these."

Jack dropped the glasses on the floor and stomped them hard.

"Why'd you do that?"

"Do you want him to be able to give the cops our descriptions, or what?"

"Oh . . . yeah."

"Let's get out of here."

"C'mon Spike," Angel said, hoisting the Chihuahua. "We're going home."

After a while, Dr. Newman dropped Bruce's tongue and stumbled out of the operating theater.

He felt his way along the wall and eventually found his office, where he bruised his thigh on the sharp corner of his desk before sinking into his plush leather chair.

Fright consumed him, but he persevered. He reached out tentatively, exploring his desktop even as his heart raced, afraid that his fingers would brush the severed tongue of a Komodo dragon.

They didn't, of course. The dragon's tongue was on the floor of the operating theater.

Eventually Dr. Newman found the telephone. He held the handset to his ear and could not hear a thing. Without his glasses, he couldn't see the keypad, either, but he started pressing buttons anyway.

Three buttons each time. Then he would say he had an emergency, and give his address, and hang up and do it again.

Eventually, he'd hit 911.

Eventually.

It was simply the law of averages.

"God, I'm glad Spike's okay." Angel hugged the Chihuahua. "I'm glad this whole thing is over."

Jack didn't say anything. He just drove.

"Jack . . . it is over, isn't it?"

"I don't know. The woman who got away . . . she's out there, somewhere. So is Harold Ticks. And the old lady and the guy with the rattlesnakes. They're out there, too."

Angel nodded. "Don't forget Tony Katt. He probably the arranged the whole thing. And the woman with the wrist braces."

"Yeah."

"So what should we do?"

"I don't know, Angel. I just don't think they'll leave it like this. You shot that woman back there. You killed her.

And her sister isn't going to forget that. She'll probably come looking for us. God help us if she brings those other freaks with her."

"You think they'll come after us?"

"Yeah," Jack said. "Unless we go after them first."

SIX

THERE WERE SEVEN RANDY TRAVIS RECORDS ON THE TRUCK STOP jukebox. Harold was sure about that. He'd heard every damn one of them, and more than once.

Still, anything was better than hanging out with Eden. Man, was she messed up. Harold didn't know how to feel about that. Deep down, he really cared about her. But to see her all torn up like that, completely out of control . . . man, it was scary. He just couldn't handle it.

Maybe things would be okay after they collected the ransom. Harold figured he could stick it out that long. Hell, he had to. The drop site was already set up. No way he could make an end run around the entire Lynch family at this late hour, even if he wanted to.

And if things didn't work out after that? Well, he'd said adios before. The word was definitely in his vocabulary.

But he'd never said adios to anyone like Eden Lynch. That would be a tough one. Of course, it was easy to say that now. Eden wasn't having a nervous breakdown right before his eyes. If she started that shit again . . . all that crying and making him feel guilty shit . . . well, watch out. That's when the rubber would meet the road.

A gear-jammer dropped a quarter in the jukebox and pressed B26. Randy Travis started singing about a love that was deeper than the holler and stronger than the river and higher than the pine trees growin' tall upon the hill.

Enough of this weepy redneck shit. Harold chugged one last swallow from his coffee cup. It wasn't quite time for the rubber to meet the road, but it was way past time for the shoe leather to hit the parquet tile.

Harold's shoe leather did. He paid the waitress and headed for the pay phones at the gas station adjacent to the restaurant. It was almost noon. Time to goose Angel Gemignani. Get her to that safe-deposit box and then give her directions to the drop site.

Harold punched in the Casbah number and the operator transferred him to Angel Gemignani's suite.

The phone rang a bunch of times. Harold was about to give up when someone answered. Some stupid Valley Girl voice. All whiny. Plus Harold could hardly hear the chick. It sounded like a party was going on or something.

"Is this Angel Gemignani?"

"No." Except the way this chick said it, "no" had two syllables. Then there was a bunch of yelling for Angel, and the next voice Harold heard belonged to the rich bitch herself.

"H'lo?"

"Listen good, bitch. It's time to pay the piper. I want you to get to your safe-deposit box. The one your grandfather gave you. Take out half a million bucks. There's a pay phone outside the bank. Wait there and I'll call you at—"

"Who is this?"

"This is the guy who's got your dog."

Harold couldn't believe it. The little bitch was actually laughing at him.

She said, "I guess you haven't been keeping up with current events."

Harold said, "Huh?"

"Wait just a second." Angel Gemignani yelled something, and someone yelled something back, followed by a chorus of laughter. Angel said, "Still there?"

"Yeah."

"Well, listen to this."

It was quiet for a second. And then the little fucking Chihuahua started barking, and Angel Gemignani slammed down the phone.

Harold started driving. He headed east. He had no idea where he was going. It really didn't matter much.

The whole deal was blown. Tony would be really pissed. Right now, Harold couldn't even face his bro. Man, they'd planned it so good, and things had gotten fucked up, and on Harold's end, too. Eden's sisters had blown it, taking the dog to that vet. Obviously. But the dog was Harold's responsibility. And so were Eden's sisters.

Man, how was he going to break the news to Tony?

Maybe he should just keep driving. He'd end up somewhere. Get something going. Start over.

The odometer notched ten miles. Then twenty. Thirty coming right up . . .

He passed the exit where he'd picked up Eden so long ago. Man, the way she looked that day. Sunburned, wearing nothing but a truck driver's shirt and a pair of dirty white go-go boots, singing "Happy Trails" like everything was okeydokey.

God, but she wanted to please him. She did everything he told her. She never questioned him. It was still that way. Even when she fucked things up, it wasn't like she did it intentionally. In fact, fucking things up nearly broke her heart, that's how scared she was of upsetting Harold.

And who the hell knew what would happen to Eden now? Her family would be pissed. They wanted that ransom money as much as Harold did, and they were about to come up empty.

Harold knew what would happen. Daddy and Mama would blame Eden for bringing Harold into the fold in the first place. And Tura and Lorelei . . . Christ, look what those crazy bitches did to Eden for stealing a bag of Fig Newtons. Harold couldn't even imagine what kind of punishment they'd dish out for something like this.

He pulled over. Man, he couldn't believe it. That fucking Randy Travis song was going round and round in his head.

He waited for a break in the traffic, and when one came he cut across the highway and headed toward the Radiation Ranch.

Harold nearly put his foot through the floorboards. That was how hard he hit the brakes.

The concrete bunker loomed before him, surrounded by a dry, stunted forest of yucca trees and scrub brush. Afternoon heat waves rolled across the desert and broke against the nuke-proof hacienda like ghostwaves of an ocean that had vanished a million years ago.

Harold pulled his .357 and got out of the car. He scanned the desert for a sign of trouble but saw nothing. No cars or trucks that didn't belong there. No tire tracks in the dirt that seemed unusual. Not one glimmer on a distant rise that would indicate a sniper's telescopic rifle sight reflecting the afternoon sun.

Fully aware of his surrounding, senses painfully acute, Harold started toward the thing that had made him stop the car so suddenly.

It was easy to miss her on first glance, because even a warped display of human flesh had a way of looking right at home in the Mojave Desert. Harold had never lived in such a weird place. In his view, every sunset looked like a bloodstain, and every empty well was a grave waiting to be filled, and every yucca tree looked strangely deformed, twisted as if it had been tortured by the Devil himself.

The woman was twisted too, but Harold figured the Devil hadn't done it. Truth be told, he didn't believe in the son of a bitch.

Mama stood against a dead yucca tree, her arms lashed to the twisted limbs with lengths of barbed wire. As usual, her mouth was open.

But she wasn't going to say a word this time. She was all done talking.

And the vultures had started in on her face.

Harold swatted at the vultures with his pistol and they flapped away on lazy black wings. He eased Mama's jacket to one side and saw the bullet wound drilled through the left cup of her black leather bikini. The blood hadn't dried. In fact, a fresh scarlet gout pumped from the hole and streamed down Mama's brown belly.

Harold stood hypnotized, watching the blood.

"Uhhhrrrhhh," Mama groaned.

Harold nearly jumped out of his skin. He stumbled back.

Mama's head bobbed, the length of barbed wire wrapped around her neck cutting a fresh trench in her suntanned flesh as she moved. Her eyelids flickered, eyes rolling blindly beneath them, eyes that were coated with a bleached-white sheen . . .

"Hellllll . . ." she groaned.

"Fuck!" Harold said. "Fuck!"

Mama gasped, a spike of barbed wire tearing her trachea. "Hellll . . ." she whispered. "Helllllppp . . ."

Then she was dead.

Harold's gaze was everywhere at once. The concrete bunker. The tumbledown chapel. The shooting range. The cars and the surrounding ridges and the old dirt road that stretched forty miles to the highway.

But there was nothing. No movement at all except the vultures circling above, patient and black and hungry.

Sweat poured off Harold's bald head and trickled down his neck. What the fuck had he been thinking, anyway? Angel Gemignani belonged to a Mafia family. He had fucked with them. Seriously. And he had come up short. And now they had found him. And when it came to blood vengeance and torture that made you pray for death, no one outdid the Mafia.

No one even came close.

The vultures circled lower and lower. Soon one landed, talons scrabbling as it balanced atop Mama's head.

Harold turned away, his gut lurching. The bunker. He had to check it out. If Eden was still alive, that's where she would be. And right now all Harold wanted was to be with her.

Even if the bunker was full of Mafia hit men. Even if Eden was already dead. He wanted to see her one last time.

He wanted to say that he was sorry before the end came.

But the bunker was empty. There was no sign of Eden or her Daddy. No sign of Tura or Lorelei. And not a single Mafia hit man, either.

Harold stepped through the front door. The sun beat down relentlessly. Man, today it was hot on top of hot. Harold couldn't remember another day like this one.

He started toward his Chevy. Maybe the Mafia guys had taken Eden with them. Maybe they were going to use her for bait so they could round up the rest of the gang.

Harold didn't know if he could rescue her. There probably wasn't much of a chance. He wasn't exactly a fucking knight in shining armor. But he had to try—

The creaking sound came from behind him. He whirled, pistol raised in his right hand just as the chapel door swung closed.

Maybe the door had been closed all along. Maybe the movement he'd seen out of the corner of his eye was just an illusion—a false image planted in his brain by rippling heat waves. With this heat, it looked like damn near everything was alive. Today had to be a real record-buster. If Harold stayed out in the sun much longer he would no doubt witness a first-class mirage—an oasis, camels, leaning palms, harem girls . . .

Harold's clothes were sticky with perspiration. The .357 was growing hot in his hand. The pistol grips were so slick with sweat he was sure he'd drop the gun any second.

No sign of movement from the chapel. The door didn't budge. Harold stared at the sign above the door, the snakeskin letters on blistered black enamel that proclaimed: HELL'S HALF ACRE CHURCH OF SATAN.

Magnum held high, Harold walked toward the chapel. His feet were heavy, like he was wearing weighted diver's boots. Walking through heat waves instead of ocean waves, kicking up little swirls of dust . . .

He knew what he was going to do before he did it. And he knew how stupid it was. But he reached up and did it anyway, because at heart he was still a good Catholic boy.

Harold Ticks crossed himself and entered Satan's church.

The place stunk of dead things. Old bones. Books bound in human flesh. Rattlesnakes frozen in threatening poses by the taxidermist's art.

And then there was the sound. The lazy buzzing of fat black flies. The insects cut slow patterns through the musty air, never leaving the chapel, always returning to the same spot.

Daddy Deke lay on the altar. Unlit candles surrounded him, trickling lazy ebony droplets as they melted in the afternoon heat. The top hat with the rattlesnake band was balanced on his chest and his string tie was cinched up tight, but he did not look at all peaceful. His eyes were open and glazed, and his thin lips were drawn back over yellow teeth, and the fat black flies buzzed in and out of his open mouth.

Harold spotted the rattlesnake bite on Daddy's cheek as he drew nearer, but he wasn't sure that the bite had killed Eden's father. Someone had bound the old satanist to the altar with barbed wire. You didn't bind a dead man.

Someone had bound Daddy, and then that someone had sliced Daddy Deke's throat from ear to ear.

Harold could see that now. A fly crawled into the open wound. A moment later the same fly buzzed out of the corpse's mouth, its black body wet with blood.

Harold retched, dropping to one knee. Coffee and bile burned his throat and he tried to choke it back but couldn't . . . his mouth opened and he vomited a hot black stream.

His pulse pounded beneath the SS tattoo on his neck. Sweat bathed his brow and burned his eyes. It was too damn hot, and the taste in his mouth was awful, and whoever had killed Mama and Daddy Lynch probably had taken Eden, and who the hell knew what the sick fuck had done to her.

Or would do . . .

But where would the killer take her?

Mama was outside, lashed to a yucca tree. Daddy was in the chapel, bound to the altar. And Eden . . .

Harold stared at the back wall of the chapel—the old mine shaft that cut a black hole in white Mojave soil.

No, he thought . . . No way I'm going in there . . . That's it. That's all.

Harold crouched on the floor. No woman was worth this. He should have never come back. He should have kept on driving east. Hell, even Salt Lake City was better than this shit.

He'd get the hell out of here. That's what he'd do. He'd drive east.

Harold stood and wiped his face. He stepped toward the open door.

Outside. A sound.

Tires whispering across Mojave soil.

Harold retreated into the darkness, clutching his .357.

Someone was here.

Tura screamed like a demon when she saw her mother's corpse cinched to the yucca tree.

Harold watched Eden's sister through a crack in the wall. Man, she'd flipped. The crazy redhead was pacing back and forth in front of the twisted yucca, that Steyr AUG gripped tightly in her hands . . .

Tura aimed it heavenward and let loose with a long burst of gunfire. "Come out, you bastards! I'm here! I'm wait-ing!"

Harold watched her. Jesus. He couldn't believe it. No way was he going out there. Not with Tura acting like this. She would probably think he fucking killed her mama . . .

And wait until she saw Daddy. *Jesus H.*—

"Hi, honey."

Harold nearly shit himself. "Eden! You're still alive!"

She stood at the mouth of the mine shaft, wearing black

leather, lace-covered wrist braces, and her carrion beetle sunglasses.

"What happened?" Harold asked. "Where have you been?"

Eden set a glowing kerosene lantern on the altar next to Daddy's head. "Daddy told me that I should take a walk. I did. I've been down in the mine. Just walking, like Daddy said. You know, he was right about the mine shaft. It leads straight to hell."

"What?" Harold glanced through the crack in the wall. Tura fired another burst and screamed. "Look, Eden, you need to get a grip on things. Your daddy's dead, honey. And we have to—"

"I saw it," Eden said. "I saw the River Styx. I bathed in its black waters. And I saw the dog." She laughed, short and hard. "I don't mean the Chihuahua. I mean the one with three heads—"

Jesus. She was gone. Gone. Harold glanced through the crack in the wall. Tura was headed this way.

"Honey." Eden held out a hand. "Come take a walk with me."

"Eden, we don't have time for this—"

"Sure we do."

She plunged the rusty knife into Harold's back again and again.

Harold dropped like a sack of potatoes.

Eden stepped to the wall and peered through a knothole. Tura was coming, reloading the Steyr AUG as she walked.

Eden picked up Harold's .357 Magnum.

"No rest for the wicked," she said.

Eden jammed the pliers into her pocket. Tura was cinched up tight, lashed to the yucca right next to Mama's. But that was only right. Tura was always Mama's favorite.

Eden sat down in the dirt. It was real hot today. She would have to put on more sunblock. Especially if Lorelei showed up. Tying a grown woman to a yucca tree with barbed wire was tough work, and the noonday sun was not at all forgiving.

Still, she hoped Lorelei would come. She wouldn't mind the extra work. Not really.

She felt strong. Really strong. For the first time in her life.

Eden sat in the spiked shade of a yucca. She squinted over her sunglasses. The sky was so very blue today. Not one cloud, only a few jet trails left by airliners headed for the bright lights of Las Vegas.

Hot, clear, and blue. She didn't much like it, so she pushed the sunglasses high on her nose. That was better. Everything was dark, dark green. Almost black.

Eden imagined that she wasn't in the desert at all. She was on the ocean floor. Dark sand stretching forever, green-black waves driving the tides . . .

It was so quiet. Eden could hear herself breathe. It seemed that all her life she'd been waiting to hear just that sound.

Mama didn't say a word. Tura kept her mouth shut. Daddy didn't preach. Harold didn't yell. It was really, really nice.

For once, everyone was doing just what Eden wanted, not the other way around.

Still, she couldn't sit out here forever. Boy, was it hot. A shower would feel real good. Cold, cold water, that nice oatmeal soap. Maybe Tura had stowed another bottle of that fancy coconut shampoo somewhere. Eden could surely use it. She'd worked up a real healthy sweat, and her hair had gone all limp.

Yes. She'd have a nice long shower. Then a glass of milk and a few Fig Newtons, and a nice long afternoon nap.

Eden rose and jammed Harold's .357 under her belt. She looped the remaining barbed wire like a cowboy's lariat.

Time for that shower.

Time to wash off Harold's blood.

SEVEN

AS FAR AS TONY KATT WAS CONCERNED, THE NEW REFRIGERATOR made one hell of a girlfriend. All you had to do was press a little lever in the door, and *voilà*, ice cubes cascaded into your glass from above.

The fridge didn't ever run out of ice, either. Tony should know. He'd been drinking kamikazes since dinnertime, and it was almost midnight now, and the fridge hadn't let him down once. Hell, it looked like he'd run out of vodka and lime juice before he ran out of ice.

Tony downed his drink and fixed another. He couldn't imagine what had gone wrong. Harold should have phoned hours ago. The ransom drop was scheduled to take place no later than five o'clock. Harold was supposed to call when he had Angel and the dog, at which point Tony would rendezvous with the gang at the Radiation Ranch.

If the drop had gone down the way it was supposed to, Harold was now sitting plush with half a million bucks. That was enough filthy lucre to change a guy, sure. But Tony didn't think a double cross was likely in Harold's case. Tony and Harold were blood brothers. Aryan Brotherhood brothers from Corcoran State. Harold wouldn't cash out on him like some jailhouse snitch.

So it had to be that something had gone wrong with the drop. What that something was, Tony couldn't imagine. It didn't make a bit of difference, anyway. Something had fucked up, and that was for sure, and all it meant was that Angel Gemignani and her poocherino were somewhere besides the place they were supposed to be right now—in the fucking palm of Tony Katt's hand.

Man, the baddest tag team in the history of the Shoe had planned it good, too. Harold coming out of the deal with five hundred bills large, and Tony getting the rich bitch and her little Chihuahua.

And how he wanted that fucking dog. So bad he could taste it. Worse than he wanted the Gemignani bitch, even.

Tony had no idea why Angel G pulled that shit on him last New Year's Eve. Man, everybody in town said that she was a little starfucker. And there he was, heavyweight champion of the world, ready to show her a good time. What did she want, roses or something?

So he'd come on a little rough. So what? Plenty of women actually *liked* that kind of stuff.

Not Angel Gemignani, though. And not her little poocherino. Man, that Chihuahua was a terror. Worse than a jealous husband who caught another guy with his wife, *in flagrante delicto*.

But the way it went down, Tony's *in flagrante* hadn't gotten anywhere near *delicto*. That didn't stop the Chihuahua, though. The little mutt got between the baddest man on the planet's legs and . . .

CHOMP! CHOMP! CHOMP!

. . . Tony had come up short one testicle.

The heavyweight champion of the world had an itch, and

he scratched it. The plastic surgeon had fixed him up with a prosthetic nut, but it just didn't feel right.

Jesus. A plastic testicle. Like the doc joked—hahahaha—that, indeed, was one tough nut to crack. And sure the ordeal had given Tony the opportunity to get his Johnson stretched, but man, that didn't change the fact that some little starfucker's Chihuahua had gobbled his left nut.

A man couldn't lose his left nut and not do anything about it, especially if that man was the heavyweight champion of the world.

Tony wanted that Chihuahua so bad he could taste it. He'd planned his revenge months ago. He'd lain awake many nights dreaming about it. And just a few hours ago he was sure that his fantasy was about to become a reality.

Boning knives and butcher knives waited in the kitchen. Charcoal was piled high in the barbecue out back. Lighter fluid and wooden matches stood ready and waiting.

Blackened Chihuahua, coming right up. You want red or white wine with that, my dear?

The ice had melted in Tony's kamikaze. He didn't fucking care. He wasn't fixing one more fucking drink for himself.

Shit. Bitches. What more did they want from him, anyhow? He'd enlarged his vocabulary. He'd enlarged his dick, too. He'd evolved as a person. But that didn't stop Porschia from walking out on him.

And look what had happened since Porschia left. Some geriatric light-heavyweight beat the shit out of him. The fight scheduled three weeks hence was canceled as a result. He had fucking Popsicle sticks taped to his fucking busted nose, and his voice was so whiny and nasal and terminally white that he couldn't even recognize it.

Porschia. Man, but he missed her. Even if she did give him shit about ice cubes and stuff like that. But now he had the new refrigerator. Hey, that was a big change right there.

Maybe he could call Porschia, tell her about it. Tell her about his fucked-up nose, too. Maybe she'd even feel sorry for him—

Tony glanced at his watch. The last show at Skull Island would be over by now. Porschia would be in the dressing room, changing with all the other bitches. Tony snatched up the phone and dialed Skull Island.

The switchboard operator put him through. "H'lo," he said in his fucked-up voice. "Borschia Gees, bleeze."

"Who?"

"Borschia Gees."

"You mean Porschia Keyes?"

"Yes," Tony said, trying hard to enunciate.

"Who's calling?"

"Tony Katt."

"Oh, gee." The woman on the other end of the line paused. "I guess you haven't heard, Tony. There's been an accident."

"Huh? Is Borschia otay?"

"What?"

"Is Porschia okay?"

"Well, we're waiting to hear. See, Porschia danced the lead tonight. She was doing that big number with the animatronic King Kong, the one where they dance the macarena. Everything went fine until the part where Kong picks her up . . ." The woman sobbed. "It was horrible, Tony. The engineers think there was some kind of computer glitch. They couldn't get the monkey's paw to open . . . instead it kept on closing and Porschia was squeezed something awful . . . we could hear her ribs breaking and the way she screamed . . ."

The woman started crying. Tony hung up the phone.

Wow. Porschia was in the hospital.

But, hey, those were the breaks.

Tony picked up the phone and dialed Caligula Tate's number.

Tate said, "How's it going, champ?"

"Good. The nose feels better. You get in touch with Baddalach yet?"

"No. But I've got a deal all ironed out with Skull Island. Baddalach will bite as soon as I pass on the offer. Believe me. He can't turn down this kind of money. You'll have the chump in the ring just in time for your birthday, and you know that ain't far off."

"All right," Tony said. "I'll hit him once for you."

"Good. I never liked the son of a bitch."

"Is the money good?"

Tate whistled. "Astro-fucking-nomical. Everyone wants to see this fight. You'll clear twenty million. Maybe thirty."

"I love my job." Tony laughed. "Thirty million bucks to bust up a guy I'd meet in an alley for free."

"Only in America."

"Amen, brother."

"So how's everything going?" Tate asked. "The new fridge okay?"

"Yeah. The fridge is fine. But my girlfriend got hurt."

"What happened?"

"Porschia got squeezed by a robot monkey. You know— that one she dances with at Skull Island. She's in the hospital."

"Sorry to hear it. You want me to send some flowers for you, champ?"

"Sure. Maybe some candy, too."

"Anything else?"

"Yeah," Tony said. "Send me another girl."

"Any particular kind?"

"As long as she can make a kamikaze, she'll be all right with me."

•   •   •

Man, it didn't take long at all.

A car pulled up in the driveway just as Tony climbed out of a hot shower. He toweled off and peeked through the window.

Check that. It wasn't a car at all. It was a truck. A beat-up piece of shit Chevy. This had to be a mistake—

No. It wasn't a mistake.

The woman who climbed out of the truck was fine. Tony watched from above as she appeared, section by foxy section.

Black stiletto heels.

Black fishnet stockings.

Black leather miniskirt.

Black bikini top.

Raven hair.

Tony smiled at his reflection in the mirror.

"Brother," he said, "it's going to be one long night."

PART FOUR

Feast of
the Mau Mau

In the place where dogs licked the blood of Naboth, shall
dogs lick thy blood, even thine.

—THE OLD TESTAMENT,
1 KINGS, XXI, 19

ONE

AFTER A DISCREET VISIT TO A VETERINARIAN IN HENDERSON, SPIKE the Chihuahua was resting comfortably. Angel Gemignani could rest easy, too, but of course that wasn't Angel's style. She shifted into slam-dance overdrive. After all, her girlfriends had come to Vegas for a bachelorette party. Under Angel's direction the affair became a forty-eight-hour non-stop marathon of indulge-o-matic bliss.

Jack was invited, of course. He bowed out politely, mostly because he wanted to give Angel some breathing room. The secrets they had shared at Jack's condo gave them a special bond of intimacy. Jack had told damn few people *anything* about Kate Benteen, and Angel was certainly the first person who forced him to admit that he loved Kate. And Jack was pretty sure that there weren't too many people who knew about Angel's run-in with Tony Katt or the insecurities she hid beneath a rattlesnake tattoo.

Besides that, Angel had plugged the redhead at the Frank Newman's office. Jack knew he owed her for that.

The feeling of mutual attraction that had burned between Jack and Angel the first couple of times they bumped up against each other had turned into something special. Not romance, and certainly not love. But something that might, given time, become friendship. Angel had called him just last night, saying that she wanted to get together for lunch before she headed back to Palm Springs. She didn't say anything directly, but her tone of voice told Jack that she hoped they could be friends, too.

Jack felt good about that. There wasn't any doubt that he'd gotten off to a rocky start with Angel. Things were working out okay, though. Spike was safe, and Angel hadn't heard another word from the dognappers. The police were investigating the shooting at the vet's office, but so far no one had connected Jack or Angel to the trouble. The police couldn't identify the dead redhead, either—she wasn't carrying ID, and computer searches of several law enforcement databases had failed to match her fingerprints.

Not that the media were screaming for more info about the dead redhead. In fact, the news reports of the incident hardly mentioned her. Journalists seemed more interested in the "murdered" Komodo dragon. Several animal rights groups were offering rewards for the endangered lizard's assassin.

But Jack wasn't worried about Tarzan the bounty hunter showing up on his doorstep. For now, he was willing to leave the dognapping gang to Freddy G's hotshot investigator. The guy was trying to track Harold Ticks through the California Department of Corrections computers, but it looked like Harold had jumped parole some time back. The investigator hadn't been able to get in touch with Tony Katt, either. Not that Jack figured the guy could sweat Tony. If Jack was any judge of human nature, the baddest man on the planet wasn't going to give up his buddy, not now.

Jack took it easy for a couple of days. He didn't do much

more than sit on his couch and read paperbacks. Anybody called, he let the answering machine pick up.

Every once in a while he made himself a couple of White Castle Burgers or Pop Tarts. He watched some television, too. The Tony Katt/Jack Baddalach story was still going strong. Caligula Tate was lobbying for a big money fight between the two men. He had phoned Jack several times.

Jack had spoken to the sports reporter from CNN, just to get the guy off his doorstep. He pretty much spent his five minutes of prime time ducking and dodging the reporter's questions like bothersome jabs. But the reporter couldn't get a word out of Tony Katt. No one had seen him. His bruised ego and busted nose were obviously in hiding.

Katt's disappearing act bothered Jack. It interfered with a decision he had made.

He wanted Tony Katt.

In the ring.

Jack wanted to make Katt pay for what he'd done to Angel. Sure, that was part of the reason he wanted a fight with Tony the Tiger.

But Jack was motivated by more than revenge. And it wasn't just the money, either. Which was looking pretty spectacular, by the way. Johnny Da Nang was turning out to be one hell of a negotiator. He had jacked Caligula Tate's initial offer of five million to nine million two, plus a healthy percentage of the pay-per-view action, rebroadcast rights, and live gate. The plan was to let Tate sweat for a couple more days, at least until Tony Katt showed his ugly face again. When that happened, Jack would sign on the dotted line . . . he'd take a Katt fight anywhere, anytime, anyplace.

Money was nice, but it could be a pain in the ass, too.

And in the boxing world, it brought out the leeches. But Jack could deal with them. He'd dealt with them before. He wasn't some kid who would spend a fortune before he even made one.

So he could handle the money, and the revenge angle would be sweet . . . but there was more to Jack's decision.

It was almost kind of funny, because Jack felt that the whole Tony Katt thing was the first conscious decision he'd made in a long time. Since Spike was dognapped, Jack's run-in with Katt was the one action he had actually planned. Everything else was like one big adrenaline rush, immediate responses demanded by stimuli that were dangerous in varying degrees.

To put it another way: Jack never acted, he always reacted.

Angel kisses him in Palm Springs, and he kisses her before he can even decide if it's a good idea or not. Dognappers lock him up with a rattlesnake, he's got to escape or die. Punkers attack his dog, he steps in and takes the punishment. Angel puts the moves on him in a hot tub, he makes the same mistake he made when they kissed. One of the dognappers pulls his chain, he gets into a shootout at a veterinarian's office. A Komodo dragon goes into rampage overdrive, he has to shoot it before someone gets eaten.

But the fight with Katt was different. Jack had time to think about it. He weighed all the options. The advantages and disadvantages.

And in the end his decision didn't have much to do with Tony Katt. It had a lot to do with Jack Baddalach and how he defined himself.

Once upon a time he defined himself as the light-heavyweight champion of the world. Then he defined himself as a problem solver for the mob. Just lately he had defined himself in varying degrees as a Chihuahua's baby-sitter, a lover ignored, and Jack the Giant Killer.

Back there somewhere, behind ego and pride and all the rest of that bullshit, Jack knew better. He knew that he should define himself as Jack Baddalach. Just plain old Jack. Whatever happened to him, that's who he was.

It was a healthy attitude. Some would call it a Zen kind of thing.

Jack figured, *later for that.*

Because he had to admit that he wanted one last definition on top of all those others. One that would stick until the day they put him in his grave, and then some.

Jack Baddalach, heavyweight champion of the world.

Jack took a shower and got dressed. It was Angel's last day in town. They were going to do lunch at Bertolini's in the mall at Caesars Palace.

The phone rang as Jack was headed out the door. Johnny Da Nang's voice came over the answering machine speaker.

Jack picked up. "Hey, Johnny."

"Good news and bad news, champ. I got Tate up to ten million five."

"All right. You're earning your percentage. What's the bad news?"

"Tony Katt's still the Invisible Man. No one has seen him. Tate's worried about it. So am I. If the story starts to cool off before we sign a contract, I figure Tate's offer will go soft."

"Okay," Jack said. "I'll make a few calls later today. I know a couple of Katt's sparring partners. Maybe they know what rock he's hiding under."

"Sounds good."

They said their good-byes and Jack headed for the parking lot, swinging by his mailbox on the way.

A couple bills. An Archie McPhee catalog. The new

Sports Illustrated featuring cover boy Jack Baddalach over the punch line, GIANT KILLER!

A large Express Mail envelope, too. Jack recognized the return address as that of the Casbah Hotel & Casino.

But he knew the address was a phony as soon as he opened the envelope and pulled out the ransom note:

> HEY HERO: YOUR MEAL TICKET IS
> ALIVE 4 THE MOMENT. TEN MIL-
> LION & HE'S YOURS. SKULL IS-
> LAND PAYS & YOU DELIVER.
> DETAILS TO COME.
>
> REMEMBER, THE DIFFERENCE BE-
> TWEEN CHAMP & CHUMP IS U.
>
> YOUR FRIEND

> *P.S. Hope you can use the enclosed. They make nice lamp shades.*

Jack stared at the note. The kidnapper—for this note was signed in the singular instead of plural—had used the same font as the previous note. And the smiley face looked identical, too.

But the postscript—*they make nice lamp shades*—what the hell did that mean? Jack peered into the open envelope. Something was stuck to the paper, glued there . . .

. . . . glued there with blood.

The tattooed face of Colonel Harlan Sanders smiled up at him from a torn canvas of human flesh.

Jack shivered as he saw the words:

Finger Lickin' Good . . .

TWO

JACK TOSSED THE ENVELOPE ONTO HIS DESK. MAN, HE COULDN'T even get a break. His brief foray into action mode was over. The reaction express had just chugged back into town.

Only this time he didn't know how to react. He figured he should make a phone call. But to whom? The corporate bigwigs at Skull Island . . . or Freddy G . . . or Caligula Tate . . . or, hell, the Las Vegas cops?

No, he couldn't call the cops. That was definitely out. There was too much back story that he couldn't explain— the dognapped Chihuahua and the reason behind Jack's run-in with Tony Katt, for starters. And if the cops talked him into a corner . . . well, Angel *had* killed the red-headed dognapper at Dr. Newman's office. Jack didn't want her to end up as Court TV's designated celebrity murder defendant of the season.

Jack's hands weren't exactly clean, either. After all, he had assassinated a rampaging Komodo dragon. According to some people, that made him Public Enemy Number One. Jesus, he didn't want animal rights activists picketing outside his door.

A chill iced Jack's spine. At least he hadn't skinned

anyone alive. Tony Katt, Jack's only link to the gang, was learning some serious lessons about honor among thieves. Man, there were easier ways to get rid of a tattoo.

Hardball time, that's what this was. The main event. The road to hell wasn't paved with good intentions; it was paved with ten million bucks. In an effort to collect that kind of scratch, the dognappers had turned on one of their own.

Now they were Kattnappers.

Or Kattnapper, singular. That's what the ransom note indicated. Still, Jack had a hard time believing that one person could pull off something like this.

Jack sat and stewed, playing it over and over in his mind. Who to call—

He glanced at his watch. First of all, he had to cancel his lunch date. He dialed the Casbah and the operator put him through to Angel Gemignani's suite.

"Jack," she said, "I was just going to call you, but I figured you'd be on your way over."

"I kind of got sidetracked. Something pretty important. I'm going to have to take a rain check on our lunch."

"No. You've got to come over here."

"Sorry, Angel. I'm serious—"

"So am I." She paused. "This is really important, Jack. See, we were sitting around, drinking champagne, doing the bachelorette party thing, and Evie—she's the one who's getting married—put on this porno video she bought at a shop near Fremont Street—"

"A porno movie? C'mon, Angel, I don't have time for this. Someone has snatched Tony Katt. I think it's the same bunch who kidnapped Spike. They sent me one of his tattoos in the mail. They want ten million dollars for the rest of him."

"Jesus, Jack."

"Anyway, I've got to call the bosses at Skull Island, or maybe Caligula Tate—"

"Settle down, Jack," Angel said. "Grow some patience, huh?"

"I don't have *time* for patience. Especially when it comes to porno movies. If you've got something to tell me, make it fast."

"Okay . . . I recognized one of the actresses in the movie—a redhead in black leather."

"Oh shit. You're kidding."

"Jack, I couldn't forget this woman if I tried," Angel said. "Because the last time I saw her, I put a bullet in her head."

The movie was called *Little Bitches*. A costume piece featuring three-way action, early American style. Louisa May Alcott was probably rotating in her grave.

"Recognize them with their clothes off?" Angel asked.

"I can make them out." Jack sat on the bed, watching the screen. "Jo and Amy are definitely the two we ran into at the vet's office. And the one with the wrist braces, Beth, she's the one I knocked out when the gang grabbed Spike."

Angel nodded. "So what are we going to do about it?"

"I don't know." Jack looked at the video box, but the only address he found was a Las Vegas post office box. "I guess we could get in touch with the investigator Freddy was using. Maybe the guy could use the video to track them down."

On screen, Jo and Amy and Beth were taking turns with Professor Bhaer.

Angel shook her head in disbelief. "I guess they left this part out of the Winona Ryder version."

Jack grabbed the telephone. "I'll give Freddy a call."

"Wait a minute." Angel snatched up the remote control

and thumbed the rewind button. "There's something else you need to see. Something I forgot about."

Oh, man, Jack thought. Don't tell me Grandma plays the mother . . .

Angel restarted the tape. She fast-forwarded through several phone sex advertisements and hit the pause button when a notice from the producer appeared on screen:

WARNING! ADULTS ONLY!

Not to be sold to or viewed by minors. This videocassette contains adult viewing material and is rated X. All actors and actresses are 18 years of age or older. Proof of age is on file at:

EVIL EYE PRODUCTIONS
36 Arroyo Blanco Drive
Las Vegas, NV 89030

Jack headed for the door. Angel followed him. "Where are you going?"

"Thirty-six Arroyo Blanco Drive," Jack said.

"Don't you think it would be smarter to let Grandpa handle this?"

Jack stopped short and turned to face her, his voice registering exasperation when he spoke. "I haven't always been a Chihuahua baby-sitter, Angel. In fact, when your granddad has a problem of this nature, I'm the guy who usually handles it."

"I'm sorry. I didn't mean—"

"You don't need to apologize." Jack put a hand on her shoulder. "You got your dog back, Angel. This really doesn't have anything to do with you or your granddad anymore. It has to do with me."

"Wait a minute." Angel turned off the television. "God

knows I'd love to see you knock out Tony Katt. God knows I'd love to see you break his nose all over again. But to risk your life for him? That's crazy, Jack."

"Yeah. I guess it is." Jack looked at her long and hard. "Almost as crazy as risking your life for a consumptive Chihuahua."

"You're really going to go through with this."

"Yeah." Jack sighed. "It's hard to explain, Angel. I guess it comes down to who I am and who I want to be. I don't want to be the guy who lost the boss's granddaughter's puppy. I want to be the heavyweight champion of the world. I've got my reasons . . . and, well, they're *my* reasons. I want to win that belt, and I can't do that without Tony Katt."

"Okay, then. Let's go."

Jack shook his head. "I'm doing this alone."

"No, you're not. Like you said, you risked your life for a dog. My dog. I guess I can risk mine for your dream."

"Forget it, Angel. You're not coming with me."

Her backbone turned to steel. "I guess that I should go ahead and call Grandpa Freddy, then. Maybe he'd like to know that Jack Baddalach is about to get his ass blown away."

Angel shoved a brand new .45 into her purse. Her other gun—the one she'd used to kill the redhead—was now at the bottom of Lake Mead.

"Let's go," Jack said.

Angel opened the top dresser drawer and pulled out a pair of nylons. She tossed one of the stockings to Jack.

"What's this for?" Jack asked.

"Trust me." Angel laughed. "You're gonna need it."

THREE

DRY . . . PARCHED . . . DESICCATED . . . BARREN . . .

Like the vast Sahara. Like a mummy baked in desert catacombs. Like a creature with peeling wallpaper skin hung by the Devil himself. Like something that had been dead, yet conscious, for a very long time.

Tony Katt tried to swallow. His Adam's apple bobbed against a barbed-wire spike. He wanted to scream, but his parched throat wouldn't allow more than a rattling whisper.

God, but he was thirsty. The woman had removed the bandages and cotton from his broken nose, but it didn't do any good. He could get more air sucking on a crimped straw.

So Tony breathed through his mouth . . . Every inhalation flared like wildfire in his tortured throat . . . His mouth became a dry desert burrow, a trap-door spider's hole . . .

Tony could almost feel it. The spider. Crawling over his chest, along his neck, furry legs crossing the pulsing carotid artery and the SS lightning bolts tattoo, fat arachnid body squeezing between Tony's cracked lips and over his tongue, down his throat until its fat body became stuck and he started to suffocate—

Sharp sliver cuts split Tony's dry lips as he opened his mouth. This time, the scream had to come out, no matter how dry his throat. Hot air baked in his lungs tore his windpipe like a dull razor.

The scream was short, and not very loud.

Tony was awake again. So was his kidnapper.

She had been dozing in the shade by the tumbledown shack. She raised her chin and looked at him, eyes invisible behind dark sunglasses.

"Okay, Tiger," she said. "Don't get your shorts in a bunch." Then she grabbed the canteen and walked in his direction.

Tony couldn't move, of course. She'd tied him to a yucca tree with a length of barbed wire that speared him every time he so much as wriggled. His arms were bent at odd angles, mimicking the twisted branches. Thick, sharp leaves and gnarled scabs of bark dug into his naked back.

Tony heard water slosh in the canteen as the woman approached. Instinctively, he leaned forward, barbed-wire spikes tearing his flesh.

"Want another drink?" the woman asked.

Tony only moaned.

"You know the price."

Tony remembered. He opened his mouth. Her gloved fingers brushed his dry tongue as she jammed several pills between his bleeding lips. He thought they were Percodans, the pain pills he was taking for his broken nose. But it seemed like he was hallucinating, too. All that shit with the spider. Maybe the heat was the cause of that. Or maybe his captor was feeding him world-class mind-benders, too.

She tilted the canteen and gave him a long drink. He swallowed thankfully. Then she returned to the shade.

Leaning against one wall of the dilapidated shack, she unscrewed a dark bottle and oiled her pale skin with creamy white sunblock.

Tony's tattoos flared like melting neon on sunburned flesh. The woman had stripped off his shirt while he was unconscious. He figured he was out of it for a good long while. She must have drugged him at his house, slipped something into the kamikaze she mixed soon after he invited her inside.

Tony didn't regain consciousness until she peeled the Colonel Sanders tattoo off his shoulder with a combat knife, and by that time it was too late. He was already wired to the tree.

His kidnapper had placed some kind of mask over his head. The mask had openings for his mouth, his eyes, and his nose. It was terribly hot, tight as a second skin, but for the most part the mask kept the sun off of his face.

Other parts of his body were painfully exposed. His naked chest had begun to blister. His arms burned, biceps and triceps fiery slabs of useless meat. In a strange way, it was the barbed-wire cuts that saved him. Dried blood wasn't the best sunblock in the world, but it was doing its job. Anything was better than flesh roasted by unforgiving Mojave Desert sunshine.

Anything was better . . . anything . . . because pride was useless here. Without strength, pride couldn't exist.

It didn't exist.

"More water," Tony whispered. "Please."

The woman sighed and capped the bottle of sunblock. "Okay, but not too much. I don't want you getting any ideas." She smiled, walking toward him, the canteen sloshing with every step. "After all, you *are* the baddest man on the planet, and I'm just a weak and frail woman. I certainly wouldn't stand a chance if you managed to get loose. Right?"

The kidnapper held the canteen just short of Tony's torn lips. He wanted to tell her exactly what he'd do to her if he got loose. He wanted to say that he'd rip her limb from limb and piss on her corpse.

But Tony couldn't say that at all. All he could say was, "Unnngh . . . *Wattttterrrrr* . . ."

"First things first. I asked you a question, Tiger. A girl like me, I wouldn't stand a chance against the heavyweight champion of the whole wide world. Right?"

"You . . . you would." Tony said those words, all the while telling himself, *Pride doesn't exist.*

"I couldn't quite hear you, Tiger."

She was so close. If he could just get his hands on her . . .

"You want a drink, you'd better answer me."

Tony could barely remember the question.

"The other night." She slapped his cheek. "Who was stronger? You or me?"

"You were," Tony began, because he really needed that fucking drink. "You outsmarted me . . . and you were stronger."

"I guess I did get the better of you that night, Tiger." She laughed. "But you were drunk. And you weren't expecting any trouble." She patted his skinned shoulder very lightly, and an electric jolt of pain threatened to blow several circuits in Tony's brain. "That's why I've got to keep you weak," she said. "I wouldn't want you getting any ideas about escaping."

"I won't get ideas," Tony said. "I can't escape . . . but I need a drink . . ."

No pride. Not here. Pride doesn't exist. Only the tree

exists, only the barbed wire and the memory of the knife . . .

The woman tipped the canteen against Tony's lips. He sucked greedily, managing a long swallow. His tongue was wet now. It felt wonderful. Water cooled his aching throat. For a moment he felt a little stronger.

A cool oasis nestled under his ribs as the water hit his stomach . . . cool . . . and inviting . . . the waters deep, and dark . . .

Tony remembered the price he'd paid for a drink of water. The pills were dissolving in his gut. Soon a slow numbness spread to his arms and legs and iced his flayed shoulder.

Tony started to drift.

No, he couldn't let that happen. He had to fight. God. If he could just get loose. If he could only wrap his hands around this bitch's slender neck. If he could manage one hard twist, just one . . .

The yucca trees stretched far in the distance.

The sun burned down.

Tony blinked against the great white ball, head lolling on his thick neck.

A blinding glint as sunlight slapped the woman's knife.

She touched the blade to Tony's other shoulder and began to carve.

Tony couldn't move. He moaned, soft and low, because his throat was dry all over again.

The woman didn't say a word as she worked. Tony closed his eyes. He moaned low . . . a seashell moan . . . and his blood flowed hot and wet, droplets raining on dry desert sand . . . pattering, pattering in the seashell silence.

Jack drove through a quiet neighborhood—industrial park redux—which was okay with him. He didn't say a word. Neither did Angel.

He pulled to the curb just as a starved-looking brunette stepped though the glass doors at 36 Arroyo Blanco. She yawned, pulled at her microminiskirt, and slipped behind the wheel of a battered Malibu.

A moment later she was gone. One vehicle remained in the parking lot. A Jeep Cherokee. Jack hoped the owner of the Jeep would know something about the kidnappers.

Jack figured the faster he could get to the gang, the better. He needed Tony Katt in one piece. Was that selfish? Sure. But Tony Katt was no prince. If the Tiger didn't have the heavyweight title, Jack would let the kidnappers have their way with him. It wouldn't be any skin off Jack's ass. Or Tony's shoulder, as it were.

But Jack really wanted that title. And he had to admit that he wanted the kidnappers, too. They had screwed him once, with Angel's dog. That was plenty. They'd damn near killed him with a rattlesnake. And now they were trying to screw him again. Jack didn't like that much. He didn't want anyone thinking that they could make a habit of doing him like some chump.

He remembered the kidnapper's note. *Remember, the difference between champ and chump is "U."* Jesus. These people were nuts. Either that, or they wrote *Rocky* movies for a living.

Jack pulled into the lot and parked the Celica. The air conditioner kicked off as he killed the engine.

"I guess this is it," Angel said.

"Yeah. I guess."

Jack grabbed his pistol and stepped out of the car. Man, it was hot. He started sweating almost immediately.

Angel glanced around to make sure no one was watching. Then she pulled the nylon stocking over her head.

"You're kidding, right?" Jack said. "Angel, its too hot for

this shit. I put one of your stockings over my head, I'm gonna suffocate."

Angel checked her .45 and walked toward the building. "Do what you want, Jack. Just remember that you've been on television all week long. Anyone with an IQ above plant life is bound to recognize your face, even an idiot who makes porno movies for a living."

Jack pulled on the stocking. Man oh man, he could hardly breathe—

Angel angled toward the door, peeking through a window, her gun raised.

Jack adjusted the stocking, smiling as he filled his lungs with nylon-filtered air.

Calvin Klein's Obsession.

Angel Gemignani. She was something.

When it came to perfume, she had really nice taste.

As the sun settled low in the sky, Eden finished peeling the tattoo from Tony Katt's shoulder. The heavyweight champion of the world was unconscious, his body a study in sunburned flesh and spilled blood. So too were the heavens, violent shades of red staining the horizon the color of a dark bloody smear.

Eden entered the chapel. Daddy lay on the altar. Oh, but his expression was so peaceful. She brushed flies from his wounds and straightened his arms. She opened his hands and pressed them together at waist level, palms facing upward, gnarled fingers slightly bent.

Two hands. Daddy's right hand. The Devil's left hand. And now they were one. A callused cup that lay open and waiting on Daddy's belly.

Eden laid the tattoo in Daddy's palm. An odd-looking man, staring at her from a patch of singed flesh. And those words below his face: *That which does not destroy us makes us stronger.*

Yes. These words were indeed true. Eden recognized that. For she was much stronger now.

But not nearly as strong as she wanted to be.

Eden opened the old spell book. It was written in the last century by Estrellita Dolores Refugio Cavendish, a blind witch of some notoriety who had spent her last days in Truth or Consequences, New Mexico.

Eden flipped to the correct page and studied the text. *For mortar and pestle: a dead man's hands and a reprobate's thumb.*

She had Harold's thumb. It would do.

Combine the tattooed flesh of a crucified sinner. A green pear and a whore's hair—

Eden had a lock of Tura's hair, fragrant with coconut shampoo. She'd bought the green pear at a grocery store on her way to kidnap Tony Katt.

—the powdered tongue of a hyena that has laughed its last . . . and fat from the back of a baboon, boiled down to a pound dinner spoon.

Daddy's shelves were jammed with elixirs and nostrums and potions of every description. Magical ingredients gathered from the four corners of the earth stood next to prosaic products such as Ban Roll-On, Del Monte Prunes, and Poligrip. A wide assortment of prescription drugs filled one shelf. Daddy had stolen these from sacrifice victims, hijacked truckers, and other unfortunates who had crossed his path over the years.

Eden ignored the drugs. Impatiently, she sorted through jars and phials and cruets until she found the magical ingredients she wanted.

Baboon fat and hyena tongue. Daddy had them both, two

small jars jammed in a small wooden casket bearing African stamps.

Eden sliced the pear into small bits and laid it on the face of Friedrich Nietzsche. She added her sister's hair, powdered hyena tongue, and baboon fat. Gripping Harold's thumb tightly, she mixed the ingredients in Daddy's weather-beaten palms.

Eden glanced at the yellowed page. One last time, just to be sure.

She was sure. Tonight, true strength would be hers. Satan's strength would protect her forevermore. No one would ever hurt her again.

She closed the book and left the chapel, but she took the witch's words with her.

> *The fat will fire and flare so bright,*
> *Burn cinder and ash the center,*
> *Satan's hot breath rides the pale moonlight,*
> *His strength, a demon, will enter.*

The place was a warehouse filled with sets for porno movies. B & D stuff . . . a trapeze . . . lots of couches with peculiar stains. Jack didn't *even* want to think about it.

The guy was holed up in a little office the size of a broom closet. He wore black Armani slacks and a shiny Lurex shirt, the kind you could use to wrap leftovers if you ran out of plastic wrap.

He didn't even look up when Jack and Angel entered the room. "No more auditions today, Sheri," he said. "Tell 'em I'm too tired."

Jack said, "I think Sheri went home early."

Angel nodded. "She looked kind of tired herself."

The guy looked up and saw their guns.

"Oh, Jesus. Whatever it is, I didn't do it."

Jack tossed the *Little Bitches* video onto the guy's desk. "Jo, Amy, and Beth. We want to know where they live, and we want to know right now."

The guy stared at the box. "I made this one last year. The girls have moved since then. They're sisters. I know that much."

Angel laughed. "You're telling us that you don't know where they went?"

"Yeah . . . that's what I'm saying. Jesus, they were a weird bunch. It wasn't like I was going to send them Christmas cards or anything."

"Weird how?" Jack asked.

"Every which way. The two older sisters were gun nuts. Real *Soldier of Fortune* centerfold girls. The younger one was okay, but she had problems, too. Carpal tunnel syndrome. It got so bad that she could hardly give a guy a hand job without whimpering, so I had to let her go—"

Jack laughed, and so did Angel. She said, "Do you believe this?"

"Not hardly," Jack said.

The guy threw up his hands. "It's true! I swear to God! Every word!"

"I don't know." Angel looked at Jack. He hardly recognized her with that stocking pulled over her head. Her features were all mashed up. She kind of looked like Ellen Barkin.

Angel said, "I guess we're wasting our time. You want to go?"

"No." Jack shook his head. "We'd better kill him first."

"You want to do it?" Angel asked.

"No. I killed the last one."

"No, you didn't," Angel insisted. "You killed a Komodo dragon. That doesn't count. I killed the redhead."

They looked at the guy. He was all thawed out under that

plastic-wrap shirt, sweating like he'd just stepped out of a microwave.

Angel pointed her gun at the guy's head. Jack aimed for the heart.

The guy nearly sprang out of his chair. "They live out in the fucking desert, okay? I've never been there, okay?"

"Never?" Jack cocked his Colt Python. "You sure about that?"

"Okay!" The guy sputtered. "Okay! I took Eden's boy-friend some money one time. His name is Harold Ticks. I met him at this highway off-ramp. I got there early. He drove down this dirt road. He said that Eden and her sisters lived on some kind of ranch or something about forty miles out. Maybe fifty. But he didn't invite me for a fucking visit . . . Okay? I'll draw you a fucking map if you want."

Jack turned to Angel. "What do you think, partner?"

She smiled. "A map would be good."

The sun was down, and the woman was gone.

And Tony Katt was conscious again. The doped-up feeling was almost gone. He had sweated it out or bled it out.

But that was dangerous, because Tony was beginning to feel the pain.

He knew he couldn't take it once it hit him full force. He pulled at his bonds. Barbed wire tore his skin and he grunted but made himself pull again. Yucca leaves scratched his flesh and broke loose, skittering down the tree trunk. The great yucca groaned . . . and pain seared Tony's flesh . . . pain he could *feel* . . .

He eased off, sweating hard now, bleeding from fresh wounds. He sucked a deep breath through his mouth.

That was when he saw it. The canteen. His captor had left it by the tumbledown shack.

Maybe it was empty. Probably it was. But if it wasn't. And if he could get to it . . . oh, how he wanted a drink right now.

Tony closed his eyes. He could do this. He was the heavyweight champion of the world. Despite the broken nose, despite the tortures he had suffered while lashed to the tree, he was strong. He'd been training for six weeks. Running six or seven miles a day in the desert sun. Sparring with guys who could take your head off with a single punch. Pounding the bags, doing drills for speed and endurance . . .

During that time, he thought he was training for a fight. Now he knew that he had been training for something else.

This was the main event. In this corner: Tony Katt. And across the ring, in the opposite corner: a fucking yucca tree.

And to the winner? Why, a canteen that might very well be empty.

Tony closed his eyes. In just a minute, he'd hear the bell, and he'd come out for round one.

But he didn't hear a bell. He heard something else.

Some kind of screech.

Tony opened his eyes.

Above him, circling in the red sky, screeching . . .

. . . circling lower . . . and lower still . . .

Vultures.

FOUR

BY THE TIME JACK AND ANGEL REACHED THE HIGHWAY OFF-RAMP, the sky was electric with colors usually only seen in tropical fish tanks.

Jack braked as the Celica reached the spot where pavement gave way to dirt. The windshield was dotted with dead insects, but the sunset was something to see. It painted the hood of the Celica in mirrored tones. The rust spots shone the way they sometimes did under the neon lights of Vegas, like deep pools of Captain Morgan's spiced rum.

"Beautiful," Jack said.

"Not now it isn't," Angel said. "But it will be later."

"Later it will be gone."

Jack punched the trip meter odometer and it registered at zero. The dirt road angled off in a straight line, spearing the great white nowhere called the Mojave Desert. The guy in the plastic-wrap shirt had said that the Lynch sisters lived forty or fifty miles out. Jack wanted to know when he was getting close to the place. He didn't want the gang to know that he was coming. He didn't want to stumble in with

227

headlights blazing. If the moon cooperated, he might even drive the last five or ten miles without lights.

Jack shifted into first gear and started out. The first five miles were pretty smooth. Jack accelerated and cruised along in fourth gear, the tac running just a little bit lower than he would have liked.

Then the potholes started.

They weren't bad at first—Jack held steady in third gear—but as sunset gave way to night the potholes became harder to see. Eleven miles from the highway, Jack took one hard. The front left shock screamed bloody murder, and Angel said, "Slow down, Jack. We'll get there."

"Okay," Jack said. And then it was the low end of third or the high end of second, dodging potholes as they came.

Twenty miles of that and he had a stiff neck from gripping the wheel while the potholes bounced him around. The Celica sure didn't have four-wheel drive. Not even close. Jack began to feel pretty stupid for bringing it.

"Maybe we should have brought your car, Angel."

"Uh-uh. I've got a rental. Mazda Miata. It's built low to the ground—a real highway hugger. We wouldn't have made it this far."

Five more miles and Jack abandoned third gear altogether. He remembered the Jeep Cherokee parked outside the porno guy's studio. He wished he'd stolen the damn thing.

A couple more potholes jarred him good and he stopped wishing. Instead, he berated himself for not stealing the Jeep.

Jack didn't mention the Jeep to Angel, though. He didn't want to give her the chance to agree that he'd made a mistake.

Jack rolled his neck and strangled the steering wheel. The

engine whined in high second gear. No use hitting third, though. The potholes wouldn't let him hold it, and he was tired of shifting back and forth.

Five more miles. Headlights washed the white road. Jack couldn't turn them off. Darkness had fallen, but the moon wasn't up yet. And he had to see those potholes.

Two more miles and Angel offered to drive.

"No," Jack said. "It can't be much further."

He glanced at the trip meter. They'd traveled thirty-eight miles since leaving the highway. Rancho Lynch couldn't be much further. They had to be—

"Jack!"

WHAM! The undercarriage of the Toyota smacked something hard and the steering wheel seemed to jump in Jack's hands.

"What was that?" he asked.

"A rock. I think so anyway. A big rock right in the middle of the road. I don't know how you missed it."

"That's the problem. I didn't."

But the car seemed okay. Jack kept his hands on the wheel and held tight to second gear.

He hadn't clicked another tenth of a mile when the engine started to knock badly.

Then the Celica died.

"Shit," Jack said. "Shit."

He got out, lay down on the road, and peered under the front end.

The Celica wasn't going anywhere.

Angel stepped out of the car. "What's the deal?"

"That rock took out the oil pan. We're screwed."

"No we're not. We can walk. How much further can it be?"

"You sure?"

"Yeah. Jesus, Jack. I'm not walking thirty-plus miles back to the highway. If we go to the Lynch place, at least we'll have a chance of swiping a car or something."

Jack thought about that. They'd notched thirty-eight miles since leaving the highway. The porno producer had said that Eden's place was forty or fifty miles off the main road.

They had to be close.

Two miles if they were lucky. Twelve if they weren't.

Jack grabbed his pistol and jammed extra ammunition into his pockets. Angel did the same.

"Let's get started," Jack said.

Eden lay in her bed, wearing nothing but a red satin sheet. Candles made from the rendered fat of a black ram guttered low on her dresser, flickers of blue flame reflected in the big mirror above. Three incense sticks stood waiting in a human skull, ready to fill Eden's bedroom with the intermingled scents of vanilla, sandalwood, and jasmine at the touch of a demon's hot claw.

For so many years she had waited to be strong. Everyone told her that she wasn't. Mama, Daddy, Tura and Lorelei . . . even Harold. Time and time again she was forced to confront her weaknesses, each time accepting lies from the lips of those who claimed to love her. She was weak. She was no child of Satan. She was not even a child of her own mother, who disowned her with the last words she spoke on this earth.

Mama's words couldn't hurt her now. Eden was too strong for that. But the words had cut her when Mama spoke them in the chapel, just as so many other slights and reprimands had cut her over the years.

Eden was a good girl. She accepted every slight. Every

reprimand. Every punishment and reproach. Until the very last one that spilled from her mother's lips.

If I had it to do over again I'd rip you from my belly with a coat hanger. That's what I'd do. By Satan, I would.

Those words broke Eden. In their wake, she *was* weak. Too weak to do anything. Too weak to fight the sisters who abused her. Harold saw that when he undid the handcuffs Tura and Lorelei used to chain Eden to her bed.

And then Eden lost Harold too, breaking down in front of him, so that his only recourse was to flee into the night.

That was the greatest blow of all. The pit of weakness called to her, and she plunged into it. She hit bottom. And it was only then that she heard His voice. Only then, for the first time in her life, that she truly took Satan's hand.

For it was Satan's hand who guided her own.

Satan fitted Eden's hand with a pistol, and she shot her mother in the heart, and she was strong. Satan slipped a straight razor into her waiting palm, and she slit her father's throat, and she was stronger still. With a rusty knife from Satan's pit she stabbed her lover in the back and felt his strength quiver on the blade as she spilled his blood. And with a dead man's pistol she killed her sister—yes, even this she did—and strength fairly pulsed in her veins.

And soon she would crucify the heavyweight champion of the world to the glory of Satan. Surely the dark one could not receive a greater gift than this. Eden had stolen this prize for Him. Alone, she had captured the strongest of all men. And she would slay him and revel in Satan's glory, but she would not do these things alone.

Satan would send her a demon, for no man could satisfy her now. No mere mortal could hold sway with a woman of her strength.

Of course, the mere mortals in Las Vegas did not

recognize the true nature of Eden's plan. The fools would pay her ten million dollars for Tony Katt's safe return, and she would pocket the ransom money and sacrifice her captive.

Eden would sacrifice Jack Baddalach, as well. For she would demand that he alone deliver the ransom.

She had not forgotten the Harold Ticks Shuffle. Harold might be gone, but she would keep something of him, even if it were only his treachery.

And when she had that ten million dollars and Jack Baddalach was dead, she would burn his bones and sow his grave with salt. And her demon lover would dine on Tony Katt's flesh and grow strong, and from Katt's naked bones Eden would fashion a gate to the great pit of hell which yawned in a Mojave Desert chapel. And all who came to worship at the place called Hell's Half Acre would see this gate. And all who came would know of Eden's strength . . .

Hot as hell's promise, the night air drifted through the open pillbox window. The moon hung high in the sky, a ball of fierce blue light shining upon the earth, fierce blue light that licked Eden's body like the flickering flames of black ram candles.

Upon the desert sands, she heard a heavy tread.

A shadow passed before the moon.

Eden sat up, fearing an intruder. She almost reached for Harold's .357 Magnum, but the hot breeze blowing through the pillbox window stilled her hand, for carried upon it was the scent of hell.

The smell of balms known to Satan's children filled Eden's lungs. Oil of dog and attar of black roses. Eau de Sodom and essence of iniquity.

Eden breathed deeply and tossed back the red silk sheet.

Down the hall, the front door swung open.

Naked, she waited. Her chest rising and falling as anticipation pounded in her blood, the scent of demonflesh searing her lungs.

A heavy tread slapped the tiled hallway floor. Eden smiled and stared into the darkness.

The hallway stretched before her, a study in gray and black slivers of light. Then a huge silhouette appeared, coming closer, closer . . .

"Here, my lord," Eden said. "I await—"

He came to her, his great arms outstretched.

"Yes, my lord," she said. "I have waited so very—"

Tony Katt snapped the crazy bitch's neck.

"Who's stronger now?" he whispered. "Huh, bitch? Who's stronger—"

Oh, God. That was it. Tony dropped onto the bed. He had burned himself down to cinders. He didn't have an ounce of strength left.

Weird. Tony felt every damn thing. Every ache, every pain. Every cut, every blister, every open wound. That fucking tree had rubbed him raw. But he felt the satin sheets, too. Cool on his tortured flesh, slicked tight against his back by ribbons of blood.

It fucking hurt. Sure it hurt. But pain was the only thing that had kept him alive.

The buzzards had pushed him over the edge. Oh, he'd known pain before they came. He remembered that.

Hell, he would never forget it.

The dull Percodan edge fading . . . fresh waves of pain sharpening his senses . . . from the tiniest discomforts on up to nuclear shockwaves of misery . . . from chapped lips and dry mouth through blistered skin right on up to barbed-wire punctures and flayed flesh, Tony felt it all . . . and just when he thought he couldn't stand one more sliver of agony the vultures swooped down, pecking his head with stony beaks . . . sharp knifing nips on his busted nose until it was almost like he could breathe through the damn thing . . . nip nip nip . . . and the taste of blood wetting his lips as the vultures tore through the leather mask and ripped at his cheek, their talons digging into the flayed flesh of his shoulders as the birds' clawed feet fought for purchase and Tony couldn't stand it anymore, not one second more because the pain was Jesus on the cross kind of shit . . . and he couldn't even scream, all he could do was tell himself that he was the heavyweight champion of the world the baddest man on the planet Tony the fucking Tiger King of the fucking Jungle and it was way past time for him to rear up with every ounce of strength he had and . . .

One of the yucca limbs broke loose and slipped from his arm in a bloody tangle of barbed wire. Tony started to fight. He slammed those damn birds with his fist, grabbed one by the throat and squeezed its fucking avian neck and it shit all over his shoulder but he squeezed and squeezed until its fucking black scavenger eyes nearly popped out.

He tossed its dead scavenger ass into the dust. Yeah. He was Tony the Tiger. He was King of this fucking Jungle. Nothing with a brain the size of a walnut was going to treat him like so much fucking carrion. No butt-ugly bird was going to make a meal of his eyeballs.

Soon the Tiger was loose. He stumbled to the canteen. Thank God it was still half full. Tony drank thirstily, then dropped the empty canteen in the dirt.

It landed with a sound like a bell stoppered with cotton.

It was only then that Tony noticed how quiet it was. Eden Lynch was nowhere in sight. Only those dead women bound to the other trees. Christ, he didn't want to end up like them.

He almost had ended up that way. He wouldn't now.

He needed to get out of sight. Just long enough to catch his breath. He stumbled into the shack. Jesus. Another dead guy. This one with his throat slit from ear to ear. It was some old guy. Not Harold. Tony wondered what had happened to his homeboy. But he couldn't think about that now. He had to worry about his own ass.

Quickly he looked around. A knife lay on the floor. Yeah. Bloodstained and rusty, but at least it was something. And there was a jug of water in one corner. Tony took a deep drink and kept it close.

A bunch of shelves on one wall. Crazy labels on this shit. Dried leaves and herbs, mostly . . . but there were some lotions, too. Tony unstoppered a few bottles and smelled the contents. Not bad. He oiled up his sunburned flesh, greasing his wounds. Oh, man, that felt good. Cool as ice. Oh, man . . .

Some other bottles on a low shelf. Prescription bottles. Tony sorted through them. Shit. Some of this stuff was real nasty. He hoped the bitch hadn't fed him any of it.

All right. There it was. His Percodan.

He'd just take one. Only one, and then he'd rest some. That cave on the back wall . . . even if Eden noticed his escape, she wouldn't look for him there. He'd sit in the dark, drink some more water. Drink it slow so it wouldn't make him sick. Then get the hell out of here. There was a truck parked by the bunker, a couple cars, too. Maybe one of them had the keys in the ignition. If not, he'd find the keys. And if that meant going in the big concrete house and killing the bitch, so much the better.

He had to check out that house, anyway. Maybe the bitch had trapped Harold in there. His brother might still be alive. And Tony wouldn't pussy out on him. He remembered Harold taking that bullet for him in the slams. So he needed to get up, get started, and he needed to do it right now . . .

For a second Tony was back there in that cave, thinking these thoughts all over again. Like he hadn't done any of it yet. But he knew he had. The bitch lay next to him on satin sheets, and she was dead.

Tony thought about getting up. Oh, man. He hadn't seen any sign of Harold, but he had to look. His brother might be bound and gagged, might be suffocating this very minute . . .

Maybe if he slept. Just a little . . . No. *Hell no.* He wasn't going to sleep with any dead bitch. He had to find Harold and get the hell out of here.

All he had to do was get up. Yeah. That was all he had to do . . .

Tony lay on red satin sheets with a dead bitch at his side. He couldn't move at all.

Burned down, man. That's what he was.

Cinders. Just cinders.

"This must be the place," Angel said. "Here's another one."

Jack looked away from the redhead's crucified corpse. Angel stood before another yucca tree. The old woman with the cantilevered breasts was tied to this one. Again, the killer had used barbed wire.

"She was one of the dognappers," Jack said. "I think she was running the show. She had a voice like a drill sergeant."

"She's not going to be using it now."

"Yeah."

Jack held tight to his Colt. Angel was sweating, and so was he. They'd had a long walk. Nearly six miles separated the Celica from this spot.

Jack shook his head. As they humped the last two, Angel had complained of blisters. Vociferously. And she was wearing those Doc Martens. She wore hiking boots, but she'd never hiked a day in her life. Her boots weren't even broken in.

The way Jack saw it, you just couldn't figure people. There wasn't any use trying. Like these corpses. Man. Who would do something like this? Murder was murder, but this was overkill. Some kind of rage killing. The killer wanted to make a point.

What that point was, Jack didn't know. But he wasn't going to figure it out by standing in the middle of nowhere.

The moon was large and white, and the desert was painted with an indigo glow. About a quarter mile distant stood a huge concrete bunker. There was a little shack off to one side of it. It looked like a place where a kidnapper might stow a kidnappee.

Jack nodded toward the shack. "Let's check it out."

Angel agreed. Moving quickly and quietly, they threaded a path through the yucca forest. But neither one of them noticed the tree with the broken limb as they passed by or the tangle of bloodstained barbed wire that clung to its trunk.

Angel went through the door first, holding her pistol in the style of a combat shooter. Jack followed her closely, clicking on a flashlight as he entered the shack.

A dead guy lay on some kind of altar. Jack recognized the stovepipe hat that rested on the old man's chest.

"Jesus," Angel said, pointing at the deep slice on the corpse's throat. "Whoever did this nearly cut this guy's head off."

"He's the rattlesnake man," Jack said. "Another member of the gang."

"Jack, what the hell is going on here?"

"I don't know." Jack sighed. "Do you think it might be a hit? Maybe Freddy's bird dog tracked the gang, then had them killed without telling us about it."

"No way, Jack." Angel pointed to the corpse's cupped hands, which were blackened with soot. "The Mafia doesn't go in for satanic rites."

Jack nodded. He played the flashlight beam along the walls of the shack. Harsh white light revealed bottles filled with powders and potions, aged spell books coated with Mojave dust, and stripped bones, both human and animal.

Finally the flashlight beam fell on Angel. She had a death grip on her .45. "I don't know about this, Jack."

"Yeah." Jack thought it over. "Look," he said finally. "We've got three corpses right here. And you killed the other redhead at the vet's office. That leaves Pack O' Weenies and the woman with the wrist braces. Our odds are better now than they were coming in."

Angel nodded. "I guess you're right."

Jack ran his fingers through his hair. "Look, we don't have to go through with this, Angel. No one has spotted us yet. We can probably walk out of here right now——"

"Fifty miles back to the road?" Angel laughed. "My fucking feet are killing me, Jack. We leave here, we're taking a car. God knows there are enough dead bastards around this place who won't be needing their wheels anymore."

"Okay," Jack said. "Who the fuck knows, anyway? Maybe we're in the middle of Jonestown. Some kind of cult massacre. Maybe the whole gang is dead. Maybe the woman with the wrist braces did all the others and committed suicide."

Angel examined the stash of prescription drugs. "Yeah. It looks like she'd have everything she needed for a one-way trip right here. Maybe she's in that bunker, clutching a bottle of sleeping pills in her dead hand. Let's find out."

Favoring her left foot, Angel stepped through the doorway and started toward the concrete house.

Jack followed, his brain clicking away, turning the information over and over in his head.

But he wasn't thinking rationally. His imagination had kicked into overdrive.

If Tony Katt was in the middle of this . . . If the heavyweight champion of the world was chained to an altar in some big concrete snake pit, surrounded by guys in black hoods who mumbled satanic prayers . . . if they were going to sacrifice Katt to the Devil himself . . .

Shit. No. That was crazy.

Angel was getting ahead of him.

Jack hurried along.

He didn't realize the mistake he'd made.

He was holding a glowing flashlight the same way those crazy villagers held flaming torches in old Frankenstein movies.

Approaching a concrete bunker the same way those morons approached Castle Frankenstein.

He might as well have trumpeted his arrival with a Franz Waxman score.

Jack Baddalach was a sitting duck.

And so was Angel Gemignani.

Tony had checked out the house. He'd found Harold's .357 Magnum, but there was no sign of Harold anywhere. Tony hoped his partner wasn't dead, but Harold's fate wasn't exactly his first priority at the moment.

The bathroom mirror was.

Tony stared at himself in the mirror. Man, he looked pretty fucking gruesome. Some of the cuts on his arms and legs were really deep, and the sunburn was world-class. And his nose . . . Jesus. A red mess. What was left of it, anyway.

He fingered the hole in the side of the mask—one of those black leather S & M jobs with all the zippers and shit. God, it was like he hardly had a cheek under there.

This was awful. And the mirror didn't lie. Tony recognized his eyes all right, but he didn't recognize the fear that burned in his irises. Man, he was afraid to take off the mask, just like that monster under the opera house in the old creature feature—

Tony heard voices . . . someone was outside. He snatched up the .357 Magnum and returned to the bedroom, where he peered through the open pillbox window.

Two people were headed his way.

He recognized both of them.

Angel Gemignani led the way, limping, carrying a .45.

One look at her and Tony's nut started to ache.

That little bitch Jack Baddalach brought up the rear, carrying a flashlight. He was packing heat, as well.

Both of them, right here on Tony's fucking plate.

The Tiger could serve them up raw and bloody. Snuff them with some other guy's gun. No one would ever figure out just who'd done who in the middle of this fucking abattoir. The joint was a chamber of horrors. Mickey Spillane couldn't sort this one out.

Yeah, it was open season.

Tony checked the Magnum. It was packed. Six cartridges. He headed for the front door.

• • •

She had that gimpy walk, but she wouldn't slow down.

"Angel," Jack said. "Wait a minute—"

It was like she didn't hear him.

Her hand was on the knob.

She opened the door.

And something grabbed Angel just that fast. It was a bloody fucking mess, big as Frankenstein, and it twisted the .45 from her hand and let the gun drop as it spun her around—

Angel stared at Jack, eyes wide as the monster's left hand squeezed her throat. The flashlight beam scorched the thing's head with white light . . . a black head covered with silver stitches . . . some kind of mask . . . and Angel's mouth was open but she couldn't say a word . . .

And neither could Jack. There wasn't enough time . . .

The thing had a .357 Magnum. The barrel arced toward Angel's head . . .

From twin black leather pits, a pair of crazy eyes stared at Jack. He didn't recognize them. But he recognized the smiling lips beneath the eyes . . .

That baddest man on the planet smile, nestled in black leather . . .

The .357 Magnum neared Angel's temple . . .

The Colt Python bucked in Jack's hand before he had time to think.

Black leather, flesh, and bone exploded in the night.

Tony Katt's corpse crumpled against the open door.

Jack didn't say a word.

Neither did Angel.

They didn't have to.

She ran to him and they embraced.

She looked into his eyes, and he looked into hers.

And then her hands drifted away from his shoulders, and

his fingers slipped away from her hips. And in a moment he wasn't touching her, and she wasn't touching him.

But they stood side by side for a long time, the bright moon hanging above, the warm breeze rushing down from the mountains, the indigo night holding strong.

FIVE

JACK UNSCREWED THE CELICA'S LICENSE PLATES AND TOSSED THEM in the back of the Chevy Apache.

Angel sat behind the wheel of the truck. "Sure your car will be okay?"

Jack nodded. They had pushed the Celica off the main road. Tomorrow he would borrow a tow truck from his mechanic buddy, Pablo Morales, and retrieve the Toy. If anyone showed up at Hell's Half Acre in the meantime, Jack didn't want them connecting him to the bloodbath at the Lynch family compound through a broken-down Celica. That's why he was taking the license plates.

Hidden among the yucca trees, the Toy would be safe. From above, the root beer foam paint job blended with the light Mojave earth. And hell, those rust spots on the hood made good camouflage. A couple more excuses like that and Jack would *never* paint the Celica.

Jack climbed into the Chevy and Angel gunned the engine. "How much further?"

"A mile. Maybe two."

They bumped along in silence. The sun was rising outside Angel's window. Jack studied her profile as she drove, her features haloed by the glow of the coming day.

Sunny and hot. That's what daylight would bring to the Mojave Desert. Pushing a hundred degrees and pushing it hard.

Just another day in hell.

They shadowed an arroyo for a quarter of a mile. On the other side of the dry creek bed, a coyote padded along with a jackrabbit clenched in its muzzle. Angel pulled to a stop and watched the predator.

The coyote glanced at them but didn't hurry its pace.

"Want me to keep driving?" she asked.

"No," Jack said. "This should do it."

Jack grabbed a shovel from the truck bed. He started to dig. And he started to sweat, too. The morning heat was baking him good.

He peeled off his T-shirt and kept at it. Angel sat on the hood of the Apache and watched him, picking at a hole in her jeans.

"You think anyone will ever find him?"

Jack almost laughed. "It's a big desert, Angel. You don't even want to know how many guys your granddad buried out here in the old days."

Angel was quiet for a minute. "I guess it's really no different than that coyote. Not really. Everything dies sooner or later. Today that jackrabbit took it hard. But one of these days, it'll be the coyote's turn." She smiled the same peculiar smile Jack had seen before, the one devoid of pleasure. "And one of these days it'll be our turn, too."

"There's a cheery thought."

"I said *one of these days*." She laughed. "But not fuckin' today."

"Amen."

They hauled Tony Katt's corpse from the truck bed. The heels of his boots dug trenches in the dirt as they dragged him to the grave and dropped him in. Nobody was going to find Tony out here. He would always be the heavyweight champion of the world who disappeared without a trace.

"You want to say anything?" Angel asked.

"Are you kidding?"

"Let me do it then." She took the shovel from Jack.

Angel looked down, into the grave.

She said, "See you later, Mr. Coyote."

Then she heaped the shovel with loose dirt and flung it into Tony Katt's tattered face. Angel worked hard, and soon sweat poured off her the way it had poured off Jack, and the scent of Calvin Klein's Obsession was gone gone gone . . .

Angel Gemignani was doing what she needed to do, and she didn't need any help from Jack Baddalach. He wandered along the arroyo. Once in a while he'd turn and look at his footprints. It didn't matter how many times he looked; he was always surprised to see them there, following along behind him.

The sky was way past blue, the flip side of the indigo night. A lone jet trail split the heavens. Another load of tourists headed for the land of the dollar slot.

Jack walked among the yucca trees, looping back toward Angel. He kept expecting to come upon Pack O' Weenies, wired to a tree.

He didn't, of course. Who knew what had become of Harold Ticks? Jack wondered why he should even care.

Still, he thought about the bald-headed son of a bitch. Harold Ticks, bound with barbed wire, watching the sun rise, feeling the heat.

Pack O' Weenies, roasting in the Mojave Desert.
All alone.

But Harold wasn't roasting. Not at all.

He lay at the bottom of a mine shaft, the one that began in the Hell's Half Acre Church of Satan.

After stabbing Harold in the back and hacking off his left thumb, Eden lit a kerosene lantern and pushed Harold down the tunnel in an old mining cart. Harold wasn't stupid. He saw the handwriting on the wall. He tried to talk Eden out of it. He tried to figure out what was wrong with her. But Eden dumped him down a deep shaft before he even had a chance to say that he was sorry.

What he could possibly be sorry for, he didn't know. After all, Eden was the one who had fucked everything up and cost them half a million bucks. She was the goddamn tater queen in a family full of goddamn spuds. But, hell, Harold couldn't tell her that when she was about to dump him down a mine shaft. He was a little bit smarter than that. He would have apologized for anything if only Eden would let him remain above ground.

Creak! Dump! Wham! Not a chance, Harold.

Harold was cold. He'd lost a lot of blood. He knew that. And his back was busted. At least he thought it was. He couldn't move his legs at all.

He couldn't see anything in the dark, but he knew that he wasn't alone. Sometimes he heard a whispering hiss that seemed very near his ear. And now and then he heard a stuttering rattle.

Harold didn't like those sounds.

He tried not to think about them, but that was pretty hard. Because he had to think of something. He couldn't just . . . well, wait to *die*.

So he lay there at the bottom of a mine shaft, and he tried to think.

But only one thought entered his head, over and over, again and again.

Eden . . . Eden . . . Why . . . Why?

EPILOGUE

Viva Lost Wages

I feel like one who treads alone
Some banquet-hall deserted,
Whose lights are fled, whose garlands dead,
And all but he departed!

—THOMAS MOORE
OFT, IN THE STILLY NIGHT

EPILOGUE

A WEEK LATER, JACK WOKE UP AT FOUR IN THE MORNING.

Wide awake, staring at the ceiling. Visions of Tony Katt and piranha and suckling pigs dancing in his head.

He decided, *What the hell, I'll go for a run.*

Many moons had passed since he'd done that. These days he never ran unless someone was chasing him.

But in the old days he could really run. Man, he loved the burn. Notch four or five miles and he was floating in the rhythm. He always did his running early in the morning, before the rest of the world was awake. The light-heavyweight champion of the world, putting in the time.

Jack pulled on some old jeans and a sweatshirt, filled Frankenstein's bowl with dog food, and headed for the golf course. The one by Tony Katt's mansion.

He checked in with the guard at the gate. A fighter running on a golf course in the predawn hours was not an unusual thing. In Vegas, the boxing capital of the world, it happened all the time.

The guard wasn't about to turn away Jack the Giant Killer. Besides, he wanted to know if there was anything new with Tony Katt.

"Still missing," Jack said.

"I guess you scared him but good," the guard said.

"Yeah."

The guard flashed Jack the old thumbs up. "I know you'll beat him in the ring. I'm lookin' at the next heavyweight champ. I'll bet green money on that."

Jack only grinned at that last part. He parked the Celica and started across the green. It wasn't even five A.M. Not a soul in sight.

The air was still a little crisp, but Jack could tell that it was going to be a hot one. He threw punches in the air as he ran, short hooks and uppercuts that bunched his shoulders. His breathing hit a ragged rhythm, but he loved it. His lungs hadn't felt this kind of burn in a long, long time.

The grass was wet, and soon Jack's shoes were soaked through. He headed toward a little grove of fruit trees about a mile distant.

He picked a couple of oranges and ate them in silence. The sugar hit his empty belly and it was heaven. The black sky smeared gray as he ate, and then the dawn came on.

Jack grabbed another orange for the road. He ran another mile, and suddenly he felt like walking.

He passed the Skull Island corporate mansion where he had danced his dance with Tony Katt. Porschia Keyes was recuperating there after her accident. At least that's what Jack had heard. Skull Island management was being especially nice to Porschia. They didn't want to get sued.

So Porschia was sitting pretty. But Tony Katt would never walk through those mansion doors again.

And Jack would never meet the heavyweight champion in the ring.

He would never get up at four in the morning and run because he was set to face Tony Katt in a month, or three weeks, or six days . . .

He would never sit under a tree and eat an orange while he planned the traps he'd set for Katt with his quick jab . . . how he'd stick and move, bip bip bip, in and out . . .

And he would never buckle that heavyweight championship belt around his waist.

Jack peeled the orange as he walked toward the parking lot. There was no sense thinking about any of it. Just lately, it didn't seem that thinking had gotten him anywhere, anyway.

Because every time he needed to think things through, there wasn't enough time for it.

When Angel Gemignani opened that door, and Tony Katt grabbed her, Jack chose his path in less than a finger snap.

He didn't think about money, or the heavyweight championship of the world, or his place in the universe. He didn't spare a second questioning the fate of his immortal soul. He didn't wonder if killing another human being was immoral. He didn't ask himself if a slime like Tony Katt even *was* a human being.

No. When Tony Katt grabbed Angel Gemignani, Jack shot the motherfucker in the head.

He didn't need to think about it. He only needed to react. He only needed to draw on something that was hard-wired into his soul a long time ago.

Jack trusted that thing, whatever it was. He really did.

He finished the orange and tossed the peel into a garbage can. The morning was coming on fast, orange sherbet riding the flip side of indigo blue.

Jack felt good. He didn't know why. But he went with it.

He wasn't the heavyweight champion of the world. Hell, he wasn't even the light-heavyweight champion of the world. He was just a guy named Baddalach who occasionally baby-sat consumptive Chihuahuas.

Shaking his head, Jack unclipped the cellular phone from his belt and tossed it into the Celica. Man, was he a case.

Maybe that phone would never ring.

But Kate Benteen was out there somewhere. At least he hoped that she was. He still had her picture on his desk. Maybe she thought about him once in a while. Maybe one day she would stop thinking and just go with it and dial his number.

Maybe, one of these days, Jack's phone would ring.

If that ever happened, he knew exactly how he'd react.

Exactly.

About the Author

Stephen King says that Norman Partridge is "a major new talent."

Joe R. Lansdale calls Partridge "the hottest new writer going."

High praise, indeed. Here's what earned it: Partridge's first novel, *Slippin' into Darkness*, was heralded as "nitro-laced, in-your-face fiction for the '90s" (*Locus*). His short fiction has made regular appearances in the "year's best" anthologies for suspense, mystery, and horror. A collection of short stories, *Mr. Fox and Other Feral Tales*, won the Bram Stoker Award and was a World Fantasy nominee. Another collection of short fiction, *Bad Intentions*, was published in May 1996 to rave reviews. Partridge's second novel, *Saguaro Riptide*, was published by Berkley Prime Crime in May 1997.

Partridge has worked in libraries and steel mills. He loves fifties rock 'n' roll, drive-in movies, and old paperbacks where the bad guys get away with murder.